CONSEQUENCE

Also by Eli Yance:

House 23

CONSEQUENCE

a thriller

ELI YANCE

Skyhorse Publishing

Skyhorse Publishing books may be purchased in bulk at special discounts for sales promotion, corporate gifts, fund-raising, or educational purposes. Special editions can also be created to specifications. For details, contact the Special Sales Department, Skyhorse Publishing, 307 West 36th Street, 11th Floor, New York, NY 10018 or info@skyhorsepublishing.com.

Skyhorse® and Skyhorse Publishing® are registered trademarks of Skyhorse Publishing, Inc.®, a Delaware corporation.

Visit our website at www.skyhorsepublishing.com.

10 9 8 7 6 5 4 3 2 1

Library of Congress Cataloging-in-Publication Data is available on file.

Cover design by Lilith_C (lilithcgraphics)

Print ISBN: 978-1-5107-0438-1
Ebook ISBN: 978-1-5107-0445-9

Printed in the United States

To Hugo, Sheldon, Beatrice & Rincewind

1

Darren Morris sat still in the parked silver Ford Mondeo, his body comforted by the plush leather interior, his eyes fixed firmly through the windshield. The winter afternoon had chilled the skies an eerie gray; the clouds swamped the fading sun and spread a silvery glow over the gray cobbled pier.

His hardened eyes, sliced with a web of deep wrinkles, wandered from the empty area ahead of him and glanced over the metal railings, into the silky black sea.

"What a fucking mess." His voice growled out the words with a deep layer of disgust.

James Roach sat behind the steering wheel, a firm look of determination on his face and an unfaltering straightness in his spine. He gave an apathetic glance out the passenger window before regarding his partner unsurely. "The pier? I think it looks okay," he replied.

"The sea, you fucking idiot," Morris snapped.

"Yes . . ." Roach agreed, turning back to concentrate on the world beyond the steering wheel, his indifference intact. "Beats living in the city though, I wouldn't mind moving out to a place like this someday."

Morris shrugged and fixed his eyes on the concrete pier, waves splashed the gray ground, spilling frothy flecks onto the surface.

The sound of a car engine rumbled through the salty air. A blue Porsche rolled into view several yards ahead of them. The driver, unseen through tinted windows, pulled the car to a stop about twenty yards from the edge of the pier.

The men in the Mondeo glared at the vehicle.

"Fucking bastard," Morris said through clenched teeth.

They watched as a man in his mid-twenties clambered out of the car. His face was drawn and pale, his attitude confident. He rested against the hood of the sports car and stared at the distant waves.

He wore an expensive leather jacket which had been unzipped to expose a wealth of silver medallions and chains around his neck. His baggy jeans, hanging loosely from his pencil-thin frame, had been scribbled with threads of graffiti. The slack denim material was covered with hip-hop lyrics and declarations, including a stitched picture of three rappers.

Silently the two men exited their vehicle—parked out of sight under the shade of a dilapidated warehouse—and carefully closed the doors. They both embraced the cold sea air, digging their hands into their pockets as they strode toward the Porsche.

The youngster didn't see them as they approached.

"Nice view isn't it, Dean?" Morris asked.

The comment startled him and he slipped off the hood, immediately shooting a glance at the two men.

"You scared the fucking shit out of me," he muttered through heavy breaths.

"How's tricks?" Roach asked.

The younger man smirked and directed their attention towards his car. "It's all good," he declared smugly.

A frown pulled at Morris's lips as he surveyed the car and the youngster's expression. "OK. That's enough small talk for one day," he said. "You got the cash?"

The younger man nodded. He walked to the passenger side of the car and removed a briefcase. Walking back around the front of the vehicle he paused in front of Morris.

"It's all here," he tapped the case and then looked concerned, noticing that the two men carried nothing. "You got the gear?"

Morris grabbed the case, gently nudged the youngster out of the way and rested it on top of the car. He opened it to reveal a mass of used notes, carefully tied together in elastic bands. He picked up one of the piles and flicked through.

"It's all there, twenty grand, you got the dope?" Dean repeated.

"Nice down here is it, Harris?" Morris asked.

"Yeah . . . plenty of fucking junkies, keeps me in whores and champagne," he laughed. The gesture wasn't returned.

"Been through our neck of the woods recently?" Morris inquired.

Dean Harris hesitated for a moment, his eyes moved from Morris to Roach.

"No. The last time I went up there was to meet up with Sanderson . . . w—w—why d'you ask?"

Morris slammed the lid of the case and glared at Dean, "Word is you're peddling your shit on Sanderson's turf."

"What? No, I wouldn't."

"You deal your shit *here* and only *here*," Morris began.

"I am—" he pleaded, but his words were cut short.

"The boss gives you a good deal. He set you up, he gave you all of this." He gestured to Dean's expensive chains and luxurious car. "He started you in this game."

"I know . . . I'm grateful—"

"He picked you off the streets, gave you the dope and only took a cut from your earnings. You've made a lot of money, Dean."

"Yes, and I've—"

Morris continued, "Freebase, straight from the factories, you can cut it as much as you want and sell it for whatever you fucking want, as long as you keep out of the city. He gives you a good deal. You make a tidy sum. You have it easy, if there's any trouble you come to us and we deal with it. How long you been working this area, Dean?"

"Two, maybe two and a half years." Dean's voice cracked as he spoke.

"Pure, uncut cocaine and heroin," Morris continued, his mind already set on a speech, "and the entire fucking southeast coast to peddle it to, yet you insisted on coming to London, and selling Sanderson's shit to Sanderson's clients right under his nose."

"I swear . . . I didn't," Dean's voice was becoming increasingly anxious.

Morris shot out an arm and grabbed him by the lapels of his jacket. He threw him over the car as Roach, unmoving and silent until that point, looked around to see if anyone was watching.

"He's losing customers; business is slipping, want to hazard a guess why that is?"

"I don't know, please—"

"He's losing customers because you're selling them *your* fucking shit, which also just so happens to be *his*."

"Look, I'm sorry, I just—" Dean gagged.

"You know the score, you cut and sell and you stay away from the city, but you got greedy didn't you?"

"I didn't think it would do any harm."

"You see, Dean . . . we have a dilemma. The boss was willing to let you go, maybe with a few more broken bones than usual."

A moan escaped Dean Harris's lips.

"But it seems that not only are you selling his gear on his turf, but you also turned in one of his boys."

"I swear I didn't know he worked for Sanders." Dean said.

"Every fucking dealer in the city works for Sanders, you idiot!"

Morris looked calmly across at the briefcase. "Get up," he released his grip on Dean's jacket and allowed him to stand.

Dean brushed his jacket down and, with tears of fear welling in his eyes, began to spit out an apology, "Look . . ."

"Save it," Morris said. "Come with us, Sanders wants a word."

Roach had already stalked around the back of the car, making sure to grab the briefcase as he did so. He shoved the youngster forward. Harris stumbled in shock, his quivering legs struggling to hold firm. He looked back at the two men and then continued walking.

"Our car is parked near the warehouse," Roach assured, as Dean kept glancing over his shoulder.

As he walked into the shadows behind the warehouse and spotted the Mondeo, a wave of relief washed over his panicked face. He turned to speak to the two men with a relaxed smile.

He barely had time to blink before Morris's fist crashed into his face, breaking his nose and dribbling a fountain of red from the appendage.

He stumbled backwards, but his move was matched by James Roach. The older man grabbed him by the arm and yanked the limb with deadly accuracy, pulling it free of its socket.

Harris opened his mouth to yelp as the pain soared with burning white heat through his body. Morris threw another punch, catching him just as he opened his mouth. The impact caused his head to jolt so hard his neck nearly snapped. Two of his teeth shattered and spilling blood into his mouth. One chipped, sending the enamel shrapnel into his upper lip.

He gurgled blood, his screams stifled by the crimson fluid curdling in his throat. Roach, still with a firm grip on the wounded arm, pulled him over to the railings. Dean's eyes widened as he stared down at the water below.

He tried to struggle out of Roach's firm grip, but to no avail. The older man grabbed his head and, in one strong and deadly movement, slammed it down onto the iron railing.

Both men recognized the sickening sound as Harris's skull cracked against the fatal force. His lifeless body slumped against the railings, a mass of blood spilling from a split in his head.

Roach watched indifferently as the blood seeped from the body in his hands.

"I'll drive back," Morris said, walking to the driver's side of the Mondeo while he examined a small cut on his right knuckle.

Roach nodded. Then, grabbing hold of Dean Harris's legs he propelled him over the railings and let go. He watched, his face devoid of emotion, as the broken body of the dealer crashed into the rocky waves and disappeared.

2

Michael Richards rapped his bony hand against the solid double-glazed glass. The impact reverberated through his knuckles. He recoiled, grasping his hand tightly to his chest.

"What the fuck is wrong with you?" Johnny Phillips looked across at his friend with little sympathy, his hard-edged brow arched with distaste.

"I bruised my knuckles," Michael Richards replied, his high-pitched voice chirping the sounds of a Cockney accent.

Phillips rolled his eyes and turned away from his friend. He peered through the smeared glass in the solid wooden door. He could see only smudges and distorted outlines of various furniture: a carpeted floor, heavy shaded walls, and what looked to be a staircase further down a long hallway.

"How'd you manage to do that?" he asked, his eyes still scanning the door.

"Boxing," came the hesitant reply from his friend.

Phillips turned; his eyebrows raised, "Boxing?"

"Yeah, what's so surprising about that?" Richards spat as he examined his hand.

"You're built like a fucking anorexic jockey," Phillips said, glancing at his friend's frail appearance despite his large protruding gut. "You couldn't punch your way out of a wet paper bag."

"I'm learning, okay?"

"If you say so."

Phillips turned his attention back to the door. He raised his hand and knocked three times, his knuckles slamming hard on the wood below the glass.

"So when did you start?" he added when the thuds of his fists had faded.

"About a week ago."

"A week? And you've cracked your fucking knuckles already? How the hell did you manage that?"

"They ain't fucking cracked okay? They're just a bit tender."

Phillips rolled his eyes. Through the glass he could see a large silhouette approaching, when it got to the door, he heard the metallic sound of a key clicking against a lock.

"Look sharp, Cinderella," he mumbled.

The door swung open and both men were greeted by a middle-aged woman dressed in a loose-fitting robe. Her short blonde hair had been ruffled; locks of dirty gold sprayed over her face. Her eyes were sunken and her lips were dry and cracked.

She looked at the two young men with hazy, sleepy eyes, concentrating on Johnny Phillips—the heavier built and more intimidating of the two.

"Can I help you?" she asked, allowing a yawn to escape her lips.

Phillips smiled directly into her eyes. Then, brushing particles of dust from his long suede jacket, he spoke in a formal tone.

"Mrs. J. Robinson?" he asked.

"Yes," she said, curiously.

He pulled a leather wallet from his inside pocket and held it in front of her. The wallet unfolded to reveal a silver badge next to an ID card.

"Detective Inspector Grainger," he quoted with practiced professionalism. "This is my partner," he paused as Richards half-heartedly flashed his badge to the woman, with a glare toward to his friend.

"We are here about a stolen car," he added.

The woman's face brightened up, "Stolen? What are you talking about? I . . . I didn't steal any car . . . I've—" Her hesitant remarks were cut short by Michael Richards.

"We know you didn't steal anything Mrs. Robinson," he assured her, his professional tone overlapping his accent. "*Unfortunately,* we believe one may have been stolen from *you.*"

"What? What do you mean?" she asked, her voice breaking.

Phillips pulled a notebook from his pocket and began leafing through. He stopped on an empty page and pretended to read.

"Do you own a *red* Jaguar E-Type, License number JO5 SON?" his eyes peered up from the notebook into her worried hazel gaze.

"Yes. Yes. Why? What is it? What's wrong?" she demanded to know.

"I'm afraid your car was used in a smash and grab at four this morning."

"What!" she blurted, shocked by the news.

She stuck her head through the door and glanced past the two men, her eyes scanning an empty graveled driveway where her car was supposed to be.

"Oh my god, how did this happen?"

"It would be a lot easier if we could talk about this inside Mrs. Robinson," Richards interjected.

"Sure." She opened the door further, gesturing with a distant and disconsolate stare for them to enter.

The men needed no second invitations, they passed her and then waited for her to close the door and point them to the living room.

"Nice place you've got here," Phillips said, his eyes appreciating the vast amount of crystal ornaments and porcelain dolls that decorated a marbled fireplace.

"Thanks," she replied with little enthusiasm.

He reached into his pocket and felt a small device touch his fingertips. He kept his eyes on the woman as he worked his fingers around the solid object, waiting for the right moment.

He sat himself down on a black leather sofa, watching as his companion walked to his side. A glance passed between the pair, unseen by the homeowner. She stared at her own twiddling thumbs, nearly jumping out of her skin when a chirping ringtone cut through the silence.

Michael Richards smiled as the sound of the tubular bells lifted from inside his jacket. He pushed his hand inside the cotton material and pulled out a cell phone, alight with a blue screen and alive with a melodic tune.

"Sorry," he said to the woman. "I have to take this. You don't mind, do you?" he asked pleasantly, gesturing to the door.

She shook her head with as much politeness as she could muster and Richards walked out of the room, moving the phone to his ear as he disappeared.

Phillips smiled reassuringly at the older woman and lifted his hand out of his pocket. "As I was saying," he began, "your car was involved in a smash and grab at a jewelry store—"

"I didn't . . ."

"It's okay. We know you have nothing to do with the robbery. The thieves were caught by the security cameras; they both have extensive criminal backgrounds and are well known to us." He paused to admire a large landscape painting of the Cumbrian countryside, hanging next to a fifty-inch 3D television.

"That's a very nice painting. I've always admired the Lake District, have you been there recently Mrs. Robinson?"

A look of bewilderment crossed the woman's face; she followed his gaze and shook her head. "No, no it was a gift. Look, can we please get back to the car?"

"Of course," Phillips paused glance admiringly at the painting once more. "We have yet to track down the two criminals involved. I'm afraid there is a high risk that they have dumped, burned, or resprayed your car by now."

"Oh God," she uttered in disgust.

"Yep, life's just one big kick in the balls ain't it," Phillips mumbled, glancing passed her and admiring a large collection of vintage LPs—perfectly manicured in plastic wrap and dotted along a large oak bookcase.

"Excuse me?"

"Nothing Mrs. Robinson. Now, I'm afraid I will need details of your whereabouts from last night to, well . . . now really."

"But why? You know it wasn't anything to do with me, don't you?"

"Of course, but we still need to run checks, routine business that's all. I'm sure you understand."

"Yes, yes. Of course."

Phillips pulled out his notebook again and flipped to one of the many blank pages. "Right Mrs. Robinson. First off, where were you at 8 o'clock last night?"

He listened as she spoke, nodding every now and then when he felt appropriate. His hand constantly scribbled on the notepad, drawing unrecognizable pictures and patterns.

"Thanks for all your help Mrs. Robinson; we will get in touch when we have more information."

Johnny Phillips and Michael Richards walked briskly down the graveled driveway, the soft pebbles crunched noisily beneath their feet. Only when they heard the front door slam shut behind them did they speak.

"So, did you get it?" Phillips asked.

"Yes, I got it," Richards said smugly, tapping his heaving gut. Phillips smiled broadly.

"Why do I always have to be your *partner*?" Richards queried.

"What?"

"You get to be the fucking *Detective Inspector,* I have to be your *partner*, you could at least introduce me, give me a name, or a title, not just a fucking *partner*."

"Stop bitching would you, does it really matter?" Phillips said as they exited through the house's large gate, their feet finding concrete.

10

"I guess not."

They halted next to a parked car. Both men clambered into the vehicle with Phillips sliding into the driver's seat.

"Well, let's see it *fat boy*," Phillips joked inside the confines of the car.

Richards smiled and took off his jacket. Underneath he wore a white shirt, wrapped over what appeared to be a large beer belly.

Unzipping his shirt, Richards revealed a large cast around his midsection, made from a mixture of latex, cardboard, and plastic, it had been tied to his stomach with thick string and a line of masking tape. It served as a large Kangaroo pouch underneath his clothes; it had no top and was completely hollowed out down to his groin.

Johnny Phillips's eyes lit up when he saw the contents of the pouch. "There's gotta be at least ten grand in there!" he said excitedly, staring at the piles of bound notes inside the papier-mâché pouch. "Did you get in okay?" he asked, his eyes still fixed on the money.

"Yes. It was pathetic, any idiot could have cracked it, even you," Richards said.

Phillips shook his head, "If you weren't carrying all that cash I'd kill you for saying that."

They both laughed. Phillips rolled his chair back and ducked below the steering wheel. Seconds later he emerged with the engine roaring; both men were grinning widely as the stolen Jaguar pulled away down the quiet country road.

3

Howard Price drummed his fingers impatiently on the desk. The oak construction cushioned each blow, absorbing the sound. He released a long sigh, and lifted his eyes from his musical exploits.

His office was immaculate, as usual. The claret carpet was as fresh and colorful as the day he'd bought it. The pristine furniture looked laminated through the thick varnish and the manila walls shone with pride, donning Howard's achievements.

He ran his eyes over the framed articles and certificates on display.

HOWARD PRICE INHERITS SIGHTSYS declared the bold words on the oldest newspaper clipping. The front-page article pictured Howard in his early twenties, a look of contentment on his face as he stood in front of a multi-story building.

RECORD PROFITS FOR SIGHTSYS read the next, a couple of years younger than the first, this time only the building could be seen.

SIGHTSYS SETS PLANS FOR LARGER HEADQUARTERS

SOFTWARE COMPANY SIGHTSYS BREAKS THE MOLD

HOWARD PRICE ENTERS THE RICH LIST

The wall was like a timeline, from left to right, with the declarations of news-printed success ending at the door. Howard's eyes scanned the final one.

The article had been taken from an international magazine and chartered his success. He had inherited the business from his father, a man whom Howard hardly knew and a man who had put his work before his child—he had died in a hit and run incident twenty years ago, leaving the business to Howard, his only son.

All of this, and Howard's rise to greater power and fortune with the software company, had been documented in the article. A picture accompanied it. In it, he was standing outside his mansion, a look of great pride in his eyes, his wife and daughter by his side.

He smiled at the sight of his pretty seven-year-old child, who had been incredibly excited at the time, so much so that Howard had been talked into buying over thirty copies of the magazine so she could show her friends at school.

A static voice bellowed out from the surface of the solid oak desk, "Mr. Price, your wife Elizabeth is on line one. Should I put her through?"

Howard frowned and pushed the intercom. "Just tell her I'm on my way. I'll be there in half an hour." A buzz greeted him when he released his finger from the button.

His gaze fell onto a framed picture by the intercom, looming proudly over the silent device. The picture inside the silver frame had been taken on his daughter's seventh birthday party. She was dressed in a pink ballerina's outfit, with two small yellow flowers entwined in her long golden hair. Her mouth grinned widely while her bright blue eyes stared straight at the camera. Her mouth was covered in chocolate cake and some had even reached her dimpled cheek and the tip of her nose.

Howard grinned at the picture and at the memory, but that smile faded when he caught sight of his own reflection in the polished silver frame. Signs of stress and sleep deprivation screamed out from the deepest recesses of his middle-aged face. Pits of the deepest black dug into the soft, wrinkled flesh under his eyes, the whites of which were speckled with red blotches.

His strong cheekbones and heavy jaw hid a tired man. He was only forty-three but his rough skin, pale lips, and red-lined eyes displayed the portrait of a man at least ten years older.

He turned his face away from his fatigued reflection and slowly stood up. He could feel his legs and lower back stiffen as he rose, creaking like a farmhouse door.

Walking across the plush flooring, which indented like wool beneath his feet, he took his coat from the sleek metallic coat stand in the corner of the room and slowly slipped it on.

He glanced around the office as his arms slid through the satin-lined sleeves. His eyes fell upon the many plaques and framed items on the other side of the room.

Certificates awarded in the company's name.

Framed covers of successful software programs.

Certificates for his personal achievements, including his college and university degrees.

He stopped to admire a colorful painting behind his desk. It was a picture of the company headquarters drawn in crayon. In front of the clearly unstable, scraggly building stood two matchstick figures holding hands, one was almost taller than the building, the other was much smaller, its head decorated with yellow crayon to emphasize an abundance of blonde hair.

The grin returned to his ragged face.

4

Phillips yanked the steering wheel, violently dragging the car to one side. Richards slammed against the passenger-side door, his body unprepared for the instant action. His face slammed into the window, leaving an imprint of his cheek on the humidity freckled glass.

"What the fuck?" he rasped, bringing his hand to his throbbing jaw.

Phillips regained control of the car just as quickly as he had lost it. He continued to drive at a steady pace.

"*I said:* We only need another fifty-thousand and we're set," Phillips repeated.

"Why the fuck did you swerve?" Richards asked, ignoring the comment.

"Because you weren't fucking listening, you've done nothing but stare at that fucking money since we left the house."

Richards nodded in agreement. "Fifty grand," he muttered to himself, watching the empty road ahead. "Reckon we'll do it?" he asked, turning towards his friend.

"Of course we fucking will." Phillips stated confidently. "Seven years of this shit, hundreds of fucking cons and fuck all to show for it. We'll make it because we *need* to fucking make it."

"Seven years and nearly one hundred thousand in the bank," Richards corrected.

"It's not enough."

"We have the house and the apartment as well."

"Still not enough," Phillips's eyes were fixed on the road ahead. "The house is worth one hundred and fifty at the most, and the apartment is worth fuck all. Fifty more and we can start work on the shop. Put some decent money in our hands."

Richards nodded and drifted back to his thoughts. For two years, they had aspired to something bigger, something better. Tired of a lifetime of small cons and cheap thrills, they decided to open up a betting shop. They had sought a location and thought of countless ideas to make extra profit, none of which were legal.

The legal business venture would not only help to hide their illegal earnings from the tax man but would give them a valuable source for new cons and tricks. Phillips had always said that gambling was a fool's game, and in the world of professional gambling, the fools carried credit cards and left their rational thinking at home.

A gambling license wouldn't be hard for them to acquire; the world stank of corruption and Phillips had his nose in every crevice.

"We can get some cash for this," Richards said, hooking a thumb over his shoulder to indicate the car.

"Not much, you know the score: Pritchard will give us seven hundred tops. There are too many two-bit, fucking lowlife car thieves around here; he can afford to pay peanuts."

"We could ask for more," Richards said.

"It's a fucking chop shop not a pawn shop; we get what we're offered."

"But—"

"But nothing," Phillips cut in. "If you want more you ask him your fucking self."

The image of Robert Pritchard's aggressive personality and intimidating frame popped into Richards's head. He could almost feel himself being castrated as he imagined himself asking the madman for more money.

"Seven hundred it is."

5

Price slammed the door of the Mercedes shut behind him.

He checked his watch: 5:36

Somehow he'd managed to shave ten minutes off his journey, one he had become accustomed to over the years. He knew every landmark, every stretch of road, the best places to overtake, and, more importantly, he knew where all the speed cameras were.

He wasn't a fast driver; he usually stuck to the speed limits, his great punctuality and ability to stick to a strict timetable meant that he never needed to rush. But, this afternoon his mind had been elsewhere, and his speed had matched the thumping drums of classic rock as he allowed the sounds of his music collection to swamp his instincts.

The air had grown colder as the day progressed. A light fog clouded the distance and dragged a musky humidity through the air.

The facade of the mansion before him was decorated with an expansive, colorful garden, donning a variety of beautiful plants, bushes, and even a solitary tree standing tall near the entrance, its long branches dangling over a tall iron gate.

The gravel driveway stretched a hundred yards from the gate to the white front of the garage. In front of Price's expensive vehicle sat a compact and sporty Toyota. Its sapphire paint dulled by the grayed afternoon sky.

The house itself stood out like a diamond in sun drenched water. The garden revolved around the beautiful three story edifice. Every flower, bush, and garden ornament was more of a declaration to the beauty of the house than an addition to it.

On entering the house—stepping across a pine-scented threshold where a succulent and pleasant warmth greeted him—a sweet voice beckoned him.

"In here, Howard."

Walking into the kitchen he saw his wife standing by a tall, sleek fridge. She was arched over one of the kitchen counters, slowly chopping vegetables.

His eyes traced her body from foot to head. Her long, slender, toned legs were wrapped snugly in softly shaded tights. She wore a short black skirt which hung just over her thighs, her firm buttocks protruded seductively through the material. A thin and short silk blouse delicately housed her upper body, when she bent over it lifted to reveal the soft, browned flesh on her lower back. He could see her supple skin through the material.

When she turned Howard saw that she wore a red apron with the words 'Hot Stuff' embroidered on it.

"Are you just going to stand there?" Elizabeth Price asked with a smile, knowing where her husband's eyes had been traveling.

His smile spread into a grin. The apron covered her body, allowing his vision no access to the sights of her form from the front, but he was just as happy to stare at her face.

She was wearing makeup as she always did, but not too much, it was never too much. Her eyebrows were shadowed with a green tint that brought out her deep blue eyes. A light, glossy shade of crimson colored her lips, giving them a sweet and sticky appeal.

She always managed to look beautiful, from the moment she woke to the minute she fell asleep. Howard often found it amazing how she could pull off such a feat; even when she was ill or drunk and violently vomiting she still managed to shine.

Everyone admired her. Men wanted to be with her, and because of her great, warm personality, women wanted to be her friend. Howard had been her first and only love, they had met in a nightclub, she was twenty-one and he was twenty-five. The first time he laid eyes on her he wanted her, and if there was something he wanted, he always got it.

"Well?" She said with a smile.

Howard returned the gesture. He walked up to her, kissed her, and then wrapped his arms around her. He closed his eyes and sunk his face into her thick blonde hair. He sucked in a deep breath and filled his lungs with the flowery fragrance lingering there, before slowly letting her go.

"What are you cooking?" he asked, looking past her at the mass of chopped vegetables.

"It's a surprise," she replied.

Howard raised his eyebrows, "Surprise? Your cooking's always a surprise darling," he joked. She lightly slapped his shoulder.

"You'll like it, trust me."

Howard nodded and sat down at the kitchen table. He picked up the local newspaper from the surface and tried to focus on the articles.

"This must be a record," she said looking at a sleek metallic clock above the sink.

"What?"

"You're on time for once," she smiled widely at him but he didn't return the gesture.

"You look shattered," Elizabeth said after a moment's silence, a hint of concern in her voice.

Howard dropped the paper on the table and slumped lazily over it.

"I am," he confirmed. "I always am."

"Maybe you should take a few days off," she offered. "There are plenty of qualified people who can run the place without you there."

"I feel better when I'm in control."

Elizabeth nodded.

After a long silence, he asked, "How was work today?"

"It was fine." Elizabeth paused and smiled, a look of reminiscence flickered across her eyes. "You know little Peter?"

"Not really."

"You know, short kid with a lisp, very quiet. His dad owns the local newsstand."

Howard merely shrugged.

"Well, anyway," she continued, undeterred. "We were painting today, I told them to paint something they had seen recently, something on their minds, their memories. All the other kids were drawing their houses, pets, parents, you know . . . the usual. But Peter . . . well his was a little more pornographic."

"Really?" Price said, shocked. "He's what? Four, five?"

"I know, but it wasn't like that. He had drawn a bed and what looked like two matchstick men getting a little . . . heated." Elizabeth smiled. "I asked him what it was and he said it was his parents last night," she laughed. "The poor kid said he went in to ask if he could watch television because he couldn't sleep, but they seemed 'busy' so he went back to bed."

Price smiled, "And he didn't realize?"

"Of course not, he's four for God's sake."

"Well, I don't know, do I? You work in a nursery; you're the expert on children. I've only ever worked with rich idiots and adolescent wannabes all my life."

"What about Lisa?" Elizabeth asked.

"That's different."

"How?"

"I'm her father; if she wants to ask questions about sex or babies . . . she goes to you," he smiled.

Elizabeth also smiled, "Well, I'm finished with work for a while now, anyway."

"I don't know why you don't go full-time. You're good at what you do; you should be working more than one or two days a week. You enjoy it, right?"

"I do, but I also enjoy looking after Lisa and the house. I prefer being home," Elizabeth said warmly. "Plus, I've got the next three weeks off work, I'm on my vacation."

"You work two days a week and they still give you a vacation?"

Elizabeth smiled and shrugged it off. "Dinner will be ready in half an hour, darling."

Howard stood, loitering, his eyes wandering, "Is the babysitter arranged for tonight?"

"Yes, darling." She walked away from the counter and embraced her husband. "Ten years," she said with a grin. "I hope you're getting me something big . . . and expensive, I deserve it being married to *you* for *this* long."

Howard laughed. "You'll see tonight," he confirmed.

He held her tightly for a second longer, then let her go and kissed her gently on the cheek.

"Happy anniversary, darling."

6

Phillips rolled the Jaguar onto the sparsely populated parking lot of an apartment complex, its tires crunching against the old pavement, hitting divots, stones, and shards of glass as he parked the car in one of the many empty spaces.

Next to the stolen Jaguar was a silver Vauxhall owned by the pair. The car was five-years-old and had been bought by the two friends over four months ago, replacing an equally inconspicuous and cheap vehicle.

Richards hopped out of the car like an excited kid, the money from his pouch now packed into a duffel bag. He sucked in the afternoon air, a smug expression filling his features.

Three teenagers gathered close to the ground floor of a large apartment building, surrounding an area made to store bikes. They were huddled together against the graffiti stained walls, nervously looking over their shoulders, alerted to the sound of the approaching Jaguar. After a few idle glances—weighing up the two conmen—they continued to talk quietly amongst themselves; pillows of smoke drifted out of the huddled circle.

Richards felt something slam into his leg, almost bringing him to his knees. The bag spilled out of his hands and he groaned in frustration as the money-filled sack dropped onto the floor.

He looked up to see four young kids staring at him, no more than ten-years-old. They were playing soccer in the center of the enclosure, using the door to an unoccupied apartment as a goal. They were grinning widely at him, amused by his reaction.

"Hey, throw us the fucking ball back, you pussy," one of them bellowed, encouraging cheers of laughter from his friends.

Richards looked down to see that the item that struck him was a soccer ball, the stitching ripped and the panels worn.

"Give the little bastards the fucking ball back, would you, Mickey," Phillips said as he clambered out of the car.

Richards looked down at the soccer ball, his heart still pounding.

"You fucking deaf?" another kid added.

Phillips shot an angry glance their way, "Watch your fucking mouth, you little shit, or I'll come over there and fucking rip you a new one."

"You wouldn't dare," the kid said, clearly unsure of his own words.

Phillips glared at him and began walking toward him.

The kid held up his hand and took an instinctive step backwards. "Sorry man, look . . . just give us the ball back," he pleaded.

Phillips laughed, turned, and began walking past the car and to a flight of stairs. "Give the little inbred fuckwit his ball, Mickey," he said as he turned a corner—his footfalls bounding on the metal stairs in the distance.

When Phillips disappeared from view, the kids returned to taunting Richards. The con man just smiled. He rolled the ball forward, clear of the car. Then, resting his foot on its rough surface, he flicked it up, juggled it between his feet and smacked it high and hard, past the entrance and into the road beyond.

He grinned as he heard the sound of the ball bouncing on the downhill road.

The youngsters looked towards the entrance in surprise. They stood motionless for fleeting seconds then exploded all at once.

"What the fuck did you do that for?"

"Asshole!"

"Get the fucking ball!"

With a smile spread wide across his face, Richards picked up the bag, holstered it over his shoulder then headed for the stairs.

Rokers Court was filled with drug addicts, petty thieves, single mothers, and uncontrollable kids. The three story building with its thirty apartments circled around a large car park and a concrete play area. The stairs and elevators to access the higher tiers of the apartment building were decorated with graffiti, cigarette butts, beer cans, burned foil, and the odd hypodermic needle.

In every niche and sheltered hole around the apartment building, addicts could be found shooting heroin, snorting cocaine, popping pills, and drinking themselves to oblivion. Kids from the age of ten were getting high in the bike sheds or on the balconies.

It had a law of its own. The residents rarely called the police, and outsiders wanted nothing to do with the place.

Occasionally, someone would be dropped off in the back of a police van or escorted to the station for violating probation or missing curfews, but the residents saw a lot more crime than police.

That suited Phillips and Richards. They had hooked up an elaborate security system to their apartment, but, as of yet, no one had attempted to gain access. The apartment was cheap—rented for the price of a fix from an unscrupulous council-house tenant—and expendable, nothing inside could be linked to them. They didn't live there. Neither of them could bring themselves to do that; they were criminals, but they still wanted some semblance of peace and safety. The apartment was just a hideout, a safe place, a glorified storage unit.

Phillips climbed the final step and turned the corner on the second floor, passing three doors before halting at the one he sought. The door was covered in graffiti, burn marks, and flaked paint like the rest of the apartments. It was like that when they bought it, and they had decided that if they were to fit in, they wouldn't change the rotting exterior.

He stuck the key in the lock and turned to his friend, crossing the walkway noisily behind him. "I heard the kids shouting. What the fuck did you do?"

Richards shrugged.

"Just be careful, would you? We need to keep a low profile. Those kids have parents . . . I think. It just takes one little runt to start spreading news and the next thing we know we have a group of junkies throwing bricks through our windows." Phillips waited until Richards stood beside him before he turned the key and allowed his friend to enter the apartment first.

He glanced down both sides of the long, second floor balcony. Two youths were smoking cigarettes and drinking cans of beer at the far end but took little notice of the con men. After studying them for a moment, Phillips walked into the apartment and slammed the door shut behind him.

Richards had dropped the duffel bag in the small corridor entrance. Phillips watched as his friend unhooked a landscape painting from the brown-tinged walls to reveal a keypad.

He jabbed at the pad, punching out seven digits. A digital beep sounded from the bottom of the two walls which led into the living room and the rest of the apartment.

Richards replaced the landscape picture, picked up the bag and, with Phillips on his tail, walked through the corridor and into the living room. Phillips's steps were slow and deliberate as he strode through the apartment, his eyes on his feet as they made their way into a dingy room.

"Two years," Richards said as he dropped the sack onto a beige sofa, "and you still watch your footing every time you come through."

"It's hard to get used to the idea of walking through a laser trip line attached to ten pounds of fucking Semtex," Phillips said.

"There's nowhere near ten pounds in there."

"I don't give a fuck how much there is," Phillips threw himself onto the sofa. "It'll still gonna blow me to shit."

"It's safe."

"I don't trust technology," Phillips confessed.

"It was your idea," Richards reminded him.

"But you set it up."

"What's that supposed to mean?"

"If it goes wrong, you're to blame."

"Fair enough," Richards reached over and unzipped the bag. "When your brains have decorated the walls and your balls are halfway down the corridor, you can blame me all you fucking like."

"Twenty fucking five," Phillips mumbled, his eyes staring at the contents of the glass tumbler in his hand. He paused to take a sip of the Jack Daniels, sighing in delight as the liquid worked its warmth through his body. "Twenty fucking five," he repeated, "and we still live together like we did when we were eighteen." He looked across at Michael Richards who was taking a sip from his own glass—half filled with Coke.

"Nothing wrong with it," Richards said, slurring slightly. "If we lived with girlfriends or wives—if we had any that is—then we wouldn't have gotten this far, we wouldn't have been this successful."

"Successful? We're fucking con men Mickey. We're liars. Anyone could do this shit."

"Maybe so . . . but we haven't been caught. That takes a different class."

"Good point," Phillips said, his eyes had wandered to the large window at the far side of the room. The world outside was still and dark, the moon had covered the foliage bundled close to the window with a deathly glow. "But maybe that's been our problem."

"What d'you mean?"

"I mean, if we aimed higher, took a bigger risk. If we tried for a big score, if we—"

Richards slumped back in the recliner, "We'd be in jail" he said, finishing his friend's sentence.

Phillips merely shook his head.

"We have it good," Richards slurred. "I mean look at this house," he paused and glanced around the living room of the detached three-bedroom house. This was their real home. The apartment was a cover, a place to stash the cash and to hide out on occasion. It was too exposed, too risky, and Richards also couldn't live in the same house as several pounds of explosive—active or not. The house was just as inconspicuous, situated in a nothing piece of suburbia in an estate that the police only ever visited to turn down a stereo or respond to complaints about footballs in gardens, missed garbage pick-ups, and neighborly disputes.

The walls of the house had been decorated in a gray tint and adorned with many paintings, photographs, and ornaments. A small marble fireplace rested against the wall furthest away from the sofa. On the other wall, close to the large bay window, was a fifty-inch LCD screen with a sub-woofer, four tall standing speakers, a SKY box, three game consoles, and a DVD player.

The only pieces of furniture in the room was an immaculate black leather armchair and sofa.

"People work their asses off to get places like this, and then they spend the next twenty-five years paying off the fucking mortgage." Richards smiled warmly. "It certainly beats my parents place."

"Mine too." Phillips said.

"That's different, yours are in prison."

"Yep, best fucking place for them as well." He took another sip of whiskey, "You know," he began slowly, "a few of the neighbors think we're gay."

Richards burst out laughing, spilling whiskey and Coke down his chin.

"I'm serious, I was in the yard the other day, cleaning up dog shit from that fucking hound down the road, and that old lady next door popped her head over the fence. She started on about how we never speak, blah blah fucking blah, then she said, 'you and your partner should come around for dinner and drinks on Saturday.'" Phillips paused as Richards continued to laugh in his drunken stupor.

"I thought she might have seen me with that chick from the newsstand, you know, Rita . . . Rachel, whatever her name was, bit short, big tits, you know?"

Richards nodded.

"So I tried to tell her, I said that was just a friend, she wasn't my partner. Then she smiles at me . . . 'I know' she fucking says, 'I mean that young, handsome boyfriend of yours.'"

"She's just old and confused," Richards said.

"Not like I have anything against it. I'm just annoyed that she thought I couldn't do better than you. If I had my choice of men, and I'm sure I would, I wouldn't pick *you*."

"Harsh."

"But true. You'd do very well to get me, admit it."

Richards laughed his friend's comment off. "How did you get out of the dinner invitation then?"

"I told her we couldn't make it that weekend. I said we were celebrating our anniversary."

7

"Tonight was fantastic, darling," Elizabeth Price slurred her words.

Howard Price merely nodded, holding his wife's arm as she rested her weight against his shoulder.

"Ten years. This is just the start," she assured him. "We'll have many more years together."

Howard smiled and kissed her flushed cheek, sucking the warmth onto his cold lips. "Be quiet darling," he said. "We don't want to wake Lisa up."

"She'll be awake. She won't sleep unless you tuck her in. Anyway, we said we'd be back at eleven and its only ten," she said reassuringly as they both reached the door.

"It's ten past eleven darling," he said, fumbling in his pocket for the house keys.

She glanced at her new gold watch, squinted, winked, and rubbed her eyes before commenting: "Oh. So it is."

Howard unlocked the front door and carefully ushered his stumbling spouse into the house.

"I really like this," she said, her eyes still fixed on the watch.

"So you keep telling me."

"I keep telling you because I *do* really like it."

"You keep telling me because you're drunk," Price corrected her.

"That too," she agreed with a gleeful laugh. "You should have had a drink with me tonight."

"Someone had to drive," Howard reminded her.

"You always drive, why couldn't we get a taxi?" she wondered. "Or a limo."

He smiled into her glazed eyes, "You know I don't like being driven around, and the restaurant is only three miles away, I didn't think a limo would be necessary."

She shrugged. Her eyes still glared into his, but she was losing touch with reality with every passing second, night and the sedating touch of alcohol was settling in her mind and shutting it down.

He caressed her cheek, kissing her softly on the lips. She stayed motionless, her eyes still closed from the kiss as he pulled his lips away from hers. She swayed slightly.

Howard steadied her balance and helped her take her coat off. "Why don't you go on up to bed, darling," he whispered "I'll be with you soon."

She nodded and staggered to the stairs, which she climbed with great difficulty.

Howard watched her stumble and stagger her ascent, before turning his attention to the doorway and the grouchy figure standing there.

"Did you have a good night?" Joanna Walcott asked, her posture slumped and tired.

"Very nice," Howard said meekly.

"How much did it take to get her *that* wasted?" the teenaged babysitter asked, pushing her reading glasses up from her nose.

Howard smiled at the eighteen-year-old, "Not long" he looked her up and down—he always thought there was something odd about her, and not just because she dressed like an unkempt, middle-aged man.

"How was Lisa?" Howard wondered, following the teenager into the living room as she collected an assortment of textbooks and papers.

"A sweetheart as always."

"What time did she go to sleep?"

"Well, she went to bed about two hours ago," Joanna stood in front of Howard, all of her textbooks grasped tightly to her chest. "But she insisted that she'd stay awake. She wanted to see you. To read her a story she said." She smiled and brushed past him. "I'll be heading off now."

"How much do I owe you?"

"Elizabeth gave me the cash this morning."

"Do you want a ride? It's cold out."

"It's okay, the fresh air will do me good," she said without turning around. "It's only around the corner after all, I'll just walk."

Howard watched her go and then walked upstairs. He heard muffled grumbles of annoyance as he passed his bedroom door.

The door was slightly ajar, he paused to peak through. He saw his wife trying to undress herself by the side of their bed, struggling to unhook her dress before eventually conceding defeat and moving onto her socks. She lost her balance and fell flat on the bed, her face buried into the plush duvet. Within seconds he heard the sound of her snoring.

The door at the end of the corridor was also slightly ajar, a green light beamed through the opening. He pushed the door open, being careful not to make a noise, but his efforts were futile.

"Hello, daddy."

He smiled as he heard the sweet voice of his daughter. She lay on her back, watching the door with a tired smile; an assortment of shadowed shapes, thrown by the nightlight, danced on her soft face.

"What are you doing awake this late?" he asked, sitting on the edge of the bed.

"I was waiting for you," she replied with a giggle. "Where's mommy?"

Howard paused and looked into his daughter's eyes.

"She's . . . asleep."

"She's drunk you mean."

Howard smiled and nodded. "You heard her?"

"She was singing when she went to her bedroom."

She lifted her head from her pillow and sat up on the mattress, her small face inches from his. He stared at her through the soft green glow, his heart filled with warmth.

"Will you tell me a story now?"

"Sure. Which one do you want? *Cinderella*? *Snow White*?" his eyes scanned the bookshelf near her bed which was barely visible in the dull light. "What about *James and the Giant Peach*?"

"Okay," she said instantly, a twinkle of contentment in her eyes which suggested that no matter what he read it would always be the sound of his voice that offered her the most enjoyment.

8

Peter Sanderson sat back on his leather armchair, a cigar held loosely between two fingers on his right hand. He lifted his small feet, dressed in polished loafers, onto the expansive desk in front of him, digging the heels into the varnished oak.

"You boys have done me proud again," he said, pillows of gray smoke escaping from his lungs as he spoke.

James Roach stood with his head held high and his eyes fixed on a blank space in between him and his boss. His arms were folded over his chest, a look of dominance and pride in his strong stature. Darren Morris leaned against one of the far walls in the smoky office, his hands dug deep into his pockets, his eyes strained so he could hold the hollow, dark eyes of the man twenty years his senior.

"Now what?" he questioned.

Sanderson could sit for days in his office and, due to his weight and health habits, his suits were usually softened with sweat patches and cigar ash, but today, Morris noted something else on his boss's jacket. A congealed orange stain had formed on the shoulder, surrounded by a smeared smudge of crimson.

"Now . . ." the older man said with a strained pause, sinking his old and broad shoulders further back on the leather chair. "I just ask someone else."

"Someone else to deal across the coast?"

Sanderson's blackened eyes turned to the strong figure of James Roach, holding him with his gaze. Then older man nodded and turned his attention back to Morris.

"Apparently, there was someone working alongside young Dean," he said. "While you two were *disposing* of him, a little birdie told me a story."

"Was that the same *birdie* that shit on your shoulder?" Morris questioned.

The older man paused, his eyes instinctively trying to look at the patch of congealed vomit on his shoulder.

"Just a little mishap," he said with a grin. "You remember Leon? The boy Harris and his cronies turned over?"

"Sure, he was in a hell of a state last time I saw him," Morris said.

"Yes, well now he's in a worse state. The little bastard had the nerve to ask me for a loan of five kilos. He fucks up, loses my money and my fucking gear then he has the nerve to ask me for a fucking loan." A tide of anger rose and then dissipated behind his eyes.

He paused, flicked more ash into the sliver ashtray. "I had a few of the boys dispose of him last night," he brushed at the dried stain on his jacket. "The little bastard was so scared he threw up on me."

Morris nodded. He felt a tinge of anger welling up inside him.

"As I was saying," Sanderson said in a lighter tone. "Harris wasn't alone, and I wasn't the only one supplying him. He was involved with a smuggling operation, a fucking big one at that. Word is they're bringing in huge shipments of ecstasy, about a quarter mill each month. Not the usual shit either, this stuff is pure rocket fuel."

"Bullshit," Morris spat, bringing a look of distaste to the menacing brow of his boss. "Harris was small time; most what he made was from coke and smack, with the profits going back on buying more of the shit from you."

"Harris was only a pawn in this, nothing more than a runner. The pills brought him to the city, not much call for that down his way. It just so happened that while he was here he decided to sell his other supplies."

"Where is this leading?" Morris wanted to know.

"I need information," Sanderson said with a grin that displeased Morris.

"What sort of information?"

"I need to know who's bringing the pills into the country; I want to know everything about this operation. Someone is selling drugs on my turf, right under my fucking nose. I need you boys to sort them out," he regarded them both, like an officer would after giving orders to his soldiers.

"An operation that big will take more than just us two," Morris said. "We ain't fucking super sleuths, we're just hitters."

"I know, I know," Sanderson said with a reassuring smile. "I have a few others on the case; they're providing me with all the information about the wankers peddling this shit. All you two need to do is follow it, find the fuckers and get me a link to the source."

He dug the cigar between his yellowed teeth and rolled his chair backwards. Opening a drawer behind his desk he rummaged through a pile of papers, dropping one onto the surface of the desk.

"All the details I have are there," he gestured to the folder with the tip of his cigar. "A couple of my boys tracked down a few small-time dealers selling at the local clubs. I need you to finish off the work."

"Why d'you even care?" Morris inquired. "You have a supply straight out of the country. You supply all the fucking kids in the city with this shit."

"Like I said," Sanderson began. "The pills floating about now are fucking dynamite. Next to them, the stuff I sell looks like Smarties, it's cut so much. And . . ." the older man paused; Morris could see a look of extreme distaste spread across his face. "They're selling for a lot less than my gear. I can't afford to knock down the prices." He grinned his sadistic grin again, "I can't compete with the competition so I need you two to throw a wrench in it."

Roach reached for the paper and quickly stuffed it into his jacket pocket, not taking the time to read its contents.

"Here," Sanderson pointed to two large padded envelopes on the desk. "There's your cash from the Harris hit. Pull off this one and I'll consider giving you boys a little extra."

"I can't fucking believe him," Morris said as he opened the door to the Mondeo, clambering into the passenger seat as Roach seated himself behind the wheel. "We drove for five fucking hours last night to sort out Harris. All because he turned one of Sanderson's boys over—who, surprise, surprise, also ends up in a fucking body bag. What was the point?"

"It's all about respect I guess," Roach offered.

"I don't know about you but I certainly don't respect that fucking fat shit," he said bitterly. "We've been carrying out all his fucking dirty work for nine years now, and what do we get to show for it?"

"Looks like six grand," Roach held one of the padded envelopes in his hand, his piercing eyes scanning the wad of cash inside. "Each," he added, dropping the envelope onto Morris's lap and tossing the other into the back seat.

"You ever get the feeling that it isn't worth it?" Morris asked as Roach turned the keys and revved up the engine.

"Not really. It's good money and easy work."

"It's murder. If we get caught we're fucking screwed. Sanderson can pay himself off, but if *we* get caught he wouldn't bat a fucking eyelid. He'd let us rot."

"That's the risk we take. He needs people like us to do his dirty work," Roach said, his eyes on the back window as he reversed the car out of the car park surrounding the warehouse complex, "and we need people like him to pay us for doing it."

"Do we?" Morris said blankly, his eyes fixed on the bustling warehouse which operated as an import and export business and covered up Sanderson's illegal activities.

"What do you mean?"

"Nothing," Morris answered, staring off into space.

"Don't go getting any ideas, Darren—we have it good. It's easy money for people like us, it keeps my wife in fucking shoes, and it keeps you, well . . . Gambling."

Morris laughed. "How is your wife?"

"Still a fucking bitch."

"Is she still having it with the milkman?"

"I wish," Roach replied. "It would give me an excuse to get rid of her, she's fucking expensive. How about you Darren? Are you still wasting your life away at the bookies?"

"Pretty much."

"Picked any winners recently?"

"Who knows . . . I'm just—"

"Just in it for the social interaction," Roach said, finishing off Morris's sentence.

"Am I that predictable?"

"Not really, you're just a shit gambler. If you win I always fucking hear about it."

Silence veiled the car as the warehouse became a blip in the rear-view mirror.

"Here," Roach was the first to break the silence; he reached into his pocket and pulled out the crumpled piece of paper he took from Sanderson's desk. "Take a look at that, we might as well sort some of this shit out before lunch."

9

Slowly, and with great deliberation, Phillips opened his eyes—feeling every increment as his eyelashes seemed to stick to each other. Even after prying his eyes open, his vision was still blurry and dull around the edges.

"Morning."

The slurred voice came from the other side of the room and grated against his growing headache. Phillips squinted to see the slumped form of Michael Richards, his body lazily slumped over the leather armchair; his eyes half concentrating on the television, which had been turned down low.

"How long you been awake?" Phillips choked, surprised at how dry his throat felt.

"Not long enough to move, as you can see," Richards's voice was a dry rasp.

Phillips released a long yawn and pushed his body up. He had been slouched awkwardly on the sofa and as he propelled himself upright he felt a painful twinge in his left shoulder.

"Put the coffee on would you, Mickey?" he pleaded. He rubbed his shoulder, trying to restore the proper flow of blood.

"Shit," Richards muttered.

"I'm dying for a coffee," Phillips stated.

"That makes two of us, but I ain't got the strength to move yet."

Phillips shrugged and sank back into the sofa. "What are you watching?" he asked, turning his eyes to the television screen as it panned out to show an African wilderness.

"Some animal show, it was on when I woke up, we must have left the TV on last night."

Phillips nodded slowly. He looked at Richards. "You're not gonna turn it off?"

"Can't."

"Why not?"

"The remote is on the windowsill."

"Ah."

They fixed their attentions back on the television, their hazy eyes staring unblinkingly at the screen.

"Maybe there'll be something decent on after this," Richards offered.

"Maybe."

"Do you think it's wise?" Richards stood over his friend with a cup of coffee.

"Why not?" Phillips offered.

Richards shrugged. His hangover was quickly fading. He couldn't handle his drink and always suffered, but last night he hadn't drunk much before falling asleep. His brain trickled off into a spasm of thought. He instinctively took the cup from Phillips and held the hot ceramic mug in his hands.

"Two hits in two days?" Richards asked. He took a sip of coffee and reveled in its warmth as the liquid sparked life into his tired body.

"It's not really two days when you think about it," Phillips said. He had taken a seat on the leather sofa, his own cup of coffee grasped lightly in one hand. "The hit on the Robinson safe took six weeks of planning."

"It was worth it in the end," Richards said, regaining his voice as he continued to sip the scalding liquid—moistening his vocal cords with each caffeinated swig.

"I know that, but we still need more cash, we need a quick hit, something we can pull off without much hassle." Phillips leaned forward. "We need an easy earner."

"There's no such thing, you know that."

"Maybe," Phillips agreed. "But if we put our minds to it we can do it."

Phillips looked across at his friend hopefully, but a look of apathy had settled on Richards's face. "What about the construction site job we did two years ago," Phillips continued. "We pulled that off in two days"

Richards nodded his head in recollection. When he spoke, he did so over the rim of the coffee cup, his eyes gazing into space. "We stole gear from one construction site and sold them to another a mile down the road, we got lucky. What are the chances of two completely different small-time construction companies setting up developments within a mile of each other—again," Richards paused to take a long drink. "Plus, we already had a van hired from the removals job, we were lucky enough to find the two construction sites in the first place. If we hadn't taken a detour to escape the *real* removal company, we would have never latched onto the other con."

"Exactly, but as soon as we drove past the sites we came up with the idea, and hours later we were using the van to shift the tools from one site to the other."

"That was a fucking tiring day, two hours to help the family move house, a couple more to unload the gear from the van into the lockup, then back to lugging fucking bricks, slates, and tools. Took me four days to recover," Richards confessed.

"It was worth it, though, right?"

"Definitely fucking worth it," he said, a big smile on his face. "But that was a one in a million, we were lucky."

"I know, but who says we can't get lucky again?"

Phillips's words hung in the air. Richards drained the remains of his coffee, the final drops of the brown liquid still steamed with a powerful heat.

"You have any ideas?" he asked, putting the cup to one side.

"None whatsoever, but we can find something."

"Why don't we just keep playing it safe? We're still bringing in bundles of cash."

"We spend all day lying around, getting pissed, and fucking local tarts."

"Speak for yourself."

"In the old days we'd have shit loads of cons lined up, all big money."

"Most of which were half-assed and nearly landed us in jail," Richards warned.

"Times change, the hits we had back then we could pull off easy now. Then we were just kids, we always fucked up, most of the time we never even left with the money. But we worked the streets, we didn't wait for the cons to come to us, we found them."

Richards nodded. "Why the sudden change of heart? What's brought this up?"

"We need money," Phillips said without hesitation. "We need to climb the ladder, we need to open up the bookies, I'm sick of this fucking bullshit."

"You're sick of the game? You're fucking joking, aren't you?"

"I just want the money," Phillips rested his back against the plush sofa. "When we open up this shop we'll be rolling in it."

"You're rushing it."

Phillips shrugged. "We're pro's Mickey. We can pull off anything, anywhere. We could have the money by next week if we wanted."

Richards rose slowly, sighing heavily as his lower back throbbed. He shot a worried look at his friend. "You need to watch what you're doing Johnny; we'll get the shop. We just need to take our time. If we start rushing, we'll start fucking up." He wandered into the kitchen, carrying his empty mug with him.

Phillips sat motionless on the sofa, deep in thought.

10

Howard Price heartily stuffed the remains of his breakfast into his mouth. The final crumbs from a blackened piece of toast collapsed onto his blue pajama top. He took a sip from his coffee to wash them down, wincing in distaste as the hot liquid burned its way to his stomach.

"You didn't put any sugar in here love," he said.

Elizabeth Price stood at the kitchen counter, her eyes wandering over the table where her husband and daughter sat eating breakfast, her mind elsewhere. Her bloodshot eyes stared at Howard in what seemed to be confusion.

"The coffee," Howard said in confirmation, holding the cup in the air.

She nodded in recognition and walked towards the table.

"Are you still drunk, mummy?" Lisa studied her mother's sullen complexion over the rim of her cereal bowl.

Elizabeth collected the hot cup from her husband and shot her daughter a sly smile. "I'm not drunk, I'm just a little tired," she said.

"But daddy said you went out like a light last night."

Howard grinned to himself and continued to read the morning paper, listening to his daughter's words with interest.

"I was tired. I still am," Elizabeth explained.

"How much sleep have you had?" Lisa asked.

"I don't know, about eight hours I guess," Elizabeth said, scooping two mounds of sugar into Howard's coffee.

"I've had about the same, and I'm not tired," Lisa said matter of factly.

"That's different, I'm older—" her mother began to explain.

"A *lot* older," Lisa said quickly, "but you're not normally like this in the morning."

"Well, I was drinking last night."

"You can't handle your drink, can you?" She fed a spoonful of cereal into her mouth and watched her mother's slow reactions.

"Who said that?" Elizabeth asked with an eyebrow raised in suspicion.

"I just did," she spilled a drop of milk on her chin, it dribbled over her chin and dropped onto her pink night dress, she dabbed at it disinterestedly.

"How did . . ." Elizabeth began but soon stopped herself. "No, I can't handle my drink. But I *did* drink a lot."

Lisa looked at Howard who shook his head; Elizabeth saw the exchange.

"Stop ganging up on me, I'm tender," she pleaded.

Lisa giggled and continued to chomp away at her cereal.

"Half the bloody day is gone," Howard mumbled after a moment's silence. "It's past ten and I'm still not dressed."

"So, what? We had a lie in; it's our anniversary . . . or was. We deserve the rest, and you're on your vacation now remember?"

Howard grimaced, "I remember," he said, recalling a conversation the night before in which he agreed to take a couple of weeks off from work to relax and spend more time with his family. "I was just hoping you wouldn't."

Elizabeth smiled and replaced Howard's cup of coffee from which he drank immediately; the sweetened drink perked him up somewhat.

"Don't forget to call in, make sure they know you won't be there for a while."

"They already know I took a long weekend, but . . ." he allowed his sentence to trail off.

Elizabeth smiled, "Your version of a long weekend is a Saturday, which would make today your first, and last day off. You're not very good at taking a break are you? Just chill out around the house. Get some rest, watch some television."

"Sitting around all day isn't my style," Howard said, rising to his feet, leaving half a cup of coffee on the table. "What do you say we run into town?" he asked Lisa.

His daughter gave him a toothy grin. "Okay."

"Great," he dipped his head to kiss his daughter on the cheek. "I'll go get dressed, make a few phone calls, and then we can leave your mother and her hangover alone."

11

Richards shifted uncomfortably in his seat. The hard-upholstered pub bench did little to aid his aching back.

Ahead of him, beyond the empty oak table hiding his feet, a game of pool ensued between four men, two were around Richards's age—sporting casual sleeveless shirts and similarly unkempt jeans—the other two were clearly a lot older, one wore a creased suede jacket that matched his age-worn features while the other wore dirt splattered overalls.

Dinner time at the Holly and Apple pub always brought in a mixed crowd. Beyond the pool table, across from the long stretched bar, stood a row of six dinner tables, only three of which were occupied.

Richards eyed the customers curiously. At the table closest to the bar sat a young couple, they ate their meals heartily and steadily drank beer from half pint glasses. He noted how the man frequently lifted his eyes from his plate to gaze longingly into his partner's eyes. Every time he paused to take a drink he would gawk at her while she ate her lunch. Richards noticed a diamond engagement ring twinkle on her finger when she took a small sip from her glass.

The table next to the young lovers was empty. Ceramic place mats, knives, forks, spoons, and a single red rose in a thin glass vase had been neatly set on the polished oak for the ghostly customers. The flower hung over the rim of the moisture smeared vase, its petals fading and darkened; its stem browning in the dissipating water, waiting for nourishment while reaching out for company. None of the other tables donned such romantic flora, and he could only hazard a guess why this one did.

The next table was filled with laughter, loud conversation, and complaints. A couple, a few years older than Richards, sat at opposite ends of the table, but, unlike the lovers two tables away, their attention wasn't fixed on each other. At either side of the table sat two young boys. The eldest of the two ate his food carefully, poking through a mass of vegetables with the bewilderment of an archaeologist stumbling across a lost civilization; the younger child complained to his distressed mother about the food, clearly on the verge of a tantrum. The father seemed humored by his child's antics, almost encouraging him.

The next two tables were unoccupied. No silverware decorated the oak. A half empty, unwanted glass of soda had been left on one.

On the final table, tucked away in the corner of the room, sat a middle-aged man slowly eating a plate of fries. He looked well-presented but reeked of nervousness. His hair had probably been gelled and combed hours earlier, but sweat and humidity had unsettled the fair strands of black. Despite the heat and the indoor conditions, he wore a long trench coat with the collar flicked up to hide his neck.

Richards watched the man with interest. He ate very defensively. Instead of bringing the fries to his mouth he moved his mouth near the plate, a strange act which brought his head inches from the table. After stuffing some of the fried potatoes into his mouth he would then lift his head while he chewed, staring at an empty chalkboard next to the bar.

After every other bite, he would carefully move his right arm across the table to grasp a glass of orange juice—inches from his motionless left hand—untwist himself, and then slowly take two small sips before ducking into the movement again and placing the glass back on the coaster to his left.

Richards smiled in bewilderment at the strange ritual.

"What the fuck are you smiling at?"

Richards shook himself out of his trance, taking his eyes away from the nervous man.

"Nothing," he watched as Johnny Phillips moved his body around the table, arching his back and twisting his midsection as he wove himself around the stained oak and sat next to his friend.

He regarded the gathering around the pool table suspiciously, shooting a threatening glare at one of the younger players who had begun conspicuously staring at their table.

"Eyeing up that girl?" Phillips asked as the intimidated player looked away.

"What?" Richards said.

Phillips shook his head, a smile edging his lips. In each hand, he held a pint of beer; he took a sip from one and passed the other to Richards.

"The one with the blonde hair and small tits," he explained motioning towards the young couple across the room.

"No," Richards replied blankly.

"Seems like your style, you like them flat-chested, don't you?"

"What the fuck makes you say that?"

Phillips laughed, "That last slut you fucked. Brenda."

"Breena," Richards corrected.

"Really?" Phillips raised his eyebrows.

"Yes."

"What kind of fucked up name is that?"

"Her parents were—" Richards paused to search his mind for the right word but Phillips spoke before his brain finished cycling through the dictionary.

"Stupid?"

"They were intelligent."

"And they named their kid Breena?"

"It's unique I guess, maybe it means something else in a different culture," Richards guessed.

"You have got to be fucking kidding me."

"Just—"

"Okay." Phillips agreed, reverting to his initial conversation, "She had tits like a twelve-year-old."

"They were fine, they were actually kinda big, she just never wore padded bra's I guess," he sipped the froth from the pint in front of him. "You had to see her naked."

Phillips nodded and downed a large amount from his own pint as silence descended over the pair.

"Funny you should say that," he said, releasing a long and pleasurable sigh as the cold liquid filled his tired body.

Richards looked across at his grinning friend, shocked.

"You didn't . . ."

"Fuck her? Not a chance, I'd rather do it by myself. I saw her coming out of your room one morning that's all. You were still passed out in bed. She was on her way to the shower wearing nothing but a pair of your skinny ass jeans."

"She never mentioned it to me," Richards said.

"She never saw me," Phillips explained. "I heard her heading out your room and I stuck my head through the door to sneak a peek." He laughed. "They were so fucking small, at first I thought it was you."

Richards nodded. "Fair enough."

"Whatever happened to her anyway?"

"Fuck knows."

"She's taken, you know," Phillips said.

"What?"

"The titless girl over there."

"I know. I saw the ring. It wasn't her I was looking at though."

Phillips scanned the other tables, "The fat chick with the noisy brats?"

Richards suppressed a laugh at his friend's persistence. "No, the guy in the corner there," he nodded to the nervous individual who was still eating his fries.

Phillips hushed his voice, "Found a score?"

"No, not yet. We'll not get much from that guy anyway. I'm guessing single, lonely, nervous disorder . . . maybe an ex-alcoholic living in the shelter down on Newbank Street. Definitely a beggar."

"I was away for five minutes and you got all of that?"

Richards nodded.

"The single and lonely part is easy," Phillips said with his gaze fixed on the man. "No indication of a ring and he's far too uncomfortable in a quiet pub for someone who enjoys any social activity whatsoever. Nervous disorder is clear; maybe obsessive compulsive. Not sure where you got the rest from though."

"Look at his face and his glass," Richards stated. "He's shaved today; he still has the cuts to prove it, far too many cuts. He has the shakes; his hand is vibrating the liquid in the glass when he's drinking."

"Maybe that's part of his anxiety."

"No, his eyes are sunken, he doesn't sleep much. His lips are dried, caked even, he keeps licking them—he can smell the alcohol. He's here for that. He wants to smell it. He looks dazed too, chances are he hasn't been sober for long."

Phillips looked impressed, his eyes captured each movement the lonely man made and confirmed the statements.

"What about the beggar part?"

"Look at the bottom of his jacket, near the back."

Phillips did as instructed and noticed a paint stained pattern, an imprint of blue and red on his coat.

"It's a tag from one of the local gangs," Richards said. "They spray the tunnels in the area. The town's only concern is with the bypass, it's the direct link to the shopping center from the housing estates. They have workers down there every other day cleaning the graffiti, yet the taggers keep painting it; it's a game to them. It means the paint's nearly always fresh. It's a hot spot for beggars and street musicians; no one can get to the shopping center by foot without passing through the tunnel. Looks like our lonely guy picked his spot too close to the tag."

"But what makes you think he lives in the shelter?" Phillips asked.

"That part is easy. They've implemented schemes for rehab patients in there. They give them free food and drink and they put a roof over their head in exchange for a community reinstatement program, which, depending on the individual and their problems, can range from digging gardens and laying concrete to fighting fears," Richards paused, his eyes studying the lonely man. "Such as social phobias and anxieties." He took a congratulatory drink from his cold beer.

"Fuck me," Phillips said. "You're getting good at this shit."

Richards smiled.

"I'm impressed," Phillips took a long drink. "Let's see how you are with these other fuckers," he motioned around the pub, his emphasis on the men playing pool. "We came here to pull a trick, so let's get started."

Richards didn't waste any time in picking his mark. He chose one of the older men at the pool table, the one in the overalls. He was dirty, he didn't look like he had much, but he was a trades-man. They didn't live a life of luxury, but they were never short of a few bucks. He hopped to his feet as soon as he saw the man nod to his friends and then head for the bathroom.

As Richards drew near, he could smell the soil that clung to the heavy fabric of the overalls. The man was at least twenty years his senior, and it smelled like he hadn't bathed since he was Rich-ards's age. The smell was fused with a mix of alcohol and tobacco and layered with a sickening stench of body odor.

The tradesman took a turn past a narrow archway near the pool table and walked through the bathroom door that he kindly held open for Richards. They both headed for the line of stained-white urinals directly opposite the door.

"Nothing like a few beers before dinner is there?" Richards said, making polite conversation.

The man gave Richards an odd look when he picked the urinal next to his and had began to make conversation.

"More like '*instead of* dinner," he replied with a polite laugh.

"Food in here that bad?"

"No, the food's okay. It's my stomach that's the problem, ain't been able to hold anything down for two days now."

Richards nodded knowingly, "My girl has the same problem. I guess there's a bug going around."

"Nah, it's the fucking kebab shop down Queen Street and the dirty fuckers that work there, had one the other night," he explained. "Wasn't so bad at the time but I was shitting through the eye of a needle the next morning."

Richards feigned a laugh and finished urinating. He was thankful for the outburst. A job was a job, but it felt better when the target was a bigot. He began to zip up his pants as he heard the door to the toilets creak open; shooting a look over his shoulder he saw Johnny Phillips enter and glance his way.

"Never been there," Richards sighed. "Thanks for the tip."

He slid his left hand inside the older man's right pocket, grasping a large wallet. Taking another glance over his shoulder he tossed the wallet backwards; Phillips caught it on his way to one of the cubicles.

Richards finished zipping up his trousers and walked over to one of the sinks near the line of urinals. He pushed down on the hot tap and watched as the water gushed violently.

"Finished so quickly?"

"I have the bladder of an eighty-year-old," Richards lied as he shoved his hands under the warm water. "One fucking pint and I'm rushing off to the toilet every five minutes."

Moments later the chain in one of the cubicles was pulled and the sound of rushing water filled the small space. At the same time the older man finished and, disregarding the sinks, he walked past Richards, flashed him a smile, and headed for the door.

Johnny Phillips emerged from the cubical with the man in his sights—his head low and his eyes aimed at the floor. He bumped into him, quickly reached out to steady the stranger who lost his footing, and then slipped the leather wallet back into his overalls.

"Shit, sorry mate," Phillips apologized. "I didn't see you there; I was in a world of my own."

He acknowledged the apology with a disoriented smile and moved to walk away, but Phillips stopped him in his tracks.

"Harry," Phillips said with surprised delight. "Harry Allcross."

The man looked shocked. "I'm sorry, do I know you?"

"Philip Smith," Phillips stated. "We took the same drunk driving course."

"Oh," he uttered, bemused. "At the community center?"

"Yes, don't you remember? I lost my license the same time as you. I was doing ninety on the highway after drinking enough whiskey to kill a herd of elephants," Phillips laughed and nudged the other man in a friendly gesture. "What were in you there in for again . . ." he paused, feigning recollection. Harry also waited. "You were driving for a landscaper or something, weren't you? Pissed on the job in a transit van, if I remember correctly."

"That's right," he said, seeming surprised. "That was quite a few years ago now though."

"You still work in gardening?"

"I run my own business now."

"The van outside is yours I take it? Allcross Gardening Services, I thought I recognized the name, but it didn't click till just now."

Silence fell over the pair. Richards watched on from behind them, a broad smile on his face.

"So what you doing with yourself then?" Phillips noted the lack of a wedding band or tan line on his finger. "Still not married?"

"No, single as ever," he replied with a friendly laugh. "Still living by myself. The business is taking off though, I have a few boys working for me but they're out of town at the minute. Gives me an excuse to pop in here for a few drinks, eh?" he laughed and nudged Phillips who laughed along with him.

"Anyway, it was good seeing you again," Harry said. "I'll have to get back in there; don't wanna keep the lads waiting."

Phillips smiled and they exchanged awkward goodbyes.

"You want to fill me in?" Richards quizzed as the door to the toilet swung shut.

"He's a drunk, or a recovering one at that. He's been convicted for drunk driving a ton of times. His driver's license is in his wallet," Phillips explained.

"So you figured he would have been through so many drunk driving schools that he wouldn't be able to remember anyone from any of them?" Richards looked impressed.

"That and the fact that he's a fifty-four-year-old drunk; he'll have a memory like a fish." Richards smiled at the comment. "He had two credit cards," Phillips flashed his notepad which contained Harry Allcross' account numbers. "And the dumb fucker even left a spare car key in there."

"Luck is on our side. What's the plan?"

"That's where you come in. That van outside is bound to be loaded with a few grands worth of equipment and we're going to steal it."

"Are you fucking mad?"

"Probably," he took out a twenty pound note from his pocket. "Take this," he gave him the cash, "courtesy of Mr. Allcross, don't worry he won't get suspicious; he had two hundred bills in there, I only took a twenty. I need you to keep him and his friends busy while I head down to Shoddy Simons and offload the gear, he'll take anything."

"And the cards? You know how I feel about holding onto things like that."

"Simon will take those too. Allcross is a business man so his limits will be high, they should fetch a good price."

Richards nodded.

"Keep him busy until I phone you," Phillips warned. "Don't let the fat fucker out of your sight."

They returned to their seats and drank in silence for a few moments before Phillips stood, drained his drink, and declared, "Well, I better get going." He raised his voice so the pool players could hear him, noting a smile of relief from Harry Allcross.

"My phone is fully charged," Richards mumbled over the rim of his glass. "Don't be too long."

After his friend departed Richards watched the game of pool unfold. Harry Allcross, seemingly shaken by the events, had missed his shot on the black, now one of the younger men was smiling down his cue, lining up an easy shot to the center pocket.

Richards took a small sip of his drink and walked over to the table. The black ball rolled into the center pocket as he placed his lager down on the mahogany rim.

They all looked at him curiously.

"Mind if I join you guys?" he asked. "I have a few hours to kill here, either that or I go back to my nagging girlfriend and listen to her whine on for the rest of the afternoon," his smile was returned.

"No problem mate," one of them said.

"Here," Harry handed Richards a cue. "See if you can beat Lee here," he motioned towards the man who had just won the game. "It's about time someone did."

Richards took the cue and laid it against the table. He dug his hand inside his pocket and pulled out the twenty-dollar bill. "You rack them up and I'll go get the drinks," he said, nodding to the man who held the other cue. "What's everyone having?"

12

Darren Morris squinted at the rumbled paper. The bright sun beamed a threatening glare through the car's windscreen, spilling yellow spotlight over the scrunched paper.

He read the words aloud, hailing the attention of James Roach who was skillfully maneuvering the car between a large transit van and a small hatchback.

"Joseph Steiner, eighteen years old."

"Another kid," Roach grunted in distaste.

"The fuckers are getting younger," Morris said. "It says we should find him, or someone that knows him, in the Queen's Head."

Roach nodded and brought the car to a halt.

Morris finished studying the sheet of paper that had been handed to him by his boss, crumpled it back up, and stuffed it into his jacket pocket. He had already run his eyes over its contents numerous times—it contained the details and brief descriptions of a few local dealers and their likely whereabouts.

They failed to find a parking space near the pub—a dilapidated little building dropped by the side of a boarded-up alley like discarded waste loitering near the base of a rubbish bin—so they parked at the supermarket down the street.

Sighing with a great deal of mental tiredness Morris pushed open the passenger-side door with a callous shove. The door slammed into the side of the transit van with a heavy thud, the sickening screech of metal against metal rang out from the impact.

"Shit!" he scrambled out of the car to inspect the damage to his own door.

Much to his surprise it had somehow escaped any real damage. He flicked away flecks of silver paint and examined a small dent around the handle with something resembling indifference plastered on his face.

Roach sucked in a lungful of air, "That's bad," he said to his colleague.

"No," Morris disagreed. "Just a few surface scratches, here," he beckoned "come have a look if you want." He looked at James Roach who, at the other side of the vehicle, was out of sight from the damage.

"No," Roach said. "I mean that," he nodded in the direction of the transit van. With a look of confusion Morris sharply turned around and looked at the white van.

A laugh creased onto his lips as his eyes scanned the large dent and thick scratch along the rolling door of the van. "Certainly took the fucking brunt of the hit didn't it?"

A shout broke their attention and removed his smile. "What the fuck is that!"

They both turned to see a man in his twenties storm up to them with a scowl. His clothes were stained with paint and ripped in numerous places. In his hand, he carried a shopping bag from the top of which poked a large paint roller.

As he neared the van he dropped the bag, the sponge roller spilled out and rolled to Roach's feet, who stood and stared at the instrument with an amused look.

"Is this your van?" Morris queried as the man brushed passed Roach and almost pushed Morris out of the way so he could inspect the damage.

"Yes, it is my fucking van," he shouted. "What the fuck have you done to it?"

Morris could feel his tiredness stabbing at the center of his forehead. The distraught van owner was inches away from him, his strong, heavy set, beer bellied, structure bore down on him.

Roach took a step forward; Morris didn't move.

"Just a little scrape," Morris replied with a casual shrug.

"I fucking saw you, you better fucking pay for this, or else," he roared with an intimidating glare. He was at least five-inches taller than Morris and Morris could almost feel the rage reeling out of his breath and down onto him.

Morris shrugged his shoulders and dug his hand into his pocket. He pulled out a wad of cash and began flicking through, counting as he did so. "Let's see, twenty, forty, fifty—"

The man ripped the wad out of his unsuspecting grasp. "I'll take it all thank you," he said, the hint of a playground bully in his tone. "This should cover it nicely," he added, feeling like he had the upper hand over the unresponsive hitman.

Morris looked across at Roach; a question of pure bewilderment filled his eyes. Roach merely smiled and shrugged, then, glancing in all directions to check the area was clear of midday shoppers, he turned his attention back to his colleague and nodded.

With a twinkle in his eye Morris turned to the taller man who was flicking through the cash. "Excuse me."

"What do you—" the man began, lifting his eyes.

He finished his sentence with an awkward grunt. Morris's fist made full contact with his chin, sending him sprawling against his van. Somehow, despite the fall against the vehicle and the shock of being punched, he managed to keep a hold of the wad of money, tightly grasping it in his right hand as he brought both hands to his throbbing chin.

Morris reached forward and yanked the wad of cash out of his hand. He quickly stuffed it into his pocket and took a step past the wounded man, who still clasped his hands to his jaw.

"Like I said," Morris said to Roach. "They just keep getting younger," both men smiled. Morris clasped the handle on the damaged door of the Mondeo and, just as the young man pulled his hands away from his face, he yanked it open. It crashed into the man's body, sending him sprawling again. The jagged corner of the door slammed into his ribs, breaking one on impact. He bent forward as the wind gushed out of his body.

Quickly grasping the van owner by his thick matted hair, Morris shoved his head into the open doorway.

He groaned, but his agonized body failed to move.

"You think this is smart?" Roach said, interrupting his colleague's activities.

Morris paused and looked up, his eyes filled with indifference, "Probably not, but—" with his eyes still holding the gaze of James Roach, Morris slammed the door shut. The man's skull was crushed between the door and the car. The door shuck violently after the impact and the younger man, now bleeding profusely from his head, collapsed to the floor. "Fuck it, eh?"

Roach checked the car park for any onlookers as his accomplice dug his hand into the dead man's pocket. "Just find the keys, dump him in his van, and let's get the fuck out of here," he said blankly.

Morris did as he was instructed. As he lifted the limp body up and laid it down inside the van he checked the time on the dead man's wrist watch. "Come on," he slammed the rolling door of the van shut. "If we get there now we might catch them before they stop serving lunch."

Darren Morris walked through the rusted doors of the Queen's Head pub with James Roach following close behind; his stature ready and alert for any attack or confrontation.

The street outside was fresh and mild, a light breeze hung in the air. Opposite the pub stretched a long line of semi-detached houses; the large supermarket could be seen towering over the back of the Victorian structures.

The sounds from the pub brushed onto the roadside. Light echoes of music dubbed with occasional laughing and conversation, but the roaring of the passing cars overpowered any coherence.

The combined stench of alcohol fumes, cigarettes, and poorly cooked food greeted the hitmen as they entered.

A few feet from Morris two young men were playing darts with an antique board that rested in a dark alcove like a forgotten work of art. A third man stood with his back against the tables drinking a pint, his deep gray eyes bore into the new newcomers over the rim of the glass.

Morris and Roach nodded politely at the observer and he quickly turned his attention back to the badly played game of darts, spilling insults and mocking comments in between sips of beer.

The pub was small and the bar stretched half its length. To the left of the entrance stood a long bench, with small tables strategically placed in front of it. Past the bench two large tables took up considerable space, big enough to seat four drinkers—currently empty.

Beyond the tables was a large pool table, a blue nylon sheet had been draped over it and someone had dropped a white cardboard plaque on its surface declaring: Out of Order.

Besides the three men, the only other customer was an elderly gentleman who sat alone, his pint and a folded newspaper resting on the table in front of him. His wrinkled features scanned the newcomers warmly; his eyes straining to see the two men who stood less than ten feet away.

They welcomed him with a warm smile and he mumbled an inaudible, friendly greeting to them before digging in his pocket and producing a pipe and a case of tobacco.

"He reminds me of my granddad," Roach said as they walked up to the bar.

"He reminds me of *every* fucking granddad."

A barmaid in her mid-thirties, who had been watching them since they entered, greeted them with a cold stare.

Morris held her in his gaze, running his eyes over her appearance as she in turn studied him. Her long multicolored hair hung around her round face and past her shoulders, its wavy strands stopping just above her ample breasts. She was short; no more than five-feet tall, and her body was compact.

She wore a sleeveless, tight white top that exposed her curves. Her skin was strongly tanned and appeared miraculously smooth and unmarked. Through the thin material of her white top Morris could see her large breasts.

"My eyes are up here mate," she said.

"Can't blame a guy for looking."

"What can I get you?" she said, her voice devoid of any hospitality.

"Two beers." He rested his elbows onto the wooden surface, taking some weight off his feet. Roach ghosted along by his side as the woman pulled out two pint glasses.

"What do you reckon?" Roach asked, nodding in the direction of the youngsters playing darts.

Morris didn't need to follow his colleagues gaze; he had already suspected the same thing. "Possible," he muttered, catching the eye of the barmaid. "They look about his age. If he isn't one of them, chances are they'll know who he is."

They took their drinks, found a seat, and then watched. Before they exchanged another word, they watched as one of the youngsters disappeared through a door next to the bar, into the small corridor leading to the bathrooms.

The hitmen exchanged a knowing glance, and then returned to their drinks. The two remaining kids continued their game of darts, their minds set on conversation and laughter rather than the poorly played game. The old man had sunken himself into the furniture, casually smoking his pipe as he read through the local paper; the barmaid chatted noisily on a cordless phone, trying to catch Morris's eye, who made a point of refusing to acknowledge her.

"You want to go, or shall I?" Roach asked.

"I'll go," Morris said quickly. "If you leave me alone then that crazy fucking slut might try talking to me."

"She seems all right."

"I wouldn't say no," Morris agreed. "She's fuckable, that's a fact, but she's probably been around the block more times than the paperboy." They both looked at her as he spoke, she was still bellowing loudly into the phone. "Plus, her voice is giving me a headache." He drained the remainder of his pint and headed for the corridor.

The bathroom door squeaked loudly on un-oiled hinges as Morris strode through. A sickening smell of stale urine, vomit, and cigarettes hit him like a wall and he twisted his face in distaste.

There was only one cubicle inside, the door to which had been violently torn from its hinges in a drunken rage, marks and slashes in the wood remained as evidence to the pointless attack. On the far wall a small window—jammed shut and smeared—obscured the view to the outside world; it allowed no air in and no stench out.

The youngster stood at the end of a urinal stretched along the wall, he had seen the older man enter the toilets and had regarded him with little interest. Morris walked beside him and unzipped his jeans.

"Are you Joseph Steiner?" Morris asked.

"What?"

"I was told he was the man to go to for—" Morris coughed, feigning anxiety. "You know . . ."

"I don't know what you're talking about mate."

"Come on mate," Morris pleaded. "Do me a favor, would you? I just got into town and I'm dry. I'm taking my girl and a few friends clubbing tonight, I just need a few pills, that's all."

The youngster looked at him suspiciously.

"You gonna help me or not?" Morris asked.

"Who told you about Steiner?"

"A mate of mine, he was out clubbing last weekend, said he scored some great pills off him."

He regarded Morris again. They both finished, then stood by the urinal, and the man gave Morris a skeptical look.

"You're not a bit old for that shit?" the younger man said.

"When I take that shit I'm as young as I want to be, you know what I mean?"

The younger man smiled and nodded silently to himself. He glanced toward the door to make sure no one had snuck in undetected, then leaned closer to Morris.

"Okay," he surrendered, "you don't look like a cop." He paused, taking in a deep breath, "Steiner won't be in here for a while, but I can give him a ring. How many do you want?"

Morris suppressed a smile: "Twenty."

He picked a mobile phone out of his pocket and began flicking through the phone's memory to find the number he wanted.

Morris watched as the call was made. Few words were exchanged. Halfway through the conversation he asked Morris to show him the cash, Morris gladly pulled out a huge wad of notes from his pocket. They agreed on a price, and Morris was told to meet Steiner in the local park in less than an hour.

13

Through the wisps of steam rising out of his coffee cup, Howard Price watched the crowds of passing shoppers. People came and went, buzzing through the center like agitated bees carrying bags of gifts and honey for their Queen.

He heard snippets of conversations: loud, varied, and mingled voices combining into one murmured hum. He felt like he was in an airport departure lounge, listening to clusters of excited conversations and people-watching to stave off the boredom.

Lisa sat opposite him. He shot her a warm smile but her attention was elsewhere: she was staring blankly at the shoppers behind her father, her mind probably on the gifts he had bought her as she hungrily ate a cheeseburger, chewing each large mouthful with jaw aching rapidity.

Price poked at his own food. He had ordered a tuna sandwich, but the tuna had been drowned in mayonnaise before being wrapped in a disturbing amount of lettuce. He lifted the sesame seed bun and looked in disgust at the foliage that greeted him. Pushing it to one side he chose to concentrate on his coffee.

"Where to next, darling?" he asked, bringing his daughter out of her daydream.

"Can we go look for some clothes?"

"Sure, that's perfect, there's a new leather jacket and some slippers I've been wanting."

"Oh, okay."

"I'm kidding," he winked. "We'll go to that new clothes shop that you've been talking about all day."

She beamed a delighted grin and tucked into her food with more relish, keen to finish.

Price looked down at the bags of merchandise they had already purchased. He had agreed to buy her whatever she wanted and she hadn't missed a single opportunity, picking up computer games, toys, an MP3 player, and an assortment of magazines and posters.

They had also paid a brief visit to an antique shop to pick up a porcelain teddy bear for Elizabeth—one of the many things she collected—and to a sweet shop to buy a bag of Twizzlers that they had been sharing throughout the trip.

Howard was surprised at the rate in which they had shopped. When he shopped with his wife every shop and every item had to be mulled over. He would find himself stuck in one shop for over an hour as she rummaged through and debated each item. When he shopped alone he had a list, he drove to the shops bought what was on the list and drove back home. He wasn't one for lingering around and, luckily for him, his daughter had a similar attitude.

He smiled at her as a line of mayonnaise trickled down her chin before being swiped away by the sleeve of her jacket; she grinned as she pushed the last piece of the burger into her mouth.

14

An afternoon chill flushed Darren Morris's cheeks, bringing with it a light wind that toyed with his loosely hanging jacket. He shifted his feet uncomfortably and zipped up the jacket, blocking out the cold and the nuisance wind.

James Roach stood by his side, his posture firm and strong. He looked around the inactive park with trained eyes. Morris rested his back against a damaged, graffiti-covered wall and observed his colleague.

They had both been in the game for the same length of time; both had made their first hits within days of each other. They had been partners from the beginning, and had been terrorizing the inner-city gangs and law enforcement agencies for over fifteen years. They were also the same age and had relatively similar upbringings, but Morris had never considered Roach to be a friend.

They were pushed together by Sanderson. A loose cannon and a deadly efficient machine, combined to create a force feared by many local gangs.

Roach straightened up and turned to his partner. "You okay?" he asked, noticing Morris's stare.

"Fine."

They had a good agreement. They knew a lot about each other, but rarely entered into personal conversation. Morris didn't have any social skills. His ability to make friends had withered away over the years, he didn't like dealing with company and hated most people.

Roach turned to Morris again and gestured in the direction of the park entrance.

Morris woke from his trance and looked at the opening where a short concrete perimeter wall opened, serving as the entrance to the park.

Two youths strutted their way. Both wore baseball caps tipped downward to disguise their faces as they plodded along.

"Reckon this is our guy?" Roach quizzed.

Morris mumbled an inaudible reply and straightened up. He felt his stomach stiffen and he rubbed it gently.

After arranging to pick up the drugs, he had ordered two bacon sandwiches. The barmaid had said they were not serving dinner but the owner would make him something from the breakfast menu.

They arrived late and had been burned to a crisp. Morris devoured them regardless, chewing through the charred bacon with the hunger of a man who hadn't eaten for days.

The meat and grease still hadn't settled on his stomach.

"I told you not to eat so fast," Roach said, acknowledging his friend's discomfort and watching as the two boys turned toward the basketball courts.

Morris smiled and shrugged.

Someone called out from behind them, a half-shout, half-whisper that served the purpose of neither. Behind the wall, walking across the road with a confident gait, was a stocky teenager. He wore a baggy NYC hooded sweatshirt and extremely loose fitting Levi jeans. The hood on the sweatshirt was pulled over his head and shadowed half his face.

"You the guy from the bar?" he hopped over the wall and walked up to them.

"Yes, you Steiner?" Morris said.

The youngster nodded.

"Follow me, old man," he walked away from the wall, towards a dense woodland area.

Roach looked across at Morris and smiled at the scowl on his face.

"My buddy told me what you looked like, brief description an all," the youngster said as they ducked their way into the wooded area, into the cool shade and out of sight. "He didn't say you were bringing a boyfriend though," he joked.

Morris smiled. "You got the pills?"

"Sure I got 'em," he tapped a bulge in his pocket. "You got the cash?"

"How much?"

"Fifty."

"Very cheap," Morris said. "They're good pills as well, you must have a good supplier."

The kid merely shrugged, a look of impatience on his face.

"Where do they come from?" Morris wondered. "The main dealer in the city gets his stuff from up north. Fucking shit gear if you ask me, rip-off prices too, but I've heard good things about these."

"Specially shipped from abroad, you'll not get better E's than these," he replied with a smug grin.

"You know the guy who ships them?"

"If I did I wouldn't tell you, would I? Now are you gonna give me the cash or what?"

Morris smiled and nodded. "James, give the kid the cash, would you?"

Roach moved towards the teenager. His hand was in his pocket and Steiner watched with anticipation as he withdrew it. The teenager didn't even get the chance to see that the man in front of him had been reaching for a pair of knuckle dusters and not a bundle of notes, before a fist clattered into his face.

Steiner recoiled; his jaw clicked and locked in place as his body stumbled sideways. Roach reached out with his left arm and stopped the boy from falling, before driving his fist into his stomach.

He coughed violently and repeatedly. Blood trickled from each expulsion of breath, he gagged an assortment of muffled, curdled obscenities through his pained mouth.

Morris bent over to meet his eyes—the teenager was practically on his knees. "Where do you get the gear from?"

"Just take it," he yelped. He tried to reach into his pocket for the bag of pills but Roach stopped him, grasping his wrist tightly.

"We don't want your filthy fucking drugs," Morris explained. "We want to know where you get them from."

Steiner's eyes shifted nervously. "Why?"

"So we can cut out the middle man, go directly to the supplier, buy wholesale," Morris said with a smile. "Does it really matter why? What you *should* be asking is 'or what' because if you don't tell us where you get the gear then my big friend here is going to remove your appendages one by one." Morris straightened and removed a lock-back Smith & Wesson knife from his pocket. He flicked it open and aimed at the teenager's groin, "And guess where he's going to start."

He let out a gurgle of fear and tried to utter a reply but his words were rapid and jumbled by a frightened stammer.

"We haven't got all day kid, hurry up," Roach said, holding the youngster's head tightly in both of his hands.

"Pearce," the youngster stammered. "Wayne Pearce."

"That's a start. Where's he live?"

"I don't know, please, I really don't—"

Morris raised the knife to Steiner's left eye. He stuck the tip of the blade in the soft flesh below his eyebrow, drawing blood from the small wound. He then slowly brought the knife to point over his eye.

"I'll ask you again," he said, his arm steady as he held the knife in front of the rapidly blinking eye. "Where does he live?"

Roach looked down to see a large wet patch spreading over Steiner's groin. The urine dripped past his baggy jeans, over his legs and shoes before darkening the dry ground.

"Walker Street," he muttered, stumbling on each syllable. "Number thirty-two."

Morris smiled and withdrew the knife. "Is he the one who ships them into the country?"

"I don't think so, he's a big-time dealer but he's a heavy user . . . he's too fucked up to be that smart."

Morris smiled and nodded at his partner. Roach twisted Steiner's head like a bottle cap. His neck snapped instantly and he fell limp onto the floor, his face in the pool of drying urine.

"Looks like we can forget about the other name on Sanders's list," Morris said as they left the scene. "We'll check out this Pearce guy, he sounds promising."

15

Morris and Roach clambered into the silver Ford Mondeo back in the supermarket car park. Morris eyed the transit van as he passed, instinctively glancing its way. No one had tried to gain access to it, no one was hovering around.

Car crime was a big problem in that area. There were more unemployed people than employed and there had been a significant increase of commercial vehicles, like the transit van, being broken into. The crimes were usually committed by kids who didn't know how to drive and would struggle to reach the pedals if they did, so the vans were never stolen, but everything inside was.

In their eyes, vans could be holding computer gear, wholesale goods, or other expensive items. So breaking into them and stealing their contents would be just as profitable as ram-raiding a store.

Morris pondered the idea of some kids breaking into the van beside him looking for something of value. He could almost picture their horrified faces as they saw the crumpled, blood-soaked body staring back at them amid a cargo of paint brushes and cans.

Although he knew they would likely just side-step the body and steal the brushes.

A gust of wind blew through the lines of cars, kicking up the distinctive smell of putrid flesh and coppery blood. He shrugged it off and climbed into the car.

"Do you think we should give Sanders a call?" Roach asked inside the vehicle.

"He told us to sort the job out, we'll call him after we've done it."

"He told us to check the names on the list," Roach corrected. "We've already found who could be the middle man. If we give him a call maybe Sanders will know who the guy is."

Morris nodded and conceded. He knew Roach was right, if there was a change in anyone's plans Sanderson expected to be told about it, and there was a decent chance he *did* know the guy they were after. Morris pulled out his mobile phone and jabbed out the number; he knew it by heart, he had to—Sanderson didn't give his number out to many people and didn't want anyone storing it.

Sanderson answered on the second ring.

"Darren," he said with little enthusiasm. "What can I do you for?" Morris noted a tired rattle in his boss's voice.

"We checked out the list and found the first kid on there. Joseph Steiner," Morris said, getting straight to the point.

"Any luck?"

"He gave us a name to his supplier. Neither Steiner nor his supplier ship the goods into the country, but we're getting closer."

"I'm impressed; you work fast."

Morris ignored the compliment. "You ever hear of a junkie-come-seller by the name of Pearce?"

"Doesn't ring a bell," Sanderson replied firmly. "Why?"

"That's where Steiner is getting his gear from; he gave us an address."

"A name *and* an address . . . you boys really *do* work fast," Sanderson took a puff from his cigar, Morris could almost taste the smoke down the phone line. "Where's this Steiner kid now?"

"Face to face with his own piss at the local park."

"I expect you didn't leave any evidence?"

"None at all," Morris said with little care. "So, do you want us to scrap the list and head for this Pearce guy?"

"Yes. The other kid on the list is a nobody like Steiner. We need to climb the chain," Sanderson said, making Morris wonder where the *we* fit in. "You say you have his address?"

"Yes."

"Head over there, stake it out if necessary, I want him dealt with today. If he's a junkie it shouldn't take much doing, get as much information from him as you can."

"We just finished on Steiner, what about your other boys?" Morris wondered. "Can't you send them in?"

"Darren. Darren. Darren." Sanderson said, sounding disappointed. "You and James are the best I have. The other idiots I have with me would fuck it up; I wouldn't trust them as far as I can throw them. You two are the best in the business, that's why I hired you." He paused to take another puff of his cigar. "Head over to this fucking junkie's house, do what needs to be done and report back to me."

Morris nodded as the line went dead. He sealed the phone and dropped it back inside his pocket.

"Another fucking job," he muttered. "We don't get paid enough for this shit."

"Sanderson watches our back, he pays us enough to keep us going," Roach disagreed.

Morris turned to his colleague and shrugged. "We could be doing a lot better than this," he pleaded. "If we worked for ourselves we'd be making fifty-times more than we do now."

"Sanders is a fucking gang lord," Roach argued. "It took him years to build up what he has." He glanced across at his friend, "You like your job, you always have, so what's your problem?"

Morris shrugged. "We need a job of our own, something away from Sanders; something that can sort us out for life."

"Cut out the middleman?" Roach smiled.

"Yes. Something like that."

Roach revved up the engine of the Ford. "Only there's one slight problem," he said as he reversed the car out of the small space. "Sanders is the middleman *and* the front man. If we cut him out of anything we do, he'll cut us out of anything we *ever* want to do." He rolled the car out of the space and picked up pace as he weaved through the car park, "And I plan to have kids someday."

Morris smiled, but his mind continued to whir with ideas.

"What did he say anyway?" Roach wanted to know. "Are we to head straight for this Pearce guy?"

"Yes."

"Thought as much. No rest for the wicked," he remarked coldly.

16

Michael Richards had made new friends and they liked him. They talked to him like they had known him for years, sharing stories about their girlfriends, wives, habits, and even their petty criminal endeavors.

He cringed internally at every word they spoke, hating them more by the second. When he eventually told them he was leaving he promised to return to the pub on another occasion to share a few drinks, he had also made plans to join them on a night out — he would be doing neither.

He was relieved to be away from them, his eagerness unconsciously translated into a fast walking pace that was two strides short of a jog.

He found Phillips in another pub half a mile away. He was steadily sipping from a beer, idly staring out of the window.

After ordering a glass of Coke, Richards trudged over to one of the seats by the window. He sat down opposite Johnny Phillips, who was watching the road outside—flicking over each car that occasionally drifted by with a thought-filled twinkle in his eye.

"You walk?" Phillips said without looking away from the window.

Richards nodded and took a sip from his glass.

The pub was empty. Richards had never been inside before and had been given directions from Phillips. He could hear commotion past a doorway next to the bar—looking through a glass panel in the door he could see a few small pool tables, a large television screen, and a gathering of customers.

The area where Richards and Phillips were seated was quiet and small. There were only two tables and three bar stools and they were the only customers.

"Been here before?" Richards quizzed.

"Once. I was seeing a girl not too far from here, big ass, but she had a decent set of tits on her. We came here one weekend for a drink. Through the door," Phillips motioned to the source of the commotion. "There are a few pool tables, bigger bar, television ... not a very exciting place but the drinks are cheap. Had some fun in the toilets, too."

Richards shook his head in disbelief, "Is there anywhere or anyone you haven't fucked?" he quizzed. "You get more action than the A-Team. We've been friends for, well, nearly forever; you'd think that would work in my favor," Richards paused and took a sip from his glass. "Last fuck I got was from a drunk slut I met at a nightclub six months ago," he explained. "She walked me to her house, we spent half an hour fucking ... she passed out, then she woke up in the morning asking me who I was and telling me to get the fuck out of her house."

Phillips shifted his eyes away from the window, turning towards his friend, "Yeah. I remember you telling me that," he laughed. "You came home with stiletto wounds on your face and scratches all over your neck."

Richards nodded, "I wasn't even fully awake when I heard her start screaming. Next thing I knew, she'd picked up her fucking heels and was slamming them into my face."

"You always manage to find the crazy ones."

"Yeah . . . anyone would do at the moment," he mumbled. "I'm getting so desperate even you're starting to look attractive."

"Get a hooker or something," Phillips said.

"Nah, fuck that, I ain't paying for sex."

"Well, you ain't getting it for free either, are you?"

Richards shrugged and changed the subject, "So, how much did we get?"

Phillips looked cautiously around the bar before answering: "Four grand."

Richards nearly choked on his pint. The action caught the attention of the sour faced bartender but he quickly lost interest and continued to clean glasses. "Four K? What the fuck was in the van?"

"Paving slabs mostly, we had to clear those out of the way to get to the good stuff."

"Which was?" Richards jumped in eagerly.

"Allcross was working on two landscaping jobs in the area, I found the receipts in the glove compartment. Up on Hedgefield Drive, all those fucking posh palaces. Fuck knows how a lowlife like him got the job." Phillips seemed to perk up somewhat, "Marble stones, a couple of little fancy fucking fountains, silly fucking cherubs, gnomes, fairies, and a ton of equipment. All looked useless to me but I think I caught Simon in a good mood."

"He was stoned again?"

"Completely out of it."

"What about the cards?"

"Five hundred. Dumb fucker probably won't get that much when he sells them on but that's his loss."

"That's a lot of money for one take. So why you looking so down?" Richard wondered.

Phillips shrugged his shoulders, paused and then answered, "I just want something . . . bigger."

17

The silver Ford twisted through the tight roads. Semi-detached houses lined each side of every road; no matter where the hitmen turned, the Victorian edifices glared out at them as they maneuvered through the small town.

They drove past a crowded fish and chip shop, it was small, no larger than a simple corner shop, yet people were lining up halfway down the road. Darren Morris glanced inside the building as the car struggled on at a slow pace. There were more than a dozen people inside, all crammed together, waiting to be served one at a time by a buff and sweaty woman in white.

"Must be something they put in the sauce," Roach said, watching his friend's bewilderment at the capacity of customers.

Morris nodded and turned his attention further down the line. Teenagers and young adults gathered towards the back, wearing baseball caps and hoodies to shelter themselves from the breeze. They were drinking cans of beer and chatting loudly; their antics clearly annoying an agitated elderly couple in front of them who seemed too scared to say anything.

"Should be around here somewhere," Roach said as the car rolled past the brimming fast food shop and turned a sharp right at a T-junction.

"Have you been to the place before?" Morris said.

"Heard of it. Supposed to be a right shit hole, the rest of the town is bad enough but it seems they dumped all the real fucking lowlifes in one street."

They rounded a corner and the houses disappeared. The sides of the roads littered with teenagers and children. Ahead, Morris could see a brimming cul-de-sac engraved into a half circle; after that there was nowhere to turn, the street was a dead end.

It felt like they had entered a different dimension as they pulled into the circular street. Kids were sitting on the side of the road smoking and drinking. A group of adults gathered around a battered Vauxhall; the windows and doors were open—as was the trunk—and the stereo blared out a heavy drum and bass soundtrack.

Morris mused at the sight of the neglected car—a car worth at least ten times less than the pulse shattering speakers and subwoofers within. A group of kids no more than ten-years-old gathered around a bike shed openly smoking a joint. Near them, youngsters not much older cradled cheap fireworks, plotting as they hugged the explosive devices to their chests like fragile newborns.

"What a fucking hole," he grumbled as the car stopped.

He looked out at the houses; fifty-year-old terraces lined all the way around the street, bending into a semi-circle. The windows on most were boarded up and covered in the detritus of spray-paint and vandalism. Driveways sat in between every other house, but besides the Vauxhall in the middle of the street the only car in the area was a Morris Minor—minus the wheels and dumped in one of the gardens.

Roach and Morris noted the intimidating glares they received upon entering the cul-de-sac, they exchanged a glance inside the car before stepping out simultaneously.

They ignored the questioning stares from the residents and headed straight for Pearce's house.

The garden to number 32 Walker Street was sprouting into a forest. Inside the four foot clumps of weeds and grass a variety of junk and decayed rubbish nestled—from a wheel-less mountain bike to a rusted lawnmower.

Morris could feel the hard grass rubbing against the tops of his legs as he headed for the front door. He reached for the blistered wood and paused, turning an ear to the door, trying to make sense of the incoherent mumbles beyond the skimpy wooden frame.

Roach walked up to his side, brushing at the bottom of his coat as if to dispel the decrepit garden air from its fibers. "If any of those fuckers even look at the car I'll string them up by their balls," he said bitterly, glancing towards the street.

18

Michael Richards stared into the bottom of his glass. He had been cradling a pint of Coke for nearly an hour and the small amount of liquid that remained seemed to be growing skin.

He downed the final drops. The drink had lost its fizz, which, combined with its dormant state, gave it an extra sugary kick. He lolled his tongue around his mouth as the sweet drink soaked his glands and slid down his throat.

A door slammed loudly behind him and he turned his attention to the noise. Through the glass panel in the door opposite he could see Johnny Phillips entering his view.

He watched with a sly smile as his friend struggled through half a dozen people, weaving in and out of the human slalom course. He inevitably bumped into a few but he was quick to apologize, but one man, at the end of the line, didn't take kindly to his apology.

The drunken man turned towards Phillips with an angry growl.

Richards readied himself in his seat, waiting to see if the incident caused uproar. He listened to their conversation.

"Sorry, mate," Phillips said.

"You should watch where you're fucking going," the man spat in a drunken fury.

"Like I said, I'm sorry. Accidents happen," Phillips replied,

"You want your face fucking smashed in, mate?" the man snapped, his mind clearly on one track.

"Why would I want that?"

"Are you trying to be funny?"

"No, of course not, how could I do such a thing? I'm absolutely petrified. Humor is the last thing on my mind."

"You think you're better than me?" The man spat.

"I would hope so, yes."

The man advanced, his drunken face raging with fury. He picked up a cue from a nearby pool table and swung it at Phillips.

Phillips casually moved out of the way and watched as the cue handle crashed into the shoulder of a nearby drinker. The man turned, grabbed the end of the cue, and pulled it free of the drunken man's grasp. He laid it back onto the table and rushed the drunk. Soon three people were holding the drunk back as he struggled frantically to get free of their grasp, shouting abuse at Phillips.

"I think you better leave," the bartender commanded. "He gets like this when he's had a bit to drink."

Phillips nodded and walked away from the babbling drunk. He noticed Richards standing by the door. "Come on Mickey," he said. "Let's get going."

"The world is full of fucking drunks and assholes," Phillips said as they exited the stifled bar and braced the cool afternoon air.

Richards nodded and they continued in silence, walking to the back of the building where Phillips had parked the car. He stopped as they reached the corner, out of sight of the pub windows, he leaned up against the wall of the building.

"What're you doing?" Richards said, stopping and watching as his friend dug his hand into the inside of his jacket pocket.

Phillips pulled out a small wad of cash, "Took it off that drunken bastard," he declared. "He was buying a round of drinks when I went to the toilet. I saw him pull out a bundle of notes and figured I'd score us some easy cash on our way out of the pub. Didn't bank on the bastard trying to start a fucking fight though."

"I saw it all," Richards noted. "He was just drunk. It's a good thing his mates didn't join in."

"I'd have been okay. I had my bodyguard waiting for me at the door, didn't I?" he grinned mockingly.

"Hey! I'm a decent fighter, I could have helped you out," Richards assured.

Phillips smiled and counted the money before stuffing it in his back pocket.

"Fifty bucks," he announced. "Not great, but it'll do."

"Every little bit counts huh?"

19

The door to number 32 Walker Street slowly creaked open. A pasty and creased face appeared in the dimly lit doorway and stared at James Roach, who glared back.

"What?" it asked through thin cracked lips, its voice harsh and laden with a chesty thickness and a sour touch of thirst.

Darren Morris smiled awkwardly at him. The door had been opened enough to expose the gaunt face of the man; his glazed, heavy eyes seemed to protrude from his skull, popping out from his tight skin in a comical and disturbing manner. He shifted the bloodshot gaze from Roach to Morris then back again, before catching a beam of sunlight and recoiling like a vampire.

"Are you Wayne Pearce?" Morris asked as the pale figure ducked further into the doorway to shield his face from the light.

He continued to look the pair of assassins up and down, uncomfortable with their presence.

"Why?" he croaked in reply.

"A friend of mine told me to come see you," Morris clarified. "He said you would be able to hook me up."

He opened the door further and exposed his gawky, pasty figure. He wore a worn blue shirt which had been unbuttoned at the top, exposing a hairy chest. His ribs could be seen poking through his thin, neglected skin. A pair of jogging pants covered his lower body, clinging to his sunken form.

He glanced past Morris and looked into the street. He stared at the Ford parked just outside his house and recoiled into the confines of his doorway again.

"I don't speak to fucking pigs!" he warned in a dry tone.

"We ain't cops," Morris said calmly, rolling his eyes.

"Prove it!" the man demanded.

Morris shot a look of complete bewilderment at the pale figure in the doorway. "How?"

He contemplated this for a few seconds. "OK," the hermit continued, "let's just say I *was* Wayne Pearce—" Morris could almost see a light bulb above his head as he tried to contemplate his options, "which, of course I *'aven't* said, I might not even know the guy," the imaginary light bulb began flickering erratically. "But if I *was*, what would you want from me?"

Morris noticed that Roach had taken up a position beside him, completely blocking out the view of the doorway from the street beyond. If anyone was looking—which they no doubt were—their inquisitive eyes would see nothing but his broad frame.

"We're just here to borrow a cup of sugar, buddy," Morris said, grinning.

The pale figure began to contemplate the statement, but Morris's fist moved a lot faster than Pearce's mind ever could.

The right hook propelled him backwards, he lost his balance and crashed into a wooden shoe rack. He attempted to cushion his fall with his right hand but his movements were too slow and the appendage crippled beneath his weight, sandwiched behind the wooden rack and his own spine.

The shoe rack was small and homemade, but his small frame couldn't even crush the minor object and he paid for that disadvantage with agonizing pain. His spine twisted awkwardly over the furniture and his upper back bent over the back of the rack. He released a muffled moan as he rolled off the rack and collapsed onto the hard wood floor, unsure whether to grip his crushed wrist or care for his twisted back.

Roach and Morris didn't waste time. They quickly stepped inside the house and closed the door behind them. Roach strode into the back rooms as Morris stood over the crumpled figure in the doorway.

Pearce attempted to pull himself to his feet, using the walls and his uninjured arm to propel his body upwards. He slowly found his feet again and slouched against the wall, blinking away the pain.

Morris pounced on the stricken man again. He grabbed his injured arm and maneuvered around the back of the scrawny individual. He twisted his arm up his back and forced him forwards, shoving him hard and slamming his face into the gray walls.

Wayne Pearce moaned as his nose snapped and splattered blood across the wall.

Meanwhile, in the unkempt, smoky living room James Roach found a young girl lying drugged up on an old and tattered sofa. She looked no more than thirteen; her body was still unformed and on the slight side, her face a collage of blemishes and cheap makeup.

She wore nothing more than a tank top—the words Little Devil emblazoned in large fiery letters across her chest—and a short denim skirt, stained and marked in various places.

He shook his head as he watched her. Her eyes were gazing at the ceiling, her mind completely lost to the world. Roach doubted she knew that he, or anyone else, was even there—and by the looks of it, he thought, Pearce had been trying to take advantage of the fact.

Her underwear had been pulled down around her knees and her skirt had been pushed up around her waist. Her arms were limp and dangling by her sides, even if she did know what was going on, Roach doubted she could have done anything about it.

Her top had been lifted, exposing a black bra which had been roughly tampered with to expose one of her small breasts. Down by her side, inches from her dangling arm, lay an empty syringe. Roach sighed in disgust and quickly checked the rest of the house.

Darren Morris kicked at the limp figure of Wayne Pearce—his foot thudded into his unconscious chest and Pearce gurgled unpleasantly.

"We're not going to get much out of him if he keeps passing out," Roach said, returning to the room and studying the blood-riddled form on the floor.

Morris turned to his colleague with a distasteful look then he rammed his foot into Pearce's rib cage. "I know. He'll fucking wake up soon."

He knelt down and grabbed the injured wrist of the pale man.

"What did he tell you anyway?" Roach inquired as he watched Morris push Pearce against the wall and hold him there with a strong arm around his waist—his other hand still grasping the damaged wrist.

"He mumbled some shit about not knowing anything," Morris replied. "Then he started babbling about 'not knowing how old she was,' or some shit. Before I even asked about the shipments he was fucking telling me some bollocks about a girl on smack." Morris paused as he pushed Pearce against the wall and took a firm grip on his wrist, "Then he mumbled 'sorry,' a few dozen times. I hit him; he blacked out . . ."

"There's a young girl in there," Roach ventured with a flick of his head. "Looks like he got her doped up then tried to rape her; he probably thinks you're her father coming to castrate him."

Morris laughed, "If he doesn't wake the fuck up I might just do that." He yanked Pearce's wrist, pushing it up his back. A small popping sound echoed in the porch, followed by a muffled scream blasting from Pearce's blood-filled mouth.

"Did you find anyone else in the house?" he smiled as the drug dealer trembled—waking up to the horrific ordeal.

"No, just the young girl," Roach said. "The place is a fucking sty," he added with disgust. "For some reason there's a sleeping bag in the bathroom, and it looks like someone's been using the bedroom as a toilet."

Morris forced Pearce's head into the wall again—blood poured from his crushed nose and a large cut on his upper lip.

"I told you," the suddenly conscious addict uttered through a stream of blood, "I'm sorry, I didn't know—"

"I know what you told me and I doubt very much that you're sorry *Mr.* Pearce," Morris said. "But, luckily for you, we ain't on fucking pedo-patrol—we couldn't really give a shit about you and some underage slut."

Pearce sighed with relief.

"Although . . ." Morris continued with a tweak of sadistic pleasure, "What *we* have planned for you will be a lot worse than a pissed-off father with a machete and an eye for your crotch. If you don't tell us what we need to know, we'll turn castration into a walk in the park. You'll be wishing your father had *his* balls cut off before the fateful day when he found your mothers number in a phone box and decided he would give wanking a miss for one night and splash out a bit."

Pearce trembled like a vibrating toy in Morris's strong hands.

"What do you, you—" he stuttered as he tried to speak through the blood that curdled in his throat, "y—you want?"

Morris yanked his head away from the wall and brought it parallel with his own. Blood flowed easily down Pearce's face and he coughed it away from his mouth, spitting occasionally.

"Well," Morris began, grabbing Pearce's thin hair and pulling his head back so his eyes bore into the ceiling. "Word is, you're a dealer."

"Me? No!" Pearce blistered instinctively. "I don't touch drugs."

Morris rolled up Pearce's shirt and exposed an array of scabs, blisters and fresh holes around a slightly blued forearm.

"And this is eczema I suppose?"

Pearce struggled to regain his thoughts. For a man of low intelligence, he was surprisingly good at denying his recreational habits, but with a raging headache, a mouth loaded with blood, a nose which felt like it had been crushed in a vice, and a strong grip on his head, he was finding it difficult to cultivate lies.

"It's—it's a medical problem," he declared.

"Looks bad, does your doctor know about this?"

Pearce mulled this question over before answering. "No, I 'ate 'ospitals. I'm 'oping it will go away; it should be okay."

Morris nodded and examined the scars. "It looks bad. Any medical condition like this could need immediate attention."

"You're right," Pearce reasoned. "I'll go straight to the 'ospital, shall I?"

"No time," Morris said. "But, you're in luck. I did a bit of Biology in school." He held out his right hand to Roach as Pearce trembled in his left. "Scalpel!" he instructed.

"What are you doing?" Pearce pleaded.

"It needs immediate attention."

Roach pulled a sharp shaving blade from his pocket, flicked it open and laid it on Darren's outstretched palm.

He moved the blade to the scarred wrist. "No need to worry," he assured. "I got this," he lowered the blade until it touched skin, he could fell Pearce squirming in his grasp. He slowly poked the point of the blade into a fresh puncture wound, teasing the tip of the steel underneath the skin.

"OK! Stop! I'll tell you what you want to know, just please don't 'urt me."

Morris smiled, flicked the blade closed, passed it back to Roach then grinned directly into Pearce's face: "Excellent."

"So, are you a dealer?"

Taking the psychotic actions of his crazed captor in mind, Pearce guessed he was not a police officer. He'd be beaten up by the police before, but not to this extent, and none of them had ever threatened—with full intent—to slice open his arm. He reasoned that whoever this man was, he was not a cop—but he was clearly insane.

"Yes, I'm a dealer."

"Has anything . . . *exciting* hit the streets recently?"

"What d'you mean?"

"New drugs, new hits, new ways to fuck up the youth of today; you know what I mean."

"No," Pearce lied. "Same old shit."

Morris lifted his head and laughed aloud. He then slammed Pearce's face into the wall.

"Don't!"

Pearce's bottom lip was sliced open.

Morris pulled Pearce's head back and slammed it into the wall once again. "Fucking!"

He opened up another cut on his sweaty forehead, where his thinning hair clung to his pallid skin.

"Lie!" Again his beaten face was driven into the blood smeared wall.

"To!" The plaster began to chip away with the succession of forceful impacts.

"Me!"

Pearce now dripped blood from the cuts on his face, he trembled in fear. Tears of pain poured from his eyes and mingled with the blood dripping down his face. Morris held his head back from the wall and prepared to bring the two together again.

"I'll ask that again, shall I?" He said. Pearce's body shook with fear. "Have you had any new drugs hit the streets?"

"Yes, yes!" He cried. "Some new pills. Not long back." His words were stuttered and filled with fear. He spat a glob of blood and mucus onto the wall; it clung for a few seconds then began to slide a sticky descent. "Rocket fuel—they mix 'em with some other shit, strong stuff. Cheap to come by as well. They're better than the shit on the streets now, plus we're getting 'em so cheap we can afford to sell 'em cheap." Pearce told all for he feared another meeting with the wall.

Morris smiled, pleased with what he heard. He slammed Peace's face into the wall again and then quickly brought it back parallel with his own.

"What the hell did you do that for?" Peace spat a fountain of crimson into the air.

Morris shrugged, "Force of habit," he said. "Where do you get your gear from?"

"Why?"

His front tooth split; another chunk of plaster broke free.

"Someone down south!" Pearce bellowed, spitting mouthfuls of blood and mucus on the floor.

"How much do you know about them?" Morris inquired.

"Not much," Pearce hesitated and rushed to amend his words in fear of further redecorating. "I've been dealing with him for a long time now. I just don't know him personally."

"Do you know where he gets *his* supplies?" Morris said.

"Sort of. He has links up and down the country. He says he recently met a supplier who knows some Dutch gangsters; they've been shipping the pills in for weeks. Only one person is allowed contact with 'em though."

"Who is that?"

"No one knows, or at least me and James don't, they're tight with their business."

"Who is James?"

Pearce paused, realizing his accidental name–drop. He struggled to form a lie, and then decided against it.

"That's the name of my supplier."

"I need to find these so called, gangsters." Morris demanded.

"No one knows 'em."

"You said there was one guy."

"He's like a shadow. People only speak to 'im on the phone. Apparently 'e sends the drugs using a delivery company. They set up the company just to shift the drugs. Even the drivers don't know what they're shifting; these guys run a tight business. They're dealing all across the United Kingdom."

"If they're so tight, how do you know about all of this?"

"Word gets around."

"Bring some of it my way, then, would you?"

"I've told you all I know. Look, these guys are big business, they're untouchable."

Morris sighed and looked across at Roach who merely shrugged his shoulders.

"I need the address of this supplier," Morris ordered.

"I can't."

The wall felt the impact of Pearce's face.

"Okay!" he spat. "I don't know his address though; we don't deal like that. I phone 'im and we pick a place to meet."

Morris nodded. "Call him."

Pearce didn't resist, so far, resisting had given him two bust lips, a broken nose, half a dozen cracked teeth, a voice that could barely speak past the blood, and eyes that could barely see past it.

"My phone is in the living room," he said.

Roach was already leaving to collect the device before Morris looked his way. Seconds later he returned with a battered old Nokia.

"Number?" Roach quizzed, already flicking through the phone.

"It's under Jimmy," Pearce said, slightly surprised by Roach's voice, having forgotten there was another man in his house besides the madman intent on disfiguring him.

"I want you to tell him to meet you at The Dog & Bull on Anderson Street," Morris instructed.

"He doesn't normally come this far up; 'e meets on 'is turf."

"It's not like you're asking him to fucking drive to Scotland, I'm sure he can make it. Tell him you want to make a big deal and you're unsure about shifting all of that cash down south."

"He won't do the deal in a pub."

"Just fucking meet him there okay? You can tell him you'll both come back here to do the deal and have a cup of coffee, some cookies, a line of coke—just get the fucker here okay?"

"When?"

Morris took some time to consider this. There was no chance the dealer would want to make the deal tonight, even if he could make it. Furthermore, Morris didn't feel like running anymore errands tonight.

"Tomorrow night," he said after a short pause.

Pearce nodded and Morris released his grip on the scrawny man. Roach handed him a phone, the correct number readied on the display.

The assassins watched as a weary Wayne Pearce waited for the line to be answered.

"Hey, Jimmy," he said when the line was picked up. His eyes were boring into the two assassins as he spoke.

He spent the first few seconds talking pleasantries and explaining away his damaged voice. Morris urged him on with a push and an angry look. "I need some more gear," Pearce said into the phone. "I need you to come up 'ere, do you know where the Dog & Bull is? Meet me there at . . ." Pearce looked at Morris. Morris held up eight fingers. "Seven, meet me there at seven, then we'll move somewhere a little more personal."

"Eight fingers, you fuck," Morris snapped when the conversation had ended. "I held up eight fingers."

"I'm fucking blinking blood here; I can't see shit!"

Morris shook his head. "What does this guy look like then?" he wanted to know, "What does he drive?"

"You can't miss 'im," Pearce declared. "He's about six-foot-five, and built like a brick house. He always wears short sleeve tops and both 'is arms are covered in thorn tattoos. He's completely bald; got a snake tattoo on the top of his 'ead. He drives a red—" Pearce paused. "Why do you want to know? I can pick 'im out for you."

Morris shook his head and glanced at Roach. They both nodded and then grinned at Pearce.

"What?" the beaten dealer said. "I did what you told me to do."

Out of the addict's view, Roach flicked out the blade from the shaving knife.

"That you did," Morris agreed. "And for that, I thank you."

Roach grabbed him by the hair, lifting him up by the frail strands and yanking his fragile skull backwards.

"We can't take any risks I'm afraid," Morris told him. "And I don't like you."

Roach raised the knife. The polished steel reflected the fear in the addict's eyes as the blade slid across his throat.

20

Joyful laughs filled the air as Howard and Lisa Price walked out of the theater, clinging tight to each other and giggling all the way. Howard had been talked into going to watch an animated comedy after they finished shopping. He had immediately dismissed it as a children's movie, but it had him hooked.

He listened—with a smile spread across his face—as his daughter recounted her favorite moments from the cartoon.

Lisa beamed with pride. "I told you it would be a good movie."

Howard nodded, "I'll admit: I enjoyed it."

"We should do this more often," Lisa offered. "I had fun. Maybe we can bring mom along sometime too."

They looked at each other and paused before speaking simultaneously: "Nah."

"Mr. Price?"

Howard turned away from his smiling daughter and stared straight into the face of a young, unshaven man with gelled hair. He had an expression on his face that seemed to ask questions.

"Can I help you?" Howard quizzed, instinctively holding his daughter closer.

"I work for the Gazette," the man said, retaining his smile. "Enjoying a day out with your daughter?"

"I *was*," Howard said.

The man winked at Lisa who stuck her tongue out, showing her distaste for the journalist. He smiled at her.

"No need to be like that, Mr. Price. I'm not really here for a story," he paused and pondered his words. "Well, actually I am . . . but nothing concerning you, I have an interview with a shop owner," he gestured towards the shopping center. "Just routine stuff, you know how it is."

Howard merely nodded.

"But, seeing as I have you here, do you mind if I take a few pictures?" seemingly from nowhere he pulled out a large digital camera and began fitting an expensive zoom lens.

"For what?" Howard demanded.

"Nothing really. News is a bit slow, that's all, nothing much happening locally . . . although I'm sure a few pictures of our most famous local out shopping with his sweet little daughter would go down nicely for our readers. Everyone likes the 'local man done good' story after all."

"But you've run that story hundreds of times."

"And have we ever failed you Mr. Price? Have we ever printed lies, or discriminating stories?"

"No, oddly enough," Howard agreed, understanding that although telling the truth wasn't typically a newspaper's concern, the local paper had been very kind to him.

"So come on, do me this favor," the journalist pleaded. "Either that, or our main headline tomorrow will be about a serial shop-lifter with a fetish for rabbit food."

Howard raised his eyebrows then shrugged and agreed to the journalist's request.

Price shut the front door to his luxurious house. A fresh, warm smell aroused his senses; his nostrils twinkled with delight as an aroma of fresh baked bread and hot pastry swarmed over him.

"Looks like we made it back just in time for dinner," he said to his daughter who had already kicked off her shoes.

"Do you want to play one of my new games?" Lisa asked, seemingly oblivious to her father's statement.

"After we've had something to eat, darling." The smell of the freshly cooked food had awoken his hunger.

Lisa nodded; she could also smell the food wafting from the open kitchen door.

Elizabeth Price stood facing the kitchen door as they entered, waiting for them with a broad smile etched across her features.

"Dinner is nearly ready," she announced. "Did you have a good time?"

Howard nodded and tried to sneak a look through the oven door. Lisa exploded with delight, she raced to her mother, kissed her on the cheek and began to speed through the details of her day. Howard took a seat at the kitchen table and watched his daughter cycle through the dealings of their eventful day.

Elizabeth listened with a smile. When the computer games were mentioned she shot an unhappy glare Howard's way—they had agreed to buy her the games for Christmas.

Elizabeth flared her eyes his way a few other times as Lisa told of the many items her father had bought her, but her frustrated look—that suggested he spoiled his daughter far too much—soon turned to a pleasant smile at Lisa's enjoyment of the time she had spent with her father.

Howard always liked to buy things for her, he enjoyed seeing her smile and he loved making her happy. Money was no issue, and he knew that despite spending a fortune on her, Lisa wasn't a spoiled child. She never complained when she didn't get what she wanted and she rarely asked for anything; she was also very polite and generous. She always went out of her way to buy her parents Christmas and birthday presents, taking care to pick out the gifts and paid for them with her own pocket money.

"Which newspaper?"

Howard looked up, he had been lost in his thoughts. Elizabeth was directing a question his way.

"Sorry?" he replied.

"Lisa said someone from a newspaper took a photo of you two outside the shopping center?"

Howard nodded: "Just the Gazette, nothing important."

Elizabeth grabbed Lisa by the shoulders and squeezed her tightly, "My little darling's picture is going to be in the paper."

Lisa shook off the statement. "I've already been in the paper," she said. "*Twice*. They took pictures of me and daddy at his work, then one at the house when they did a report on granddad. And they were more important ones too, weren't they daddy?" she looked across at Howard.

Howard smiled and nodded. He remembered both occasions very well. Lisa had been very excited for the first one: a nation-wide newspaper had printed a two-page biography on Howard, his family and his work, not long after his company had declared phenomenal profits over the financial year, making it the richest software company in the country.

For the second interview—in a business and lifestyle maga-zine—Lisa had been less excited, but still managed to smile and sweet talk her way into numerous photos and quotations. The interview itself had been about Howard's father, and the family—and money—he had left behind.

Howard smiled at the memories of his daughter and her claims to fame, but rejected all recollections of his father that tried to creep into his mind. Feeling his eyes tire, he rose from his seat and headed for the coffee machine.

"It's okay, darling," Elizabeth said, pausing mid-conversation with her daughter and reading Howard's actions. "I'll make you a cup."

He smiled and sat back at the kitchen table.

"So, when is the paper due out?" Elizabeth asked, her question directed half at Lisa—who was fiddling through the carrier bags—and half at Howard.

"Tomorrow probably," Howard replied. "It's a daily paper isn't?"

Elizabeth shrugged her shoulders.

"Five days a week," Lisa said, providing the answer with her hands in the bags. "Monday to Friday" she added, confusing her parents.

"How do you know?" Howard wondered.

"Sarah Turnbull's father works there, every time I go over for tea or to play, Mrs. Turnbull is always complaining about him. He's always late for tea, leaves the house a mess, and never calls her."

Elizabeth shot a glance across at Howard. "Sounds familiar," she said.

"Here, mommy," Lisa said, bringing her hands out of the shopping bags. "We bought you this when we were out, you can add it to your collection." With a proud smile Lisa handed her mother a porcelain teddy bear and received a grateful hug.

21

The door to Wayne Pearce's house shut firmly and Darren Morris welcomed the fresh air that washed away the sickly aroma of excrement and blood. He wrapped his jacket around his body and buttoned it up all the way—sheltering himself from the cold while hiding the bloodstains on his shirt.

In the street people still lingered, but their attentions were elsewhere. The heavy bass music still pounded out from the rundown Vauxhall, the noise and the attention it sought had distracted the residents from the brutal murder of their delinquent neighbor.

"That girl is going to be in for a shock," Roach said as they made their way to their car.

"What girl?" Morris quizzed.

"The one half-naked and stoned on the sofa."

"Ah."

"She's going to wake up from her heroin paradise with a lot more then she bargained for."

"A house covered in blood and an addict lying dead in his own shit," Morris mused. "Maybe she'll be too fucked to notice." He brushed past the long uncut grass with a grimace, "Or maybe she overdosed and is picking the lock to heaven's door as we speak."

"You're a heartless bastard, aren't you?" Roach joked. "She's just a kid; she's someone's little girl."

"Look around James. She's no one's little girl, these people are heartless addicts and criminals, lowlifes." He gestured to a group of preteens sitting on the street opposite, smoking joints. "They don't give a fuck what their kids do as long as they can get their own fixes every day."

"Just because it's a rundown estate doesn't mean everyone's a lowlife or an addict."

"Doesn't matter either way," Morris said. "If you're shooting poison into your veins before you hit puberty you're just a drain on society. People like that would sell their own grandmothers for a gram, she's a kid now, but she'll be part of the next generation of shoplifters, muggers, and—" Morris paused.

"Murderers?"

He looked at his colleague and nodded, smiling slyly, "Yes," he admitted.

They entered the Ford and Roach started up the engine. They received a few looks from people in the street as he reversed the car and left the scene.

"Since when do you have a conscience?" Roach said when they were back on the road. "Since when did you even care about society?"

"I don't," Morris replied. "The world's sick and we're part of the disease—I agree with that. People can do what the fuck they like; addicts raping little girls, it's no different to what we do, and, to be honest, I don't care."

"If we cared we wouldn't do what we do," Roach agreed. "It's just . . ." he paused, struggling for words.

"Just what?"

"You seem different that's all."

"Different?"

"Bored, I guess," Roach pondered. "Fed up."

Morris sighed heavily. "I guess I am," he agreed. "I told you, I'm sick of Sanderson and his fucking games. I'm sick of running errands for a fat prick that can't piss without someone holding his cock."

"You're right."

"What?" Morris said, displaying his astonishment.

"Well, I've been thinking about what you said. We kill for a living and we're the best, Sanderson knows that and we know that, yet we get paid next to nothing for it."

Morris turned to his colleague in sheer shock. He had been prepared to launch another attack on their boss, but Roach—who Morris thought would never turn against Sanderson—was beating him to it.

"Top hitters get paid a fortune," Roach continued. "As far as the game goes, we're just thugs. We hit wannabe gangsters, drug dealers, and pathetic addicts. The only problem is, that's all we have. Sanderson is the main man here; we don't have any contacts."

"We don't need them," Morris assured. "We don't necessarily need to pull off a hit. We have the criminal knowledge and we can get all the equipment we need to pull off *any* professional job."

"Like a robbery?"

"No. That's too risky and not profitable, to make enough we'd have to hit a bank or something, and we don't have the man power or the skills to do that."

"What then?"

Morris sat in silence, shrugging his shoulders. "We'll think of something, I'm sure."

"So what about Sanderson?" Roach asked. "We can't just leave him, and if he finds out we're pulling a job behind his back he'll fucking kill us."

"He won't find out," Morris said sternly. "He doesn't follow us about, does he? He gives us a job then sets us on our way. But for now—" he pulled out his cell phone and began jabbing in a number, "—we'll see if he's going to pay us."

"Hello Darren," the smoke-ravaged voice of his boss croaked down the line, "What have you got for me? Did you check this Pearce guy out?"

"We did," Morris confirmed. "We got all we could from him. He didn't have much information for us. Apparently, his supplier doesn't even know much about the operation. He says the pills are shipped in by some Dutch gangsters and then sent around the country through a delivery company. It seems like pretty big shit."

"I don't care how fucking big it is," Sanderson said, raging at the news. "These people are fucking up my business, their gear is now all over the city, I don't care if they're dealing the rest of the country but this is my turf, and I want it dealt with!"

"It's a big operation," Morris reiterated. "We're talking gangsters, guns, and fucking corruption here, we can't sort this by ourselves."

"You work for me Darren; you do what I tell you!" Sanderson bellowed. "Did Pearce give you any information?"

Morris's eyes flared with anger but he managed to keep his composure.

"He mentioned a messenger. The only person who can contact the gangsters, he seems to work as a middleman between the dealers and the importers."

"And?"

"That's it. He said the guy's untouchable. Only a few are allowed contact with him and Pearce is certainly not one of the few."

"What about this supplier of his?" Sanderson's voice screamed down the phone, hissing in Morris's ear.

"We arranged a meeting with him. He's supposedly meeting Pearce in a nearby pub tomorrow night."

"Supposedly?"

"Pearce is dead," Morris said. "We couldn't afford to keep him alive."

"Okay," Sanderson said. "I want you two to meet up with this supplier, see what you can get from him."

Morris turned his attention towards Roach who was listening intently to Morris's side of the conversation. They exchanged a knowing glance.

"I don't think that's wise," Morris replied. "This guy is packing, and he won't be alone, he's got a little cartel of his own," he lied.

"I don't give a fuck!" Sanderson shouted so hard into the phone that Morris edged the device away from his ear. "I want you two to find him and get what information you can from him. That's what I pay you for!"

"Speaking of pay . . ."

"You'll get your pay when you sort this out for me," Sanderson cut in.

"That could take ages. This is deep and we're only scratching the surface here."

"Then keep on fucking scratching!" Sanderson shouted before hanging up. Roach turned to Morris who was staring blankly at the mobile phone. "Well?"

"The fucker ain't paying us until we sort this out."

"He wants us to take down an entire gang of drug smugglers?" Morris nodded, "Yes."

Roach shook his head in disgust, "So, what do you reckon?"

"Fuck him, I say," Morris smiled. "Let's go our own way."

Roach agreed.

They found a cheap B&B a ten-minute drive from where the body of Wayne Pearce had been left to rot. It was a converted detached house on the end of a quiet street; signposted with handwritten placards along the twisting country road that bobbed and weaved a tiresome path to its door.

The building was warm and well decorated; four bedrooms had been converted into seven—all of which were beautifully decorated. The downstairs living room and dining room had been converted into one large breakfast room, with an adjoining staff area.

Most importantly, it was cheap, out of the way, and quiet. It was perfect.

After taking their keys and requesting a bottle of whiskey, they swiftly left the reception area and met in one of the two rooms they had rented for the night.

Darren Morris sat on the edge of the single bed that had been covered in freshly washed white linen. James Roach pulled up a wooden chair and sat down with a groan of relief. There was a bedside cabinet between them and Morris used this as a makeshift bar; setting down two glass tumblers and pouring large measures of the cheap whiskey.

He handed one of the brimming glasses to Roach, took the other and sat back against the pine headboard. "Right," he took a sip of the whiskey and sighed. "Let's see what we can come up with."

22

Michael Richards stood on the second-floor balcony of Rokers Court with both his hands slowly massaging his head. He could feel a niggling hangover denting his brain. He had drunk his way through a dozen bottles of lager the night before and had little sleep—which only made his situation worse.

Ahead of him the door to the safe house was being opened by Johnny Phillips.

"I feel like shit," Richards muttered as he stumbled forward and deactivated the high-tech alarm system.

"Lightweight," Phillips uttered in reply.

Phillips felt fresh and awake. He had matched Richards drinks and had relatively the same sleep, but he rarely found himself nursing hangovers.

"You go in then," Richards grumbled, stepping back outside the apartment and welcoming the fresh air to his sickened stomach.

Phillips moaned but walked into the apartment nevertheless—taking great care to step over the deactivated laser-trip system.

Richards's stomach groaned. He needed food, he wasn't hungry and doubted he could eat much, but he was sure he needed food. He was dehydrated, his stomach was empty, and he felt like his brain had been thrown into a washing machine.

Phillips emerged from the apartment a minute later. He locked the door and then ushered Richards away.

They were sure to visit to the apartment every so often. Sometimes they stayed the night or spent the day there. It wasn't as cozy as their house, but by paying attention to the safe house they made sure everything was in order.

If the neighbors thought it was an empty flat, they would break in and try to use it as a drug den, setting off their security system. If the two conmen didn't keep up appearances in the area, they risked having it ransacked. The residents were habitual criminals and drug addicts, but they knew Phillips; he'd had words with more than a few of them, and his words intimidated people.

"What now?" Richards asked as they descended the stairs.

"Let's go get some food," Phillips said, rubbing his belly. "I'm fucking starved."

Richards nodded as his stomach groaned again.

23

Morning was an unwelcome visitor to the tired mind of James Roach. He felt its presence swarm over his dehydrated body as his brain tuned out from his deep dreams and flickered onto reality.

He opened his eyes with great difficulty.

When he moved his body, he felt hot and sticky and incredibly uncomfortable. Looking down, he realized he had fallen asleep on top of his blankets, still in his clothes from the night before. He blinked away dry tears and squinted at a digital clock by the bed. The flashing red digits told him it was 11:30 am.

He hadn't woken up that late in years.

"Finally, it's awake."

Roach recognized the discontented tone of his partner in crime. Morris had been sitting at a chair near the window; he rose and stood over the bed.

"You should have woken me," Roach said, his voice dry.

"I've just got back," Morris declared, handing his colleague a bottle of soda which was gratefully accepted.

"What time did you get up?" Roach asked.

"Early, I left at seven."

"Where have you been?" Roach snapped the bottle cap and gulped down the carbonated drink.

Morris had a proud grin on his face. "I've found us a job."

"What?" Roach blurted, a trickle of soda dribbling down his chin. "How?"

Morris's smile grew. He was holding something in his hand. Walking to the top of the bed he dropped it onto Roach's lap.

Roach stared at it in complete bemusement. It was the local paper, whose circulation didn't reach where Morris and Roach lived, but covered the area where they had spent the night.

"What the fuck am I looking at?" Roach stared.

Morris pointed at a large picture on the front page. "Howard Price," he said. "He's a big-shot businessman, lives close by."

"I know that, but what do we want with him?"

Morris smiled again, "Him? Nothing. It's his daughter we want."

"Kidnapping!" Roach choked as he stared at the picture of the seven-year-old girl holding tightly on to her father.

"Yep."

"Have you lost your mind?"

"Not that I know of," Morris said. "Look, it's an easy job. Simple snatch, big payout, what's the problem?"

Roach's gaze shifted from Morris to Lisa Price's picture on the front page of the paper. "This is not us. This is not what we do."

"Why not?"

Roach pondered but couldn't find a reasonable answer that Morris would accept.

Morris said, "If we can get away with murder, then why can't we snatch a little girl? It's just glorified babysitting."

"Babysitting with a long fucking jail sentence."

"Not as long as murder."

"That's different, Sanderson covers most of our tracks."

"Most," Morris reminded him. "The rest is all us, ruthless and efficient, that's why we're the best, that's why we're free men. Not because of a fat drug pushing bastard."

Silence descended as Roach's mind whirred.

"Are you sure you want to be trying this?" he said eventually—his tone softer.

"Why not?"

"We're fucking murderers; this is out of our league. We can't pull something like this off."

"There's nothing to it. We're hitters—compared to murder this is just a walk in the park."

"These things take a lot of planning."

"Nonsense, most of it is common sense. It's not like we're snatching the Prime Minister's kid, is it?"

"You can't just jump straight into a kidnapping," Roach argued.

"Of course we can."

"You've seriously lost your mind, haven't you?"

Morris smiled and sat down on the bed. "Listen," he instructed. "I picked up the paper from the front desk this morning, they have a bundle of them down there and they'd just been delivered; I had nothing else to do so I had a cup of coffee and flicked through. I read the article over and over before it hit me, it says what school she goes to here," he pointed to a line in the article and read it aloud. "Seven-year-old daughter Lisa Price, who attends Lady Victoria's, the local private school for girls."

"The crazy bitch at the front desk saw me reading the article and started blabbing on about Price," he continued. "She said he lives in a huge secluded house. A few niceties and I had the address."

"You went to their house?"

Morris stopped and glared at Roach before ignoring his statement and continuing with what he had to say.

"So I took the car and headed up there, it's only a few minutes away. Nice place. I used the binoculars in the trunk, checked the windows and *bam*, there she was, sitting by herself watching television, ripe for the picking." He smiled but Roach's frown didn't crease. "Anyway, I checked the rest of the house, and it seems only the three of them live there."

"Three?" Roach interrupted.

"His wife," he explained. "Saucy little number she is. I checked through some old business magazines in the library and it seems she only works part time, if at all. She just stays at the house and lives off his riches."

"You went to the library?"

"Can I finish my fucking story?"

"Okay."

"Right, so I waited there till around 8:30, then his wife walks out with the young girl, they both jumped into a Porsche—which I'm guessing is her daily driver—and drove away. I followed them to the school and saved the directions into that annoying fucking gadget of yours."

"The GPS?"

"Yes."

"I thought you didn't know how to use—" Roach paused, "Never mind. Continue."

"She dropped her off, spoke to a few of the other mothers, waited until the school opened, then she left and drove straight back home. Price was still there so I called up his work and gave some bullshit about needing to speak to him about a business proposal and the secretary tells me he's taken a vacation."

"That's a bad thing, right?"

"Not really, we don't need to snatch the girl from the house, the school is wide open, the play area is surrounded by a fence, but the gate looks like it's usually left open."

"They fence the kids in?"

"Just to keep them off the road probably, the back of the school is right next to a busy road," he explained. "So, I made a few calls, went to the library and sorted out a few other things."

"Like what?"

"I got us some phone equipment, a resprayed BMW, and a safe house."

"All this in one morning?"

"Sort-of," Morris said. "I just rang up Linders. He sorted out the car and the phone—he said they would be untraceable."

"Linders is a lowlife ex-con."

"But he has no links to Sanderson, so he's ideal."

"He's an idiot, Sanderson can't fucking stand him, that's why he has no links with him."

"He'll do. He isn't going to be involved, I didn't tell him anything and he didn't ask questions."

"How did you get the safe house, then?" Roach asked.

"You remember a few months back, when he had to hunt down that young dealer who took Sanderson's drugs and ran?"

"Yes, it took us a few weeks to catch him because he—" Roach paused, realizing, "—had been squatting in some derelict apartments . . ." he finished slowly.

"Exactly. Perfect for what we need. No one but druggies and lowlives go there, and out of the whole block only a couple of the apartments are legally occupied, the rest are there for the taking.

It's only a twenty-minute drive from here, even shorter from the school."

Roach sat up and swung his legs over the side of the bed. He felt a stabbing pain at the side of his head which he teased away with his fingers.

"Well?" Morris asked from behind him.

"Well, what?"

"Are you in or not?"

"I don't fucking harm little kids," Roach said. "She's only seven, for fuck's sake."

"We don't need to harm a hair on her head," Morris assured. "They'll pay up, she's an only child and her father's loaded."

Roach contemplated this. He turned to look into Morris's eyes, then at the smiling face of Lisa Price on the front of the newspaper. "I think you're fucking crazy and it's a risky idea, but I've worked with you for a long time and you always manage to pull through," the two men locked glances. "I'm in."

"Excellent," Morris breathed with a wide grin, "We're meeting Linders tomorrow for the gear. Now we need to check out the school again, catch them in time for their dinner break, we'll see if we can spy her running around. Then we can head across to the safe house and see what we need to do to make that place secure."

24

Howard Price jabbed at the remote control in an attempt to stifle his boredom. The satellite service he paid a small fortune for each month offered over five-hundred channels, and the law of averages maintained he should be interested in at least a few of them, but he couldn't find anything that sparked his interest.

He flipped through the channels with increasing contempt: daytime chat shows, repeats of daytime chat shows, entertainment news, sports news, local news, old sitcoms, new sitcoms, foreign sitcoms, music videos, music quizzes, matinee movies, theatrical movies, melodramatic movies.

Everything that graced his screen was greeted with distaste. He wasn't one for watching television, occasionally he would sit down at night with a drink and watch a few hours to relax before bed, but daytime TV was a different story altogether.

Finding a showing of *The Great Escape* he dropped the remote control and threw his head back on the soft sofa cushions.

"You look bored, dear." Elizabeth stood in the open doorway to the living room.

"I am," Howard admitted. "I don't know how you manage to live like this. It's so dull. How do you keep yourself occupied?"

She raised an eyebrow at him and then decided against commenting. "I work around the house," she replied with a smile. She had just left the confines of the kitchen where only an hour before she and Howard had sat down to dinner.

Howard nodded with little enthusiasm. "I'm starting to wish I'd never taken this vacation."

"You needed the break," Elizabeth said. "You took the vacation for your health and for your family."

Howard nodded again, still not convinced.

"I know you love spending time with Lisa and I know you've tried your best to make sure you spend every free minute you have with her, but lately your free minutes have dried up." She sat down next to her husband.

"You're right."

"I know I am," she said. "The stress is killing you. You need the rest, no matter how bored you are."

Howard let out a discontented sigh and then nodded in acceptance. He had recently been for a check-up with his doctor concerning intense and regular migraines. His doctor had suggested he take time off work—after Elizabeth had already insisted he do so—after further tests had shown signs of high blood pressure, which, along with the migraines, were put down to high levels of stress and tension.

Elizabeth snuggled into him and he wrapped his arm around her shoulders.

He knew the break from work would do him a great deal of good, and he adored spending time with his family, but he still stressed over every minute that he wasn't at the office, worried that his business would collapse without him.

Glancing up at a large grandfather clock—passed onto him by three generations; it would eventually go to Lisa when she got her own house—Howard smiled as the minute hand notched onto twelve and the clock rang out a polished chime to mark one o'clock.

Lisa would be home soon; that thought alone brightened his day.

25

Roach left the driving to Morris, he was tired and his energy drained, while Morris seemed to be full of it. As he raced along the highway, Roach regarded him wearily. He was smiling broadly—he could almost see the glint in his eye, the eagerness, the compassion. Roach knew that his partner really wanted to go through with the kidnapping and he also knew that Darren Morris usually got what he wanted.

The thought of kidnapping had initially hit him with concern; it was a risky thing to do, but when he mulled the idea over he reasoned that it couldn't be any riskier than the jobs they were doing for Sanderson regularly.

He had livened up to the idea. He could see the hurdles involved but couldn't see himself and Morris tripping over them. It was just a matter of common sense, confidence, a lack of morals, and a ruthless attitude—the payout would set them both up for life.

"Here it is," Morris spoke through curled lips.

The car slowed down and rolled alongside the curb. Lady Victoria's school protruded from the dull afternoon skyline and the Ford halted by the side of the curb.

The road was—as Morris had described—very close to the play area. The school itself was set further back, along with a small staff parking area. The road where the car parked was lined with large houses on one side and a fence on the other.

There were over fifty children—all young girls—in the grassed play area beyond the gate. Some were standing around talking to friends; some were playing ball games—others swung, slid and climbed on the recreational equipment.

The children themselves were at least fifty yards from the fence and in clear view of the road. In the middle of the fence stood a large gate, slightly ajar and swaying in the wind. A thick chain dangled from its handle, waiting to be tied and secured.

"The gate stays open, as far as I can gather," Morris said.

"You've only staked the place out for one morning," Roach told him. "How would you know?"

"The parents were walking their kids through it," Morris said matter-of-factly. "Then they stayed inside talking while the kids waited round the back somewhere. If they closed the gate during school hours, the parents would have talked outside the gate," he said. "You'd think a place like this would be a bit more secure."

They both watched the children playing, their eyes scouring the faces for the blonde-haired girl from the paper.

"Or maybe that rich fuck should have sent his kid to a better school," Morris said. "It's not like he hasn't got the money."

"Who cares," Roach said. "It makes it easier for us."

"True."

They both watched on in silence, before Roach asked what had been lingering on both their minds.

"So, what are we going to set the ransom at?"

In the schoolyard, Lisa Price giggled loudly as her friend kicked the plastic ball into the air, sending it spinning across the playground. She ran to catch it, but the wind took hold of the hollow ball and it spun wildly away.

She giggled again and chased after it, her school blazer flapping behind her. The ball hit the fence and rolled slowly along the metal perimeter.

She slowed her run to a walk and bent down to pick it up. A silver car, parked outside of the school, caught her eye as she picked up the colorful ball. She could see two men in the front of the car; they were talking to one another.

One of the men turned and returned Lisa's stare. She couldn't make out his features due to the sunlight glaring on the windscreen, but she could make out that he was smiling at her.

She happily smiled back at him, picked up the ball and ran back to her friend.

26

The screen on the large television glittered and flicked through highlights from an action-packed football game; below it a games console roared softly over the football chants and Indie music.

Johnny Phillips sat with his back against the leather sofa, his eyes half watching the scenes on the screen. He held a wireless controller in his hand which hung loosely by his side.

They had decided against doing anything—choosing to relax in front of the computer and watch some television instead. They had eaten well at lunchtime, both filling their empty stomachs, still fresh with alcohol from the night before, before going back to the house.

He took a small sip from a can of beer. It was only his second can and he didn't plan to have many more; he was drinking to shake away the boredom.

The sound of a flushing toilet interrupted the noise from the football game and seconds later a lock clicked, a door opened and closed, and the door leading to the living room did the same.

"You took your time," he said.

"I couldn't fucking piss," Richards said, still zipping up his pants. "I just stood there for a few minutes waiting for it to come. Then when it did come, fuck!" he gestured, sucking air in through his teeth. "It burned."

Phillips laughed over the top of his beer can, shooting small bubbles of froth into the air.

"You're probably dehydrated."

"No shit," Richards slumped onto the other side of the sofa. "That's my first piss today, it was fucking orange," he explained, much to the amusement of his friend. "I had to stop halfway through and take a hold of the door handle, the fucking burning was killing me. The longer I went, the more it burned, just my luck I had a fucking bladder full."

"It happens to the best of us."

"Come on then" he picked up the second controller left on the arm of the sofa. "Let's get back to the game"

The pause screen, with its nauseating music and graphical highlights, dropped away and a football game ensued.

"I can't believe you're drinking again," Richards said with his eyes on the screen.

"Some of us can handle our ale."

"I ain't that bad. I just drank too much last night. It's playing fucking hell with my guts, yet I've got the munchies. It hurts when I piss and I'm dehydrated yet I can't even *force* water down my throat. Beer always fucking does this to me."

"Stop complaining, maybe your body is trying to tell you something."

"That alcohol is bad for me and I shouldn't be drinking?" He suggested.

"No. That you're a pussy and you can't handle your drink."

To Roach, Darren Morris looked more than prepared for the proposed kidnapping. After hanging around the school until the children went back to their classes, the pair of assassins had departed; happy in the knowledge that they could snatch the girl without any problems.

They had driven around the area a few times and found that, on this particular day, it was reasonably empty. With the quick access to the main roads, they knew it would be easy for them to leave the scene quickly afterwards. Although, racing away didn't seem necessary as they noticed that no teachers or guardians were on patrol in the playground; the only possible witnesses to the crime would be the children themselves, but when they finally told an adult about what happened, the kidnappers would be long gone whether they raced away or not.

After leaving the area Morris drove to a hardware store to buy a kit for child proofing car doors. He bought his supplies from different stores so it wouldn't look suspicious.

He bought thin wire rope in abundance, three tumbler locks, and a large roll of duct tape and string from one small shop, and a set of solid steel padlocks and metal chains from another.

Then they headed for the safe house, unsurprised when they found it to be in an even more run-down than their previous visit.

It was a stone's throw from a small park—which had seen better days—and further back from a small council estate that looked like it was still recovering from the blitz.

It was the land that life forgot. The town itself had less than one hundred residents, most of which lived on the council estate. Near the park, past a burned-out bus shelter, were the only stores in the area: a small co-op, a diner, and a newsstand. The windows on all of them were either boarded up or completely shattered.

Morris steered the car past the busted, broken stores as he traversed his way to the apartment building which stood on the horizon like a Picasso painting on opium.

It was completely isolated. There had once been a small playground nearby, but that was now littered with beer bottles and drug paraphernalia. Even the parking area was in tatters—covered in broken glass, weeds growing between the cracked paving slabs and empty beer bottles.

They passed only four other cars, two were missing wheels and propped up on bricks. Morris steered the car in-between the two that were still mobile and they clambered out of the vehicle.

It was like a ghost town. The four-story building in front of them looked deserted, over a dozen windows decorated the outside of the building, but only two weren't boarded up.

"Want me to wait by the car?" Roach offered.

"No need," Morris said. "We won't be long."

Within minutes they found a suitable apartment. On entering the building, they were greeted by silence, occasionally they heard giggling and stomping from the two top floor apartments, but nothing that concerned them. The two apartments on the second floor and the two on the third floor were empty; the doors were missing from three of them. The insides of one looked like it had recently been the victim of a small fire while the other was filled with hypodermic needles and blankets.

They left the top floor alone as it seemed to be used more than the rest. The second apartment on the bottom floor was where they found their refuge, the key factor for their decision being that the front door was still intact.

They entered cautiously but found no one inside. The apartment had been used by squatters and druggies—needles, burned foil, and empty bottles crowded every corner, and all the furniture had been stolen except for a set of old wooden chairs and a scruffy mattress—but there was no indication of recent activity.

"Looks like the place for us," Roach noted as he ran his fingers over the edge of the plywood covering the windows, sketching a deep line in the thick dust.

Morris nodded. "Go back to the car. We left the tools in the back."

Roach nodded and left the apartment, leaving Morris to look around and admire the infested domicile. When he returned they secured the door, fitting the three tumbler locks, the metal chain, and a padlock.

They weren't disturbed.

27

"Why tomorrow?" Roach asked, his question was directed at Darren Morris, who stood over him with a remote control in his hand, only half interested in finding a decent station and half speaking to his colleague.

The bed and breakfast had filled up since their return, the other rooms were being prepared for a large family, who waited in the reception area. They had all greeted the hitmen with welcome voices, none of their greetings were returned.

"The sooner we get this done, the better," Morris replied, concentrating on finding something on the television that could alleviate his boredom and settle the nervous excitement that buzzed through him.

"We need more time," Roach argued in a tone that suggested he knew that no matter what he said, it would be overturned.

"Time is not an issue here. It's a simple snatch."

"There are more issues to cover then the grab itself. We need to sort out ransom demands, pickups, etcetera."

"Like I said James. It's all common sense. We make the snatch, head to the safe house—"

"It ain't much of a safe house, though is it?"

"Why not? It's deserted. We aren't renting it, so there's no paperwork and we've secured it. We just take the girl, dump her there, keep the noise down and the lights out, and keep an eye on her. Although, I'm sure we can handle a bunch of squatters and druggies if it comes down to that."

Roach frowned at the answer, but shrugged it off.

Morris dropped the remote control in boredom, leaving the television on a local news station.

"Why are you so uptight about the idea all of a sudden, anyway?" he wanted to know. "I thought you were up for it."

"I am, in a way. I'm just a little unsure about it. This is big for us; this could bring in a lot of money, enough for us to retire."

"Exactly, so what's the problem?"

"That *is* the problem," Roach stated. "It seems far too easy. We've been killing for years and getting away with it—yet we've hardly made a fortune from it, have we? But if we pull this off, which could be way easier than most of the jobs we've done in the past, we'll be set for life."

"Stop worrying."

"I'm not, it just seems a little too. . ." Roach was lost for words.

"Easy. I know, and that's exactly what it is. By next week, we'll have enough money to stop working for that fucking dick Sanderson, and start living for once," Morris declared with excitement.

Both men stopped mid-conversation and turned their heads towards the television screen as familiar words were spoken by the news broadcaster.

"Police say the incident on Walker Street yesterday could very well be gang related." The reporter's voice played over a camera angle focused on Wayne Pearce's house. "The murder is thought to have occurred around mid-afternoon. Mr. Pearce, a well-known drug addict and dealer, was brutally beaten to death in his home."

The camera zoomed in closer, the area was surrounded by forensic teams and a swarm of police officers and detectives. "Our reporters haven't been allowed access to the scene, but a local resident who found the massacred body gave this horrific statement."

The camera cut to recorded footage. In front of the lens stood a middle-aged, scrawny man, his bloodshot eyes and pale face a portrait of substance abuse. "The door was open," he explained to the cameras. "So I just walked straight in, when I got in there was this 'orrible smell. It was sick, like something you couldn't imagine, really 'orrible." He droned on. "It nearly blinded me, it did; I was so shocked by it. But when I opened my eyes I seen Wayne— lying there all twisted and stuff. He was covered in blood; it looked like his head had been caved in. Then I noticed the cuts—" he man paused, seemingly horrified by the recollections. "He was a mess."

"So far the police have one suspect in custody." The news reporter said as the screen offered up a photo ID of Wayne Pearce, in all his drugged-up glory. "A young girl who has yet to be named but is believed to live in the area."

The camera flashed to another interview, this time with a police detective, he read from a paper, his eyes occasionally lifting to the camera. "Mr. Pearce is a well-known addict and suspected drug dealer," the nervous officer began. "Many drugs—clearly intended for sale—were found on his premises, including a collection of banned substances found on his person. Due to his record and the severity of the crime we are treating this as a gang-related murder, and will be questioning known users in the area."

He paused to take a question from an unseen journalist, as the cameras flashed in his face.

"What about the suspect?" one journalist bellowed.

"We have a suspect in custody who we believe may have been involved in the crime; that is all I can tell you at the moment."

Darren Morris smiled at James Roach. "See," he said. "We can get away with murder; why can't we get away with a measly kidnapping?"

His smile was returned by James Roach who had been watching the report eagerly. They had seen similar events before; from here on they knew they were safe. A few druggies would be questioned, people would be arrested and released, and then the case would go cold.

They had escaped the hands of the law again.

"Okay," Roach said, still smiling. "Tomorrow it is."

28

The dice spun and flipped its way across the cardboard mat, missing a stack of cards, and landing near a silver hat.

"Three!" Lisa Price shouted in delight.

Howard Price sighed and moved a small iron three spaces across the board, it landed on a purple square marked Mayfair, decorated with a small plastic hotel.

Price, sitting opposite his daughter on the living room floor, flicked through a stack of colored money that lay by his side. He stabbed at it and flicked it away in mild distaste.

"Not enough," he announced. "You win."

Lisa smiled victoriously. She took the money from him and stacked it into piles she had already created; all neatly lined up in front of her, one stack for each denomination.

Howard rose to his feet. He had been sitting on the floor for the entire game, which had stretched past three hours and, as he stood, he felt the effects. His knees cracked awkwardly and he found himself groaning.

He slumped on the sofa. "I'm getting old."

Elizabeth, sitting next to him, smiled in his direction and nodded slyly. He pushed her playfully on her shoulders.

"You're not supposed to agree with me," he laughed, his hands holding his lower back.

"Nearly five thousand," Lisa said, flicking through her paper money.

Howard nodded, impressed. He wasn't one for letting his daughter win, he was very competitive no matter who he played, and the game of Monopoly had been no different. Even Elizabeth had been playing, until her money and assets had fallen to their daughter's growing empire.

"Are you going to put it away?" Howard asked.

She nodded pleasantly and began scooping up the mass of hotels, houses, money, and playing cards. Howard watched her every move; she had a constant smile etched on her face.

She loved spending time with him as much as he loved spending time with her. When she had returned from school she had rushed to him, offering ideas for games and things to do together. Her friend had phoned up an hour after she returned, asking if she wanted to go outside and play, an offer which she had turned down so she could spend time with her father, much to his delight.

He didn't typically get the chance to spend so much time with her due to his work obligations, so they both took advantage of the change.

They had played on her games console at first, until she tired of his lack of ability to use the controller and decided to have a catch in the backyard. After an hour or so of that, they had come inside and played the board game, settling down as a family.

Now Lisa's bedtime dawned, and she knew it, as did her mother.

"You'll have to go to bed soon," Elizabeth said as Lisa finished stacking the pieces in the box and replaced the cardboard lid. "It's past nine and you have school in the morning."

Lisa sighed and turned to her dad with a sad-puppy expression. He could offer no solace to her, so she turned back to her mother.

"Do I have to?" she said, her voice soft and manipulative.

Elizabeth exchanged stares with her daughter.

"I'll tell you what," Elizabeth conceded. "You can watch some TV first."

Lisa's face lit up and within the blink of an eye she had jumped on the sofa, nestling in between her parents.

"But just a bit," Elizabeth warned. "I'm shattered, I'll be going to bed in ten minutes or so. She turned to Howard, "And don't you go telling her that she can stay up late," she warned.

Howard put his hands up defensively.

Elizabeth rose to her feet, "I'm going to make a cup of hot chocolate and then get ready for bed." Turning to her husband, she said: "Make sure she goes to bed before ten."

Howard nodded, kissed his wife, and then watched as she left the room.

Lisa turned to him, a pleading look in her eyes. He winked at her, bringing a smile to her face. She leaned into him, cuddling him as he flicked through the television stations.

29

The two hitmen sat in one of their two rented B&B rooms; Roach on the edge of the bed, Morris on a plush chair in the corner—their attentions on the television. They had been flicking through a collection of DVDs downstairs—bought by the owner and rented out to the guests—and had picked up a copy of *The Dark Knight*. They had both seen it before but the rest of the DVDs on offer were animated comedies, sixties romance flicks, and a large collection of westerns.

Not a word had been exchanged between the pair for half an hour. They were both happy that way—in silence, singularly contemplating the days ahead.

The silence broke when Darren's cell phone began to ring.

He pulled the small device out of his pocket. He could feel Roach's eyes on him and he returned the glare.

"It says unknown number," he said with the phone still ringing in his hand.

"Sanderson," Roach said, somewhat alarmed.

Morris nodded.

"It's after ten," Roach declared. "We told him we'd be meeting up with Pearce's dealer at seven. He's going to be—"

"I know!" Morris snapped. "But it doesn't concern us anymore."

The phone continued to ring.

Roach looked annoyed. "Aren't you going to answer it?"

"And say what? 'Sorry Sanderson, but we don't wanna kill for you anymore because you're a fat, lazy, underpaying twat. We've decide to branch out and do a bit of kidnapping?'"

"If you don't answer he's going to get suspicious."

"He lives his life above the law, he's always fucking suspicious."

They sat in silence, listening to the incessant ringing.

"Just feed him some lies, it's not like it'll be the first time," Roach said.

Morris shook his head. The phone stopped ringing. He smiled and looked at Roach triumphantly.

"Problem solved," he grinned.

Just as he stuffed the mobile phone back into his pocket it started to ring again.

The noise sent a chill through the room.

He stared at it momentarily, hesitant. Then he answered it, catching sight of the worried expression on Roach's face as he did so.

"Hello," he said, his voice clear.

"Darren!" Sanderson didn't seem pleased. "What the fuck is going on there?" he spat.

"What do you mean?"

"This shit with Wayne Pearce; you said you were meeting his dealer at seven. That was over three fucking hours ago! I told you to keep in touch."

"We just finished," Morris said. He looked at Roach who gleamed back wearily. "The guy was pissing us about."

"What did you get from him?" Sanderson bellowed.

"Fuck all, he knows nothing more than Pearce did."

"But you got links, suppliers, leads, right?"

"We got nothing. He says his pills get left at drop points for him. His dealer phones him, tells him when they've received a shipment, and gives him a point to pick up the drugs. That's all he could tell us. The supplier uses an untraceable line when he contacts him, and the dumps are random and there's never anyone else there." The lies were rolling off his tongue with great ease.

"Fuck!" Sanderson screamed. "Where is this guy now?"

"Dead," Morris said. "We got all we needed from him."

The line fell silent. Morris could practically feel his boss's anger coursing through the phone.

"It just so happens I have a few other boys on the case," Sanderson announced with a deflated resignation. "And *they* haven't gone cold yet. I'm very disappointed with you boys, I expect you won't object to a pay cut, seen as you've fucked this job for me."

Morris merely mumbled into the line and then it went dead. Sanderson had hung up.

"Bastard," he spat as he stuffed the phone back in his pocket.

"What?" Roach asked.

"He's giving us a fucking pay cut. We do what he asks and he has the fucking nerve to cut our money short."

"Does it matter?" Roach asked, smiling.

Morris shrugged his shoulders, also smiling. "No, it doesn't. Fuck him."

They were awake and alert early the next morning. They had both slept in their own rooms, departing company late the night before.

At seven o'clock, they strolled downstairs, ordered their breakfast, and sat alone in the dining room, all the other tables were empty and the only noise came from the kitchen, where the clattering of pots and pans indicated that their breakfast was being cooked.

They sat opposite each other but avoided eye contact. Hardly a word had been shared between them all morning. They knew they had a big day ahead, a lot had to be done; a lot was at stake.

Morris took a sip from a hot cup of tea, served to each of them within minutes of sitting down. His eyes caught the fierce and thoughtful features of James Roach.

"I'll head over to see Linders when we've had something to eat," he said, confirming their plans for the first time. "When I get there I'll pick up the Beemer from him and head to the safe house, you go to the Price house to make sure everything is going as planned."

"Planned?" Roach said.

"Enough planning has gone into this."

Roach nodded, his eyes staring deep into a cup of black tea.

"I should be at the safe house before you. Meet me there when you've checked out the school," Morris said.

Again Roach agreed.

The dining room door flew open and a cheery-faced owner, cradling two plates, strutted into the room. She put the plates down on the table.

"There you go lads. Get that down ya. Nothing like a good breakfast to start the day."

"Thanks."

"No problem. If you need anything else just give me a shout." Her voice twinkled with pleasantness. Morris and Roach smiled at her and she left.

When the doors to the dining room slammed shut the room fell silent again.

30

"I love you, sweetheart," Howard Price kissed his daughter softly on the forehead. He embraced her briefly, feeding off her warmth.

After being released from his strong arms, Lisa Price smiled at him and walked out the front door and into the garden.

Elizabeth soon followed, she also stopped at the doorway to kiss Howard. "I'll cook you some breakfast when I get back," she said after lightly caressing his cheek with her moist red lips.

He nodded and watched as Elizabeth strolled out into the garden, following her daughter.

As the front door shut, Howard found himself deeply sighing. Boredom was already creeping up on him. He thought about heading into the living room to watch some television, but the image of happy-go-lucky, Prozac-pumped presenters eating up morning airtime was enough to put him off.

He thought about food. He hadn't had breakfast yet, but he wasn't hungry and he wasn't much of a cook. Elizabeth would come back from dropping Lisa off at school and cook him anything from an omelet to a full English breakfast. Left to his own devices he wouldn't accomplish more than toast, and he'd probably manage to burn even that.

He would wait for breakfast. He'd already drained two cups of coffee, and that was enough to keep his stomach from growling at him for at least another hour.

Sighing, he decided to call work. He wasn't working but it would be reassuring to make sure everyone else was.

Lisa Price skipped across the flower-peppered yard, dancing to a beat composed by her imagination. The sun was out bright and early and its rays bore down onto her browning skin.

Repeatedly singing a verse from a sixties song she'd heard on an advertisement, she spun underneath the morning glare in a state of childish euphoria.

In the trees at the end of the garden birds sang merrily—adding soprano to the child's soft hum. In the flower beds—ripened and glorious in the beaming sunshine—bees swarmed over the pollen, their wings buzzing with a beat of simplicity.

Among the lines of foliage, along the perimeter of the yard, a squirrel scurried nosily, frantically sniffing the ground as it raced through the dense greenery; noisily flicking dried leaves and broken twigs as its tiny feet danced across the ground.

The distant roar of cars crashed into the air. The noise spilled from the small road just beyond the yard and the adjoining highway further afield.

Past the driveway, on the small road beyond the bushes, a car—beautifully reflecting the sun from its silver surface—sat idle. Muffled sounds of music escaped from the inside where a man sat with nervous patience.

James Roach tapped his fingers on the steering wheel. He attempted to drum along to the beat of a song he'd never heard before, his attempts, unsurprisingly, failed.

Out of the driver's side window, he could see the Price house in all its splendor. He daydreamed momentarily as he watched in awe, wondering and hoping that the future would bring him a large country house of his own—his own private paradise.

The sunlight sang through the window and glared into his retinas, causing him to turn his head and blink away the light.

Through the top corner of the windscreen he watched, through cigarette burnt vision, as Lisa Price skipped merrily through the luscious front yard. He could see her smiling features and he smiled back with a twinkle of wickedness escaping his deep eyes.

He saw Elizabeth Price call to her, beckoning her to an immaculate Porsche, where she had the door propped open. He watched her with admiration, eyeing her sun-drenched face and her petite, curvy figure—pleasantly exposed when she bent down to pick up a set of dropped keys.

"Not bad," he muttered to himself. His words were captured and drowned by the sounds of the local radio station and its sugar-coated pop music.

Under the watchful eyes of James Roach, Lisa exchanged friendly words with her mother before they both climbed into the car.

He continued to smile as the Porsche and its valuable passenger reversed out of the driveway, backed to a stop a mere twenty feet in front of him, and then pulled away down the quiet road.

Turning off the radio he waited until the Porsche turned a corner and vanished from sight, only then did he accelerate.

31

Even in a city of criminals and a street of no-hopers, Peter Linder stood out as one of the most decrepit, worthless, and pointless.

Arrested at the tender age of eighteen for his involvement in a gun smuggling operation, the skinny, humorless man had gone on to serve fifteen years behind bars. Time he had put to good use.

It was common knowledge that he had made more money behind bars than he had in the free world. Using his outside contacts, he had sold everything from drugs to hardcore porn while serving his time.

He had come before the attention of gang lord Peter Sanderson while serving his sentence. Sanderson knew many men inside the prison—his dealings had landed most of them in there—and word of a youngster making a fortune while being incarcerated had traveled fast to his ears.

They had struck deals with each other. Sanderson provided protection, corruption, and an outlet for the convict's money, on condition that Linders bought all of his drugs from him. They had worked well together for years. They managed to fill one of the country's most secure and populated prison with drugs from cocaine to cannabis and Valium, to Viagra (an unsettling notion for both men, but profitable nevertheless).

Peter Linder had used his time inside constructively, there was no doubt about that. He had walked into the prison an ill-educated teenager and, thanks to the recreational and learning activities offered to the modern-day prisoner, he had left with a vast knowledge of electronics, car mechanics, and computing—all of which he exploited for illegal purposes when he was released.

He stood in front of Darren Morris with a wide grin. He wore mechanics' overalls, and held a hand-rolled cigarette loosely between two fingers on his right hand.

"Nice little motor that is," he said—his voice croaking out of his feeble throat.

Morris nodded and looked past Linders, to the black BMW. It didn't look up too much and it certainly wasn't flashy, but it would do the trick, they didn't want to stand out.

"Here," Morris said, handing a brown paper bag to the scruffy man. "The money is all there."

"I trust you," Linders immediately stuffed the bag into his overalls. "You still work for that prick Sanderson?"

Morris smiled. After Linders had been released from prison Sanderson had stopped all dealings with him. He said he didn't trust him and Sanderson didn't work with people he didn't trust. Linders held a grudge and even though he still did jobs for people who worked for Sanderson, he always resented the man who rejected his business.

"Yes," Morris replied.

Linders scowled and took a deep drag from his cigarette.

"The phone is in the back seat," he spoke through a lungful of smoke. "It's not completely untraceable, they never are, but it's as close as you're ever going to get."

Morris used the keys given to him by Linders to open the front door of the BMW. "Where's the car from?"

"You know I can't tell you that."

Morris nodded in agreement.

"It's untouchable now though," Linders added. "That much I can guarantee you. It's had new plates fitted, a full respray, and I even stripped and refitted the interior. The paperwork is in the back seat, should you need it," he took another draw from his cancer stick. "Completely untouchable."

"It fucking better be," Morris warned. "Or I'll be paying you another visit very soon. And this time I won't be so fucking friendly."

"Come on Darren," Linders said, a smile still etched onto his grizzly face. "When have I ever let you down?"

Morris stared him down—both of their features unflinching—before clambering behind the wheel of the car.

"And when have you *ever* been friendly?" Linders added with a smug grin as Morris revved up the engine.

32

The Porsche cruised along the many roads that lead to the private school. Behind, always a few lengths and at least one car away, Peter Roach followed.

The roads were busy, crammed with tired and irritated drivers rushing to their places of work or education, allowing Roach to blend in perfectly. He had kept a clean distance for the entire journey, but as the road turned sharply into a built-up area he slowed his pace and drew closer to the gleaming Porsche.

The sides of the roads were peppered with young children and their guardians. Rolling along at less than ten miles per hour Roach watched a line of children walk along the street, accompanied by two middle-aged women at the front. Further down from the walking group stood a chubby crossing guard, wielding her sign with great pride.

The Porsche rolled past the woman and stopped further down, just as the school building popped over the horizon. Roach, keeping his steady pace, watched as the walking posse halted by the side of the stubby yellow woman.

The crossing guard acknowledged the children and, with her head held high, she crossed the road, holding her sign firmly.

Roach looked past the orange-shaped, lemon-colored woman and watched as Lisa and Elizabeth Price exited the Porsche further down the road, having found a parking space by the side of the school—mere feet from where Roach and Morris had waited the previous day.

With his eye still on his target, he watched the line of children cross the road in front of him. A few looked at his car, some with blank expressions, some smiling. One, a happy-faced young boy, caught sight of Roach and offered a friendly wave; Roach smiled deeply and shot the boy a wink and a thumbs-up.

When the bulbous woman retired to the side of the road Roach continued at a leisurely pace, passing the stationary Porsche. He pulled the Ford into a parking bay further down the road and watched the bustling school building though his rear-view mirror.

Everything happened exactly as Morris had described. Lisa left the car—after exchanging a kiss with her mother—and retreated to the back of the school, into a play area where a mass of other children gathered.

Elizabeth Price, remaining outside the car, paused to speak to a cluster of other women who were dropping their children off. She seemed happy in the crowd, she seemed to know everyone. Within five minutes of watching her, Roach counted nine mothers who stopped to speak to her. Five of them gathered in a circle like teenagers outside the school building; everyone that passed exchanged brief pleasantries with the crowd, before retreating to their vehicles—lined along each side of the road.

Elizabeth Price seemed to lead them. There was something about her. Despite clearly being the wealthiest, she wasn't dressed lavishly; she wore no jewelry and dressed in casual clothes.

She didn't have an air of superiority about her; she didn't look arrogant or big headed and certainly didn't advertise the fact that her husband was one of the richest men in the country.

Yet, as she stood in the circle of chatting mothers, Roach noticed how she had inadvertently set herself apart from them. The mothers looked at her when she spoke, they looked at her when another spoke, and they looked at her when they spoke. It seemed like they needed her approval before they could act. Her laughter started theirs; her shocked expressions sent *them* into shock.

Roach was intrigued and he watched with great interest. Something about her oozed class; something about her seemed to make the other women scream, 'Be my friend. Accept me.'

He shifted his gaze when the group spilt—unsurprisingly, Elizabeth was the first to leave—and she maneuvered herself back behind the wheel of the Porsche.

33

Johnny Phillips awoke in comfort. He had slept well and, despite craving carbohydrates and something to drink, he felt refreshed and in a relatively good mood.

Throwing on his clothes from the day before—folded over a chair in his room—he descended the stairs, his soft footfalls cushioned by the pliable, thick carpet.

In the living room, he wasn't surprised to see the television on with Michael Richards sitting in a dressing gown on the sofa, his bloodshot eyes fixed on the screen.

"You're up early," Phillips said.

"Couldn't sleep." Richards yawned, emphasizing his point.

Phillips nodded and headed for the kitchen. After hungrily grabbing two slices of bread and jamming them into the toaster, he turned on the coffee machine and walked back into the living room.

"It's past eight anyway," Richards muttered.

"What?"

"It's after eight, it's not early, I'm always awake at this time."

"I know," Phillips agreed. "But I heard you scrambling around the house a few hours ago."

"Sorry."

"You didn't wake me. If you did I would have come out of my room and helped your heavy stomping ass down the stairs a bit quicker. You clambered down the fuckers like a ten-ton zombie, I heard every step."

"Sorry."

"You look bleak this morning," Phillips noticed.

"Just tired that's all, laid awake for a few hours last night, thinking."

"About how long it's been since you've had sex and if you can still get it up?"

"Fuck off. I was just trying to come up with some money-making ideas, the usual shit."

Phillips smiled and walked back into the kitchen. After buttering his toast and layering it with jam, he poured a cup of coffee and returned to the living room.

"What you watching?" he asked as he munched away on the crispy bread.

"Fucking *Today Show*," Richards replied with disgust. "Nothing else on. There never is this early."

"Then turn the fucking thing off."

"And do what?"

Phillips pondered this briefly as he chewed through his toast hungrily. Eventually he shrugged his shoulders and sunk into the seat, his eyes switching to the television set.

The nearby town was bustling with morning shoppers. Shops and paths were littered with clusters of people trying to grab retail bargains after traveling from miles around. Over one hundred stores and stalls decorated the streets which were woven through pathways, tunnels, roads, and cobbled streets.

Michael Richards and Johnny Phillips knew the place well; it was a shopping haven. You could buy anything from knock-off clothes—from sketchy dealers working in the back of vans—to expensive jewelry and real designer attire.

It was also littered with restaurants. You could dine with fine wine and Italian food at one of the most respectable restaurants in the area, buy hamburgers, hotdogs and other processed, mashed together meat products from the many food-trucks; grease up your arteries by dining at one of the two fish and chip restaurants; sugar-up in style at the high-class ice-cream parlor or grab Chinese or Indian takeout.

The town and its vast shopping community attracted everyone from middle-class shoppers to teenage shoplifters, and the numerous jewelry shops, betting shops, and large department shops also attracted the occasional armed robber.

Now, it had drawn the attention of two conmen. Michael Richards and Johnny Phillips hadn't come for the shopping *or* the food, what they hoped to find was a lot more sinister.

Leaving the Vauxhall in the parking lot of a large DIY store they crossed into the shopping district, making a detour through an underpass.

"It stinks of piss in here," Richards muttered with his nose held high like a dog as he sniffed the rank air inside the tunnel.

Phillips nodded and glanced around. The path leading into the underpass was on an incline, over the pass a small road lead to the backs of the many businesses. Passing through the tunnel made the walk from the parking lot—where the majority of shoppers left their cars—to the shopping center a lot quicker.

Most of the shoppers passed through the underpass, making it an ideal place for street musicians and beggars who could shade themselves from wind and rain and beg to thousands of shoppers.

Richards and Phillips walked past a young man. He was leaning against the side of the graffiti covered walls with an acous-
tic guitar in his hands. The guitar looked immaculate, as did the
velvet lined case at his feet which had been opened to give the
passers-by a place to throw their pity money.

There were two other beggars nearby, one strummed awkwardly on a battered banjo, the other sat in his own shame, with a
frown hidden behind his matted, bushy facial hair and a sign resting against his slumped body that declared: Need money for food.

The guitarist stood out from the other two, he even stood out
from the shoppers passing through the tunnel. He didn't look a
day over twenty. He was clean-shaven with wavy jet-black hair;
teeth as straight as a ruler and as white as a sick ghost.

His skin was dotted with blemishes and looked an eerie, yet
healthy, shade of pale.

Phillips and Richards walked over to him. He had been playing *Stairway to Heaven* and, despite some minor flaws on behalf of
his guitar playing, his voice and tone was near perfect.

He stopped when the two men approached.

Phillips looked down into the guitar case with intrigue. At
least forty dollars in coins and small bills filled it.

"What's all this about then?" Richards quizzed. The boy was
eyeing up Johnny Phillips, who glared suspiciously at his earnings.

"What do you mean?" The musician replied, his voice clean
and crisp and devoid of an accent.

"You, begging," Richards said.

"I'm sorry," the youngster said with a great deal of charm and
politeness. "Do I know you?"

Richards turned to Phillips who smiled back at him.

"You don't look much like a beggar," Richards noted, ignoring the question. "What game are you trying to pull here?"

"Game? I am simply practicing."

"La-de-fucking-da," Phillips mocked.

"Am I disturbing you?" the musician asked.

"No, we're just interested in what you're up to," Phillips said. "You don't look like a typical beggar; you stand out like a dick at a lesbian orgy."

"I am learning, if you must know. I study art and music, among other things, at college. My friends and I are here on a short shopping trip, we thought it would be quite amusing if we all did a little playing around the city. We have a small wager on the person who could collect the most money." He man smiled with a look of superiority that never seemed to leave his face, "Whoever gets the most money wins the bet," he clarified.

Phillips and Richards exchanged bewildered glances.

"Sounds like you have some wild friends," Phillips said.

The man grinned from ear to ear.

"Did you know what you are doing is illegal?" Phillips inquired with an edge to his tone.

"Excuse me?" the young man's tone quickly changed.

"The laws have changed kid, you need a permit to play music on the street," Phillips explained.

"What about them two?" the youngster demanded, pointing to the two other beggars.

"That's different, they're begging, you're not, they don't have any other income and I'm guessing that you do."

"Of course I do," the youngster affirmed.

"Sergeant," Phillips blurted. "Take this man's equipment," his words were directed at Richards but his eyes bore fiercely into the young man's gaze.

Richards slowly moved forward.

"What are you doing?" the busker pleaded.

"Arresting you," Phillips replied. He dug his hand into his pocket, pulled out his police identification and flipped it before the youngster's eyes. "If you would please accompany us down to the station sir, we can have this matter cleared up in a matter of hours."

He made a gentle reach for the youngster's arms, keeping his movements slow and purposeful.

"What? No, please. My parents will kill me, this was just a joke," he said.

"A joke? This is a serious offense," Phillips said.

The posh busker was panic stricken: "Will I be charged?"

"You will be taken to the station where you will be charged and fined. If you want your lawyer present, then that's okay—"

"No, please. I can pay the fine, just don't charge me, I'll be in *so* much trouble. Please, I didn't know I was doing wrong."

Phillips stared at the trembling youngster. The corners of his eyes were leaking fresh tears. He held his forearms lightly, showing his intent without wanting—or having the ability—to arrest the man.

"Sergeant," Phillips beckoned his partner away from the youngster with a nod of his head.

They walked a few feet away from the wannabe street player and began whispering a decision out of his earshot. The youngster watched them with pleading eyes as he waited for the verdict.

"Why do you still have that fucking police ID?" Richards said quietly, nodding his head and looking at the youngster for theatrical purposes.

"I must have left it in this jacket," Phillips said, also with a nod. "Lucky for us it's come into use."

"I'm still hungry," Richards declared with a grimace. "Are you hungry yet?"

"I told you, we'll eat later."

"Just a little—"

"Later!"

"Fine."

They parted and faced the busker, "Looks like it's your lucky day mate," Phillips declared. "You seem like a genuine, honest kid so we're going to give you a break."

"Thank you," the young musician gleamed.

"Don't get your hopes up yet," he warned. "We still need to confiscate your earnings and you will have to pay the fine, this can be done either here or down at the station—"

"Here," the young man blurted. "How much? I have plenty of money."

Phillips could barely suppress a smile, "Two-fifty," he said without hesitation.

The young man nodded and pulled out a large leather wallet.

After paying his fine and handing over his money to the two conmen, he left—but not before bombarding them with his desperate gratitude.

"Unbelievable," Richards said as the youngster disappeared in the direction of the parking lot; his guitar case swinging wildly by his side.

"One born every minute," Phillips said.

34

Darren Morris rolled the BMW up next to the Ford, parked just outside the decrepit apartment building that they would be forced to call home for the next few days. He eyed the area suspiciously, as he always did—in his line of work it paid to be suspicious about everything.

The area was empty. The wheel-less cars were still propped up on bricks nearby, but besides them and their own cars; it was empty.

He could hear noises as he entered the building—incoherent whispers, filtered from the top floor. The visitors to the building seemed to be staying in the higher levels, as they had been yesterday.

That had also been the case when they had first found the squatter's realm; the lower level apartments had been deserted while the upper levels were occupied, but even back then—when it housed more people, some legally—it was quiet.

He pushed down the brand new, solid-steel handle on the second downstairs apartment and pushed, unsurprised to find the door unlocked.

After only taking two steps into the apartment he heard a few thumps and immediately James Roach bolted around the corner to greet him with an intimidating glare and a posture ready for attack.

"It's just me," Morris said.

"You took your time," Roach said. "You should have been here before me."

"I know, but I thought I'd sort a few other things out first."

"Like what?"

He dropped a large duffel bag onto the living room floor.

"What's in there?"

"Some things to keep us going."

Roach stared at his colleague.

"Portable TV, Nintendo DS, music, food, water . . ." Morris explained.

"This isn't a fucking vacation," Roach complained.

"Look," Morris began, "this isn't an overnight job, we could be stuck here for some time. I don't know about you but I don't plan on sitting and twiddling my fucking thumbs all day."

"Fair enough."

"Plus, I want to keep track of the horse races," he added with a smile.

Roach laughed.

"I have the equipment in the car," Morris stated. "We'll keep it there for the time being."

"How *is* the car?"

"Nothing spectacular, it has four wheels and an engine. It's what we need."

Roach nodded and began digging through the bag as Morris sat down. In the bag, he found a small CD player with a set of headphones; a portable television with a seven-inch screen, a Nintendo DS with a few games, a collection of packaged, ready-to-eat meals, and a case of twenty-four bottles of water.

"You certainly came prepared," Roach noted. "Where did you get all this stuff?"

"I picked most of it up from my house. The DS and CD player are my nephews, he left them last time he came to visit me, he says he doesn't need that shit, has all his fancy fucking IPods and MP3s now. The food and water I picked up from the supermarket on the way here."

"I'm guessing the CDs are yours?" Roach said with a smile as he found a stack of classic rock CDs at the bottom of the bag.

"Actually, my nephew has the same taste in music as me," Morris proclaimed.

"I didn't even know you had a nephew," Roach said.

Both men exchanged awkward glances before turning away simultaneously.

"Everything go as planned at the school?" Morris asked.

"Yes. The mother dropped her off, gave her a kiss, spoke to a few other mothers, and then left, just as you said."

"And Howard?"

"He was still in the house when the kid left for school."

35

Howard Price glared at the clock, he was sure it was running slow just to irritate him.

It seemed to have been stuck on eleven o'clock for the last two hours. He couldn't believe how slowly time was moving, it was something he certainly wasn't used to. When he worked, he was busy, he always kept himself busy and there never seemed to be enough time. Now there was too much of it.

Elizabeth locked herself away in the kitchen where she could run through her routine of cooking and cleaning. She worked harder than he had ever given her credit for and he admired her for it, he certainly—even in his bored state—couldn't do what she did.

Yesterday, she had spent an hour preparing lunch, fifteen minutes eating it with Howard, then another twenty minutes clearing it away, before beginning her routine of making the beds, vacuuming the floors, cleaning the tables, tiles, and windowsills, and doing the laundry, before stopping to begin the preparation of another meal.

A number of times he had offered to hire a housekeeper but Elizabeth refused. It wasn't as if she enjoyed what she did, but she couldn't and wouldn't have it any other way. She was a perfectionist and an obsessive-compulsive, so everything not only had to be done right, but it had to be done her way.

Howard had barely seen her all morning. She had cooked him breakfast, sat and ate with him, then he had left her in the kitchen watching chat shows while he retired to the living room.

He knew he needed a rest. The doctor had warned him that stress was killing him, but he was sure that if he didn't go back to work soon, he would kill himself.

36

Sitting in McDonald's with a tray full of goodies in front of them, Michael Richards and Johnny Phillips watched the many people walk up and down the restaurant aisles with bags and trays of food, some choosing to eat inside the humid building, some choosing the wooden benches outside, others walking away to eat on the move or in their cars.

A crowd of hungry people stood impatiently at the counter where three pimpled teenagers took their orders at a frantic pace.

"Look at all these fat fucks," Phillips said as he gorged himself on his double cheeseburger.

Richards nearly choked on his Coke in response to the outburst. Drops of the black sugary liquid dribbled down his chin.

"You'd think these people had never heard of exercise," he continued.

"It wouldn't kill them to get off their asses every now and then to do a little, would it?"

"Looking at the size of most of them, I'd say yes," Richards said. "Put half of these people on a treadmill and they'd have a heart attack."

Phillips shrugged his shoulders callously and took a long drink from his chocolate milkshake.

"Reckon we should get another few games for the computer?" Richards muttered. "We've got shit loads for all the fucking consoles, half of which we never play on. Yet we have a super-powered gaming machine upstairs and the only game we have is Tetris."

"We don't need any more games. The less recreational activities available to us, the more work we'll get done."

"We're criminals, playing a few games is hardly going to affect our income, is it?"

"You know what I mean. We need to stop lying about the house getting pissed all the time and start stringing together another scam or two."

More people rushed through the door as the queue to the counter grew. A woman in her mid-thirties walked past Phillips and stood by Richards's side, her eyes looking forward, her back to Phillips.

He stared at her in disbelief and mouthed the words "Look at the size of that," to Richards who had to stuff his hamburger into his mouth to suppress a laugh.

He eyed up her backside and winked at Richards, "Get yourself in there, Mickey," he mocked silently before moving his hands in the air to create a slapping motion, inches from her bulbous backside.

Pulling his fingers away he licked them and sighed in a mocking gesture of pleasure. "Hmm," he said, "lard."

37

"Maybe we should have had the windows on this thing tinted," Roach offered as he and Morris stared out of the driver's side window of the black BMW.

"Why?" Morris asked, his eyes scouring the playground beyond the iron fence.

"So they can't see us looking at them. The kids will get suspicious of two men staring at them from a parked car."

"But they won't think twice about a black car with tinted windows parked alone by the side of their school?"

Roach mused over this. "Good point."

A rattling bell rang through the area. A line of children streamed out of the school and swarmed into the playground, their merry voices colliding with their stomping feet to create a wall of noise which split through the previously silent street like a hot knife through butter.

"Lunch time," Morris gleamed.

They both scanned the crowd of children as they separated into groups. Some disappeared around the back of the school, most stayed in plain sight.

"There she is," Roach noted. "Near the climbing frame."

Morris allowed his gaze to drift over a small concrete play area—home to a set of swings, a climbing frame and many hop-scotch patterns. Lisa Price, a small tennis ball in her hand, walked towards another young girl. They passed the play area and wandered away from the rest of the children, strolling closer to the poorly protected perimeter.

"Say when," Roach said with one eye on Morris.

"Not yet."

Lisa bounced the ball as she walked, thudding it off the hard ground and catching it in her right hand. As she and her friend neared the fence they broke apart; walking away from each other until a gap opened up between them. Then they began throwing the ball to each other.

Morris glanced around quickly. The children were happily playing in their own selected groups. No adults were present and the road was deserted.

"Come on," he ushered.

The two men exited the car and strode towards the open gate with purpose and with Morris taking the lead. He smiled as he walked, trying not to break into a run despite a growing impatience.

As they entered the school playground and neared their target, both girls stopped and looked at the new visitors with confused expressions.

"Lisa Price?" Morris asked as politely as he could.

"Yes."

"Hey there sweetie, I'm a friend of your father. He's sent me to come pick you up," he said, bending down to meet her eyes.

Lisa shot him an unsure stare; her friend was eyeing up James Roach with a look of indifference.

"I don't know you."

"I know you don't. We haven't met before; I work in the same building as your daddy. I do all his dirty work, you know how lazy he is," Morris smiled, trying to lighten the mood.

She still looked worried.

"Where is he?" she demanded.

Morris paused. He could tell he was dealing with a girl who'd had stories of dangerous strangers drummed into her skull, but he knew of one thing that would cast aside her firm shield.

"He's in the hospital," he announced calmly.

"What!" Lisa said, instantly shocked.

"It's nothing serious darling." He moved closer as she lowered her guard. "Your mommy is there with him. Your daddy asked me to come and get you and take you to him."

Lisa was shocked; her eyes filled with tears. She was too stricken to think or act as Morris wrapped his arm gently around her back and ushered her away.

"He's going to be okay," he said. "He just wants to see you."

"Okay," Lisa agreed. "Are you sure he's going to be okay?"

"Of course," Morris assured her as he walked her out of the school.

Roach remained. The other girl was by his side, her expression dampened more because of her vanishing playmate than the impending mortality of her friend's father.

Roach offered his widest smile, kneeled by her side and removed a small white envelope from his pocket.

"Hey there," he said, keeping one eye on Morris who was getting closer to the car. "What's your name?"

"Sarah," the timid girl said.

"Are you a good friend of Lisa?"

She nodded shyly.

Roach watched as Morris shepherded Lisa into the back seat of the BMW.

"Can you do me a big favor Sarah?" he asked.

Again, she nodded.

Roach, his hands snugly fitted into leather gloves, held out the envelope. "In here is a very important letter," he declared. "I need you to go back into the school and hand it to one of your teachers. Do you think you can do that for me Sarah?"

"Which teacher?" the girl quizzed.

"Any of them, it doesn't matter. But you must tell them how important it is. Do you understand?"

She nodded and he handed her the envelope. "If you could do that for me, Lisa and her father would appreciate it very much."

The girl smiled. "Okay," she beamed.

He watched her turn and jog away, heading towards the back of the school. As soon as she disappeared Roach walked briskly towards the BMW.

Jennifer Rose had worked at Lady Victoria's School for Girls for twenty years; she was happy there. She was born to teach and she loved kids, teaching English to seven-year-old girls was perfect for her.

She had worked in other schools in her younger days but nothing compared to Lady Victoria's. There the children had been tamed, at the public schools where she had taught previously it wasn't unusual to be sworn at or have pencils, pens and other stationery thrown at you.

Things were a lot calmer at Lady Victoria's. She had always expected that she would move around from place to place, job to job, in a continuous cycle of depressing work and low pay, but after a chance meeting with the headmistress of Lady Victoria's she had been gifted the job of her dreams.

The children were polite, young, and few in numbers, but the pay was high. It was still a teacher's wage, which was far short of spectacular, but she *was* a teacher, and this was as good as it got.

She loved the school and loved the area. It was peaceful, quiet, and friendly and nothing horrible ever happened to her during her two-decade stay.

She smiled as Sarah Connolly raced up to her, her shoes clinking on the hallway surface.

"Don't run!" Jennifer warned.

Sarah stopped running. She walked towards the teacher—who was leaning against the door of her classroom drinking a cup of coffee—with her merry face gleaming.

"I have an important letter for you Mrs. Rose," she declared politely as she handed her teacher a white envelope. "A man gave it to me in the playground."

Jennifer smiled and took the envelope.

"After he took Lisa away," Sarah continued.

Jennifer looked alarmed. She felt her heart skip a beat, "What do you mean?" she asked.

Sarah looked at her blankly, her eyes on the letter, "One of the men gave me that," she said brightly. "He said it was important."

Jennifer put the cup of coffee down on the floor and ripped open the white envelope. Inside was a single sheet of paper folded in half. She opened it up and read the large bold letters.

WE have Lisa Price.
YOU have the chance to get her back.
You should, under NO circumstances, phone the police, we do not like to be fucked around with and we wouldn't think twice about cutting her into little pieces and mailing each severed part back to you. If you want to get her back you need to comply with our demands.
This is a kidnapping. That much you have probably gathered already. You are just a teacher. You are the intermediary in this game.
Go to the Price house and show them this letter. Tell no one else, at the moment the girl's life is in your hands. Tell Howard he can contact us on the number provided below.

Jennifer Rose felt physically sick. She could see young Sarah speaking to her with a look of confusion across her innocent face but she couldn't hear her words. She felt light-headed and dizzy.

Her world turned black and she passed out on the cold floor.

38

"Fucking bastard," Phillips blurted.

Michael Richards looked away from the rows of amusing greeting cards in front of him and turned to Johnny Phillips who was standing behind him holding a business magazine.

"Look at this fucker," Phillips beckoned.

Richards peered over his friend's shoulder to glance at the open magazine in his hands.

He was reading a small article on a financial spread in the magazine. The headline stated, SIGHTSYS DECLARES RECORD PROFITS, in prominent bold lettering.

"This Howard Price guy," Phillips said as Richards began reading the article. "He owns a huge software company which made a fucking fortune last year. It says his father left him the company on his deathbed even though he didn't get along with him when he was alive." He shook his head, "What a fucking freeloader."

"Haven't you heard of him before?" Richards asked, taking his eyes away from the article.

"No. Have you?"

"Sure, he's a local. Haven't seen him or met him but apparently, he lives in a big house a few miles away."

"How do you know?"

"There aren't many multimillionaires living around here Johnny," Richards told his friend. "This guy is in the news all the time. He runs one of the biggest companies for miles around for fuck's sake, and he makes a fortune doing it."

"No shit."

Richards frowned and walked back to the card rack to glance over the greetings cards.

"People like him piss me off," Phillips continued from behind Richards.

"Why would that be?"

"Because they're lucky. People like us have to work hard for the money we make. This bastard has it handed to him."

"It isn't easy running a big company," Richards noted as he moved out of the way of a man who also wanted to glance over the vast array of cards.

"Of course it is. He was given the damn thing; it was already running when he took over. He just needed to keep the same people on the payroll and wait for the checks to come in."

Richards accidentally knocked into the man in front of him. He apologized and tapped him on the shoulder in a gesture of goodwill as he left the card rack and wandered behind Phillips.

"He didn't do that though," Richards said as he watched the man look over the cards in disappointment and then leave the shop. "He expanded. He inherited a big business and made it huge. That sort of thing takes more than skill; it takes—"

"Money," Phillips cut in. "That's what it takes, and thanks to daddy, he had plenty of it."

Richards shook his head. He stuck his right hand inside his pant pocket, clasping his fingers around the leather wallet he had just pick-pocketed. In the other pocket, with his left hand, he proudly traced his fingers over two thinner wallets.

Phillips put the magazine back on the shelf and looked at Richards with a questionable gaze. Richards nodded.

"Come on then," he muttered. "We might as well head back to the pub."

They briskly strolled through the stores and walkways, passed under the underpass where they had not long since robbed the wannabe musician of his morning monies, and headed back to the Vauxhall.

Inside the car they immediately emptied their pockets.

Richards pulled out two purses from his jacket; one was fake leather, the other one was a thick material with a tartan design. He also removed a gold watch, a gold wedding band, and three wallets from his pants pockets. He laid all the items on his lap.

Phillips looked at them, impressed. "How did you get the watch and the ring?"

"You remember the weird market-stall dealer who I haggled with to sell us the fake Rolex?"

"That's it? But I thought you threw that in the trash."

"I did. This is his watch. It isn't a Rolex, but it's gold, worth five hundred bucks at least. I snatched it when we shook hands to confirm the deal for the fake watch."

"You sly little bastard," Phillips smiled. "What about the wedding ring?"

"From the stupid drunk I helped after he fell in the middle of the street."

"And there's me thinking you were just being helpful."

"What did you manage to snatch?" Richards asked.

Phillips pulled out two wallets.

"That's it?"

"I'm not as tricky as you. I'm the brains of this operation remember."

"But I snatched those two," Richards said. "I only gave them to you because my pockets were filling up."

"Pick-pocketing isn't my game," Phillips persisted.

"It was your idea."

"And it worked, didn't it? You're good enough for both of us."

Richards sighed and shook his head. A smile creased his lips.

"What about the woman in the fake fur you followed around for ten minutes?" Richards wondered.

"I tried," Phillips pleaded. "She stopped and bent down to look at some games and I managed to slip my hand inside her bag. I even made sure I was in a dead-spot for the cameras and that my eyes and attention were fixed on a computer as not to arouse suspicion."

"And?"

"That was the problem," Phillips laughed. "Because I wasn't looking at what I was doing I ended up stealing this," he removed a small makeup bag from his jacket.

Richards erupted into laughter.

"I thought I'd stolen her purse at first," Phillips continued. "I was pleased with myself."

Richards stifled his laughter, "You're right," he said. "Let's leave the pick-pocketing to me."

39

"Why won't you tell me what's wrong with my daddy?" Lisa Price pleaded from the backseat.

Darren Morris shot a blank stare to the passenger side; James Roach shrugged a reply.

"You'll find out for yourself, won't you?" Morris said.

"Is it his stress? Mommy says he's under a lot of stress."

"I don't know."

"He has a hard job you know."

"Does he really?"

"He works in a big company," Lisa explained with pride. "He's the boss, he controls a lot of other people like you and makes a lot of money. So, was it his stress?"

"I don't know, maybe he gave himself a fucking hernia carrying his wallet around," Morris snapped.

The back seat of the BMW fell momentarily silent.

"You swore."

"No, I didn't."

"You said the F word."

"I'm a grown-up, I'm allowed to swear."

"You shouldn't swear in front of children."

"Who told you that?" Morris wondered as he steered the car through the long roads and into the dismal estate.

"My parents and my teachers."

"You shouldn't listen to your teachers."

"Why not? They never swear at me."

"You've never heard a grown-up swear?"

"Only on TV."

"I've been on TV," Morris was keen to change the subject.

James Roach looked at his colleague in bemusement.

"Really?" Lisa asked, a smile crossing her face.

"Sure."

"Which show?"

James Roach smiled; his whisper of: "*Cops,*" was hushed by Morris. "I used to be on *Sesame Street.*"

"No, you didn't," Lisa affirmed.

"How do you know?" Morris said.

"You don't look like the people on *Sesame Street.* You're old."

Morris laughed, "I was young once you know."

"You don't have the look."

"The look?"

"All the grownups on *Sesame Street* look friendly and nice. You look like a criminal."

Morris laughed again and rolled the car into the car park just outside the dilapidated apartments.

"Funny you should say that," he said.

Roach quickly jumped out of the car and rushed to the back door. A look of concern creased the young girl's features.

Morris turned towards her, his body arched over the front seat. "Because that's exactly what I am."

Before Lisa could scream, James Roach had pounced. He yanked open the back door and clasped a strong hand around her fragile mouth. In one movement he yanked her from the car.

Darren Morris calmly climbed out from behind the wheel, locked the BMW, checked around for witnesses and then followed Roach, who roughly dragged the young girl—her shoes and ankles scraping the pavement—into the building.

Jennifer Rose was conscious, but flustered. Her heart drummed heavily inside her chest, her blood buzzed rapidly through her body. She waved cool air onto her face by wafting a personal hygiene pamphlet back and forth, relishing the icy backdraft.

The school nurse had already seen to her and after checking for injury—there wasn't any—the experienced nurse had ordered her to sit and calm down.

In front of Jennifer, Howard Price and his wife spoke with a group of plainclothes police officers, to their left, near the door of the school's conference room, stood the school's principal.

Lauren Longstaff was a nervous-looking woman. Her age-worn, wrinkled features reeked of timidity. Her big gray eyes were always alert and observant; she seemed to survey her surroundings with something touching on awe.

Jennifer Rose knew from experience that the anxious exterior exposed nothing true to the real nature of the fifty-five-year-old principal. She wasn't forward but she was stern, not one to start an argument but always one to finish; she never lit up a room with her presence but was always the person everyone turned to when they needed help. Longstaff's gray eyes scoured the police officers in the room. She looked worried, behind her shy exterior and hardened soul lay a woman who feared deeply for one of her pupils.

Jennifer caught the attention of her superior and walked over to console her.

In the center of the room, Howard Price mulled over the contents of the ransom note. Reading and re-reading it until he had it memorized.

"Why were you even called?" he asked the officer in charge.

Detective Inspector Brown glanced at the principal who stood close to Jennifer Rose. "Mrs. Longstaff called us when she found the letter. She feared for your daughter."

Howard nodded, "I understand."

"It's for the best that we're here."

"For the best? They say they're going to cut her into fucking pieces if we call the police."

"It's just an empty threat, Mr. Price."

"What if they're monitoring the school?"

"We have taken the correct precautions just in case. They shouldn't suspect a thing either way."

Howard Price glared at the detective, "You'd better be fucking right."

"There is nothing to worry about."

"They have my fucking daughter. Of course there's something to worry about."

"I understand that," the detective said. "But you need to keep calm; we'll do our best to get her back safely."

Howard snarled and quelled his anger. He paced up and down, glanced at each of the occupants of the room in turn—all of them shooting him glances of pity—and then ran a sweaty hand through his thinning hair. He stopped, sighed heavily.

"What do we do now?" he asked.

"You have to call them, like it says in the letter," the detective looked toward the back of the room where a group of officers were setting up surveillance equipment. "But not just yet, first we need to set up a trace on the phone. If you keep them on the line long enough we might be able to find out their location."

Howard shook his head in disbelief. The whole situation terrified him; he wanted to retreat and cry, but his mind forced away the pain and replaced it with anger.

He read the letter again.

The ransom note had already been checked for prints by a forensics officer who had since left the scene, only three sets had been found and the detective had quickly assumed the three matches to be: Jennifer Rose, Sarah Connolly, and Lauren Longstaff. The prints would be tested anyway.

The whole note had been hand copied onto a sheet of paper torn from a school book—the original made its way back to the police station for testing. At the bottom of the note was the phone number Howard had been instructed to call.

"Sir!" the call came from the back of the room, one of the officers who had been meddling with the surveillance equipment was hooking a set of headphones over his head. "We're set," he said.

Howard took in a deep breath and looked towards the phone. Wires and devices streamed out of its rear and led to the equipment used by the officers.

"Mr. Price," the detective said. "You can make the call now."

James Roach looked across at Darren Morris who was jabbing the portable television with distaste, trying to find a signal. "Do you think they would have called the police?"

"Of course," Morris said. "It doesn't matter; the police won't be able to help them. They can't trace us and they can't stop us at the drop-off point for fear that we'll kill the kid."

Roach nodded, "I suppose so."

A muffled scream echoed into the front room, Morris looked towards the bedroom door. Roach immediately rose and walked towards the closed door.

"Leave her!"

"She might need something," Roach said.

"This isn't a fucking hotel."

"We have to take care of her; if we lose her we don't get paid."

"She's only been in there for half an hour and you've already checked on her twice."

Roach walked away from the door.

Lisa Price screamed as loud as she could, she forced her whole body into the action, but the gag around her mouth drowned out most of the noise.

She was finding it hard to breathe past the thick cloth. The room in which they had put her was dark and musty, thick dust clouds hung in the air, billowing from time to time as her breaths escaped the rag and into the dust walls.

Her throat was sore from the shouting but she forced herself into another scream.

No one came. She could hear muffled voices from the room beyond but the raging blood rushing through her head stopped her from deciphering the words of her kidnappers—it felt like she had pressed an ear to a waterfall.

Her wrist and shins stung, when they had tied her to the mattress they hadn't taken much care. The string had been tied tight and it not only restricted her movements, but also her blood flow.

Tears dripped down her face and soaked into her hair as she released another scream.

Darren Morris continued to fumble with the portable television set, shouting obscenities at the inanimate object as he poked at the controls. He was oblivious to the young girl's muffled screams.

James Roach looked towards the door again, then at Darren Morris, then at the CD player lying on the floor. He pondered over what to do but the sound of ringing decided for him.

The mobile phone, left on one of the chairs, burst to life and both men turned their attentions towards it.

Roach looked at Morris, Morris looked at the phone.

Gently putting down the useless portable television, Morris wandered over to the phone and picked it up.

"Howard Price?" he asked.

"This is Howard Price," the voice at the other end confirmed.

"Excellent," Morris said without enthusiasm.

"What do you want?"

"Money, you fucking rich bastard, what do you think?"

"Listen to me—"

"No, you listen to me," Morris cut in. "This is my fucking time to shine. I want one million in cash, unmarked notes."

"I can pay, just please don't—"

"I know you can pay, Mr. Price, and that's exactly what you'll do. You have until tomorrow night to cough up the cash, any later and I'll slit your daughter's throat, understood?"

"Understood."

"Call me at this number when you have the money. Any later than eight tomorrow night and I'll be sending your little Lisa back to you in bits," Morris said.

"Please don't hurt her," Howard pleaded.

"You know the score Mr. Price, pay up and she'll be fine. You have my word."

"Can I hear her?" Howard asked.

"Excuse me?"

"Let me hear her, I need to know she's okay."

"We're on a tight schedule here," Morris replied. "No can do I'm afraid."

"I need to know she's all right."

"How about I slit her fucking throat and you can listen to her scream?" Morris snapped with venom.

"No, please . . ." Howard begged. "Don't hurt her."

"Get the money Mr. Price and you have my word," Morris killed the conversation.

40

Howard Price had managed to restrain himself throughout the phone call, but afterwards he cried. He hurt inside and he felt the need to let it all out. Elizabeth, still in tears herself, walked up to him and wrapped her arms around him.

Detective Inspector Brown, who had been listening in to the conversation, removed his headphones. "Do you have access to that amount of money?"

"Of course," Howard said with tears pouring down his cheeks.

"Do you think you will be able to withdraw so much before tomorrow?"

He nodded.

The detective turned to the other police officers and began dishing out orders.

"Do you think she's going to be okay?" Elizabeth asked Howard.

"I'm sure she'll be fine," He said, wiping away his wife's tears while his own traced rivers down his face. "She's a strong girl."

The two embraced. Howard forced back the tears, feeling ashamed for succumbing to weakness when his daughter needed him to be strong.

"Did you get a trace?" Howard asked the detective.

"I'm afraid not."

"Now what?" He wanted to know as he continued to hug his wife.

"We suggest you get in touch with your bank, Mr. Price. Withdraw the money, and then phone them back and arrange a drop-off point."

"I don't want any fucking snipers or trigger-happy cops anywhere near my daughter or me," He warned. "I'll pay them the money and get my daughter back, after that you can do what you like. I'm not taking any risks with this."

"We understand. We won't put the lives of you or your daughter at risk but we need to monitor the situation so we can catch them after the switch is made."

41

Michael Richards twirled the stolen wedding band around his finger, the thick ring spun effortlessly around the skinny digit.

"We should do that more often," Phillips said as he approached Richards with a beer in one hand and a glass of Coke in the other.

"Do what?" Richards asked, as if awakening from a trance.

"Pocket shopping."

"It's theft."

"And?"

"We're conmen."

"Shut your shit Mickey," Phillips said, taking a seat on the chair next to him. "There's not much difference and we're good at both."

"We can make more from pulling cons."

Phillips sighed and took a long drink from his cold lager, delighting in its soothing taste.

The small pub was virtually empty. A short bartender sat on a stool behind the bar, reading a glossy magazine with unflinching concentration. She had served Phillips with a look of strained distaste on her face, taking his money without a word or a smile.

A man in his late seventies sat in the corner with his head buried in a copy of *The Racing Times*, He had a beer on the small oval table in front of him and a radio offering insights and commentary of the day's racing.

"I keep telling you Mickey, the tricks don't come along every day."

"But when they do we make a fucking fortune."

"Maybe, but we could make the same from pulling the shit we did today. Why are you so against it?"

"I don't want to end up in jail. We're close to getting what we want; we have a lot to lose."

"We won't get caught," Phillips said. "And anyway, you fucking loved it today, we used to pull off shit like that all the time when we were kids, you reveled in it. You had the same glint in your eyes today."

Richards smiled, "Okay, I admit, I fucking loved every second of it."

"It's an easy ride."

"Maybe," Richards said with a touch of belief.

"You sure you don't want a beer?" Phillips asked, noting the glass of Coke in front of Richards.

"I've got to drive us back, don't I?"

"You can have one."

"No, I'll have a couple tonight when we get back."

Phillips nodded, "Ever been to this place before?" he asked as his eyes swept over the insides of the pub that was a short drive from the market.

"No," Richards said. "Doesn't look up too much, does it?"

"It's quiet and there's a pool table in the back."

"Is there?"

"Yeah, through the glass door next to the bar," Phillips said. "I spotted it when that miserable bitch was serving me. It's empty in there too."

Richards nodded, "How much do you think Shoddy Simon will give us for the watch and the ring?"

"Not much," Phillips said. "Probably two hundred for the pair. The bastard will no doubt shift them for next to a five hundred."

"That would make a total of two and a half grand," Richards said with a sly smile curling his lips. "Not bad for a day's work."

"Shame we can't get much use out of all the credit cards," Phillips noted. "With the overdraft limits the fuckers have nowadays we could get about a hundred grand off all of them. Simon will pay peanuts."

"Don't go getting any ideas."

Phillips merely smiled. He stood up and picked up his glass, "Come on then Mickey. I'll play you in a few games of pool."

42

Evening drifted in. The apartment buildings stood motionless on the bleak horizon, noises from inside the building petered out through the mold-infested walls. The outside of the building was empty; a group of kids loitered near the shops further down the hill, and smaller group dawdled around in the park in between the two locations, drinking and smoking.

Inside the second apartment on the first floor, James Roach jabbed away with amateur intent at the buttons on the Nintendo.

A game of soccer ensued on the small screen of the handheld console; a player lit by a blue ring ran wildly about in distorted directions, before scoring an own goal and trying to tackle the referee.

"I can't figure this thing out," he muttered.

Darren Morris—putting aside a mystery novel he was struggling to enjoy—looked across at his colleague. "Have you ever played a computer game before?" he asked.

"Does Pac Man count?"

Morris laughed, "Just keep playing, you'll get the hang of it."

"How's the book?" Roach asked, putting the miniature console to one side.

"Fucking shit," Morris growled. "Not really in the mood for reading anyway."

"Television still fucked?"

"Yes."

"You should have bought a new one. They're not that expensive."

"This one worked. I had it on the other week, it must be this area," Morris looked around as if to concur with his statement. "It's fucking dead."

As he finished speaking a muffled scream floated from the bedroom into the living room—both men exchanged glance.

"Do you think Price will have the money?" Roach asked.

"He's loaded, he has it."

"You think he can get it for us by tomorrow?"

"Why not?"

"It's a lot of money to get in twenty-four hours."

"We're not asking him to make a million in twenty-four hours, James; we just want him to withdraw it."

"I hope you're right."

Morris smiled, "When have I ever let you down?"

Roach shook his head with a smile spreading across his face. Picking up the handheld console he continued with his hopeless task. "Why didn't we ask for more?" he said.

"More?"

"More money. You said he's rich and he won't have any problems withdrawing the money. So why not ask for more?"

"We agreed on a million, James."

"I know, and that's enough money. That's a lot of money don't get me wrong. I was just wondering."

"Because we need to be sure of a quick turnover. If we asked for five million we couldn't be sure he would have access to that amount of money and we'd need to give him more time to get it. People with that much money don't keep it all on hand; they put it in offshore accounts and what not. The same goes with two, three, four million. One million is an accessible amount for him; it's enough for us to retire on but easy enough to hide."

"Good point."

Darren Morris looked at his watch. "He has twenty-six hours exactly."

43

Howard Price watched a slideshow of various programs exchange places on the plasma screen in front of him.

Without realizing it he had managed to flick through the whole range of satellite stations and none had registered in his mind; he was staring hard but his mind was on other things.

Pressing the back button on the remote control he recycled through the channels, his mind still oblivious to what they offered.

Elizabeth Price sat next to him, her arm in his, her head resting lightly on his shoulder.

A detective had followed Howard and Elizabeth home. He had stayed with them for two hours while a number of plainclothes officers checked over Lisa's things. They scanned her computer, her diary, and her school books, and checked all the phone calls she had made.

Nothing appeared to be out of place.

The detective had received a call from the forensics team while he was in the house to confirm the fingerprints found on the letter. None were from the kidnappers.

The detective had moved on after ordering a car to watch the house and another to patrol the perimeter at regular intervals. Before leaving he had also informed them that young Sarah Connolly had given them a description of one of the kidnappers, but it had been too vague.

"What did the bank say?" Elizabeth asked.

"I'll have the money by tomorrow morning," Price answered. His voice seemed hollow.

Elizabeth nodded and kissed him on the cheek, "She's going to be okay, isn't she?"

"Of course she is," Howard said. "There's nothing to worry about. I'll give them the money and we'll get our baby back."

"What if something goes wrong?" Elizabeth wanted to know. "The police are involved, what if the kidnappers find out?"

"They won't find out. The police will work on the sidelines. They promised not to make a move until Lisa was safe."

"What if they hurt her anyway?"

"Why would they do that?" Howard asked, his wife's red eyes were brimming with tears again. "They're in this for the money. To them, Lisa is the money. If they lose her they won't get anything."

"I'm scared," Elizabeth admitted.

Howard held her close, "Me too, darling. Me too."

44

Lisa Price felt lost.

It had been dark for so long that she had completely lost track of time. She was still in the same dusty room, on the same grimy mattress that she had been tied to since her arrival.

She had been visited a few times by one of the men. Not the quiet one who hadn't spoken to her outside the school or in the car, but the same one who had dragged her from the back seat and tied her to the mattress.

At the beginning, his visits had been pretty frequent. He had been to see her twice at the start of her ordeal, just to give her a glass of water and tell her that she was going to be okay. After that his visits had grown few and far between.

The other man had been to see her once. He wasn't as pleasant and didn't seem to care much about her; he walked in to tell her to shut up, before turning down her demands for a glass of water.

The nicer man walked through the door to pay her another visit.

Roach shut the bedroom door behind him and flicked on a small lamp inside the room, illuminating the young girl on the bed but keeping his features in the shadows.

He sat on the edge of the bed, took off Lisa's gag and offered her a drink from a water bottle. She opened her mouth to gladly accept the fluid and he slowly poured the warm liquid onto her dry tongue. He made sure the water dripped from the bottle slowly to keep her from choking.

She was breathless when he pulled the bottle away. "Thank you."

"I'm going to untie you for a bit," he told her. "Stay calm, okay?"

Lisa nodded and Roach released the ties. Her wrists bore deep red marks where the string had been tightly tied. She rubbed at the marks, wincing as her fingers trailed the fresh wounds.

James Roach noticed her concern and squirted some of the water onto the wounds. Lisa looked at him wearily and then dabbed at the water with her sleeve, allowing it to soothe her skin.

Sitting upright Lisa took the bottle of water from her captor and gratefully drained half of its contents before taking a small breath and swallowing another two mouthfuls.

"Here," Roach handed her a bar of chocolate. "You need to eat."

Lisa studied him and then traced her eyes over the unwrapped bar of chocolate. She snatched it out of his hands and chomped into the sugary treat.

"When will you let me go home?" she asked.

"You'll be home soon," Roach said in a pleasant, calming voice.

"Is my daddy okay?"

"Your daddy is fine."

"You said he was in hospital," Lisa's concerned gaze eyed Roach over the top of the chocolate bar.

"We lied."

Lisa stared at her captor, acknowledged this information with a subtle nod and then continued: "Why am I here?"

"Business matters."

"What do you mean?"

"Your daddy owes us some money."

"Why don't you just ask him to pay you back? He has a lot of money, he would pay," Lisa explained, hoping she could resolve this situation with some advice of her own.

"Perhaps, but we need to be sure."

She nodded again and swilled some of the water around her mouth before swallowing it. "Do I have to sleep here?"

"I'm afraid so," Roach said. "But we'll try to look after you."

"You're evil men."

Roach nodded. He couldn't argue with that.

"I miss my mommy and daddy."

"I know you do."

Lisa finished the chocolate and drained the remains of the water before handing the empty bottle back to Roach.

"Are you going to tie me up again?"

"I'm afraid so."

45

Johnny Phillips and Michael Richards remained in the same pub all evening, most of its tables unoccupied. The old man and his copy of *The Racing Times* had left three hours ago, only to be replaced by a drunken duplicate.

The new old man also carried a radio and a newspaper, he seemed to be wearing the same clothes and his face was as equally wrinkled, only he was a lot more inebriated. Within five minutes of the sober clone walking purposefully out of the pub, the alcoholic one stumbled inside.

He spoke to Richards and Phillips and even played pool with them before retiring from the premises. The two conmen had used his intoxicated state to hustle him out of thirty dollars.

A couple of boys entered half an hour later, they regarded the occupied pool table and then left.

As the large clock in the pool room nudged onto seven o'clock, the only occupants were the two criminals and the bored bartender watching soap operas on the television above the bar.

"We're going to have to go back soon," Richards said.

Phillips shrugged and leaned over the table to take a long shot on a red. "Why the rush?"

"We've been here for hours," Richards said.

"Are you bored?"

"Not really."

"Then what's your problem?"

"I want a drink."

"You're in a pub. Get one."

Richards watched his friend sink the shot and then walk around the table to line up another.

"I can't," Richards said. "I have to drive us home."

"Have one," Phillips argued. "It won't do you any harm."

"I like to settle when I start to drink. Have one then another, not have one, drive the car home, then have another."

"You sound like a little girl when you complain, you know that?" Phillips observed with a grin.

"Fuck off."

"Feisty," Phillips slammed another red ball into the pocket and left the white ball in line for a long shot on the black.

"I'm getting sick of Coke," Richards said.

"What?"

"Coke. It's the soda that doesn't know what it is. I don't normally drink it on its own, unless I have no choice—like now."

"What the fuck are you bitching about?" Phillips stopped, rested his cue against the table and stared at his friend in bewilderment.

"Coke, it's becoming a flavor," Richards clarified. "There's too many knock-offs and they all taste different. So, when you order it you never know which one you're getting, is it Coca Cola, Pepsi, or some cheap shit from China. They should tell you. When you ask for orange juice they make a point of telling you it's freshly squeezed, fuck, some places will even tell you which oranges are used. But they never explain the Coke."

"What the fuck . . ."

"I'm just saying."

"If you hate it so much why didn't you get orange juice?" Phillips wondered.

"It gives me heartburn."

"Lemonade?"

"Tastes like fizzy sweat."

"Sprite."

"Fizzy sweat with a hint of lime."

"You're a picky fucker ain't you?" Phillips mused.

"Maybe I should go get a beer. Just one, then we can leave," Richards bargained with himself.

Phillips nodded.

"I'll let you take your shot first," Richards said, waiting over the pool table.

Phillips nodded, a bemused grin still etched across his face. He took his shot and then rested the cue down on the table again.

"Lucky bastard," Richards muttered. "I'll go get a beer now. Want another?"

Phillips looked down at his own glass, it was half full and surrounded by six empty glasses. The bartender had decided that she wasn't going to go around collecting glasses or cleaning tables today, so Phillips knew exactly how much he'd had to drink.

After a few more seconds of deliberation he nodded, "Get me another," he said before draining what was left in the one he already had.

46

Howard Price stared at the stranger in the mirror. In the last twenty-four hours, the well-educated, cultured, and somewhat stressed features had transformed into an almost unrecognizable portrait of despair, fear, and hate.

It was morning and he hadn't slept a wink. He'd stayed awake downstairs, watching television to try to take his mind off Lisa, but it hadn't worked. He couldn't remember what he had watched and he doubted he even knew at the time.

Around three o'clock in the morning he and Elizabeth had gone to bed. Howard found it hard to talk to her and she found it hard to talk to him, but the deathly silences hadn't discomforted either of them. They said goodnight, kissed each other, and tried to drift off to sleep.

Elizabeth had drifted off within the hour, Howard remained awake. He did, or at least thought he did, fall asleep sometime around five o'clock. He was spirited away into a soft dream, he remembered the warmth it gave but not the images it displayed, but something woke him minutes later and thrust him back into reality.

The skin below his eyes was baggy and black, he pinched it with his finger and thumb and pulled.

Shaking his head at his own sorrowful figure he turned on the cold tap and watched the gusset of water spray into the sink in front of him. Staring into the stream he felt his eyes becoming heavy, he felt tired, but he knew he couldn't sleep. He wouldn't sleep until Lisa was alive and well; until he could hold her again and assure her and himself that she was going to be okay.

Cupping his hands below the flowing tap he allowed the water to freeze his skin. He watched as the skin on his hands changed color when the water cooled his blood and numbed his fingers.

Splashing the water over his face he relished the freeze. The water continued on a downward spiral over his face, running over his bare torso and dripping onto his pajama pants, he pressed his ice-cold hands to his face.

"Are you okay darling?"

Elizabeth Price stood in the doorway of the bathroom. She also looked tired and gaunt. Her once soft, delicate features were ravaged; her eyes bloodshot, her complexion pale.

"I'm just trying to wake myself up," Howard answered without looking in her direction.

"Come downstairs," she said. "I've cooked us both breakfast."

"I'm not hungry."

"You need to eat."

Howard shook his head. He picked up a fresh towel from the rack next to the sink and sunk his head into its plush fibers.

"You need to keep your strength up," Elizabeth insisted.

"For what?" Howard said as he lowered the towel.

"It's going to be a long day."

"No shit," he snapped.

Elizabeth frowned and sunk her head into her chest, "Just have something to eat, would you?"

"I'll be down in a minute."

Elizabeth faked a smile and left. Howard listened to her footfalls on the stairs as she descended into the kitchen.

Wiping a few extra drops of cold water from his face he replaced the towel and walked into the bedroom. Grabbing a pair of tattered blue jeans, a white shirt, and a large sweatshirt, he quickly changed.

Elizabeth had woken before Howard got out of bed. He had pretended to be asleep so he could avoid conversation when she left the room. That was forty minutes ago and as he strolled into the kitchen he realized what she had been doing in that time.

The air inside the kitchen was humid and smoky; an extractor fan above the cooker tried to dry and clean the air but did little more than make a continuous, irritating noise.

Two windows and the patio doors had been opened to allow the kitchen some breathing space.

Howard's attention was fixed on the breakfast table. The large, round table was filled with fried, baked, and toasted goods. Elizabeth always cooked to take her mind off things. When her mother had been diagnosed with cancer Howard found himself coming home to large roasted dinners and three-course meals. When her mother passed away she had cooked mountains of treats. Luckily for Howard the school fair had been on at the time and Lisa and her teacher had sold all of Elizabeth's anxiety goods from one of the stalls.

On the table was an account of Elizabeth's worry and as Howard spread his eyes over the many delights he realized just how worried she was.

The table was brimming with food. In the middle, on a large plate, was a tall stack of pancakes. Howard counted fifteen, with another half dozen on the breakfast table. Next to the mountain of pancakes was a similarly large stack of toast, all buttered and spread with five different kinds of jam. Next to these was a plate of sweet waffles, a plate of potato waffles, scones, and a variety of sauces. Tomato sauce, brown sauce, sweet chili, chocolate, maple syrup, strawberry, butterscotch, as well as a jar of marmalade, strawberry jam, lemon curd, and a platter of butter.

Surrounding these delights was bacon, black pudding, fried tomatoes, fried bread, and some thick sausages.

"Like I said," Elizabeth said from behind the kitchen counter. "Eat up."

Howard looked at her and smiled. He wrapped his arms around her and pulled her close to him.

"There's beans and mushrooms in the pans," she said with tears running down her cheeks and a smile on her face. "And a fresh pot of coffee and tea on the counter. There wasn't any space left on the table."

Howard laughed and kissed her on the forehead. "I guess I can eat something," he said. "Maybe we should invite the neighbors, we could feed the whole town."

47

Darkness had come and gone for Lisa Price. The room around her remained the same musky brown color as it was when she first arrived, but her world had turned even blacker for a while. She had fallen asleep, she knew that much, but she didn't know for how long.

She had dreamed of her parents. They had all been in the house, but something about the house looked different and felt colder. Men in green suits were walking back and forth, taking furniture and belongings and loading them into a truck while her parents watched on, smiling.

Lisa had tried to reach out to them, grasp them, hold them, touch them; but all of her efforts were in vain. Instead she retreated to her room, only to find that it no longer existed. The walls had been knocked down to expand her parents' bedroom. The bathroom was stretched twice its original size and was decorated in the most elegant marble. There was a hot tub where Lisa's bed once was and a heated towel rack in place of her desk. All of her things were gone, like she had never been there at all.

She ran out of the room in shock, reaching the top of the stairs just in time to see her parents leave the house and slam the door shut behind them.

She was alone in an empty house and her parents had abandoned her.

It was then that she woke, that much she did know. She didn't usually have many nightmares but was always reassured when she woke. The horrible visions seen in her sleep would disappear and the warmth of her reality would take over, her parents were always there to console her if anything had scared or worried her.

This time it was different. She wished herself back into the nightmare.

Moving her arms and legs she realized she had more space between the string and her skin, it no longer cut into her. She reasoned that the nice man must have come in through the night to ease the tightness.

"Good morning," Morris walked into the living room of the dark apartment, stretching and greeting Roach who sat on one of the hardback chairs in discomfort.

"Is it?" Roach snapped.

"What the fuck is wrong with you?"

"Just tired."

Morris shrugged and dropped onto the chair opposite his colleague. "Did you get any sleep?"

"Not really. It's hard to sleep in here, and the fact that we don't have any beds doesn't help either."

"A cushion and your jacket, that's all you need for a good sleep."

James Roach frowned.

"Where did you go this morning?" Morris asked.

"What?"

"I heard you creeping about and when I looked you were heading out the front door."

"I went to the pay phone around the corner. The battery on my mobile is dead."

Morris paused. He watched his colleague, waiting for him to explain his actions further—he didn't speak.

"And?" Morris pushed.

Roach shook himself out of a trance, "Just to phone the wife. I told her I was staying in a hotel."

Morris nodded and looked around the apartment. Moisture clung to the walls and created damp splashes of grainy brown mold. Burn marks, cigarette stubs, ash, empty bottles, tin foil, and various wrappers were scattered on the hard floor—the air in the room stank of despair.

"Not exactly the Ritz, though, is it?" he joked.

Roach laughed. "Did you check in on the girl during the night?"

"Are you asking me or making a statement based on the fact that you saw me sneaking into her room?" Morris raised his eyebrows. Roach laughed and nodded.

"I figured I would loosen her ties," Morris said. "Poor kid won't be able to feel her arms or legs."

"Do I detect a hint of remorse?" Roach asked, surprised at the act of kindness.

"No. Just making sure our money girl remains in mint condition."

"You're a soulless fucker, aren't you?"

"It comes with the job."

Silence wrapped around them again as they both drifted into their own thoughts.

"What if she recognizes us?" Roach said, breaking the silence.

"What do you mean?"

"Well, we ain't been disguising our faces, have we? She can provide decent descriptions of us to the police."

"We've been through this before James. She's just a kid, give her a few hours and she won't be able to pick us out of a lineup of cartoon characters."

"You might be underestimating her."

"Not really. What good is a description if none of us have any police records or have never been involved with the police? They can stick black-and-white fucking drawings of our faces on as many papers and pamphlets as they want, we're ghosts in this world."

Roach agreed. "Do you plan to leave the country afterward?"

"Of course," Morris said without hesitation. "I'll put my shitty fucking house on the market and head for Spain, Italy, or France. Five hundred thousand will be enough for me to buy a house and a nice piece of land over there. I'll spend the rest of my days sitting in the sun, getting drunk, and gambling away all my money."

"The only difference to the life you have now is the sun," Roach said with a smile.

Morris laughed, "That's true. How about you?"

"Not too sure to be honest. I sorted out a place to secure the cash but never thought about what I'd spend it on. I could do with a new car I guess."

"Think big. Fine hundred grand and all you want is a car?"

"Well, I'd like a huge mansion but with today's house prices even half a million won't cover that."

"You can pick up a nice big house somewhere away from the inner cities."

"I always liked the idea of living in the states," Roach mused. "I could do with a nice big villa in Florida, but I'll need a fucking green card if I want to live there . . . I guess I've got time to mull it over anyway."

Morris nodded, "You have plenty of time to think about it. Plenty of time to lose that wife of yours too. Think of all the pussy you'll be able to pull over there," he added with a wink.

48

Howard Price glared at the titanium suitcase in resentment. Its practically indestructible exterior shone like a diamond as the glints of sunshine screamed through the cuts in the living room blinds and glazed its surface.

Beneath the thick exterior and the two steel combination locks, housed in darkness inside the thick suitcase, was one million dollars in fifty dollar bills; all neatly stacked in bundles of fifty-thousand.

He despised every sheet of paper that bore President Grant's face. This was the wealth that endangered his daughter, these stacks of green paper were the reason he wasn't sure if his daughter was alive or dead. His wealth, his status, his money, the things he had worked so hard to achieve in his lifetime, had let him down and robbed him of his daughter's safety.

"Anxious?" Detective Inspector Brown chewed slowly on a wad of gum and eyed Howard Price.

"Not really sure."

"You have every right to be anxious Mr. Price—"

"Really? Oh, well thank you, now that I know that I can really let my fucking hair down eh?"

"If you would let me finish Mr. Price," the detective asserted. "You have every right to be anxious, but, you should know that we will strive to make sure you and your daughter are safe. We are behind you all the way."

"A long fucking way behind me," Howard mumbled. "I don't want you lot fucking this up."

"I can assure—"

"You can't assure me anything; you can just lie and tell me what I want to hear, but I'll tell you one thing . . ." he snarled and took a step closer to the officer. "If you or any of your officers start shooting, I'll hold *you* fully responsible."

The two men held each other's stares.

"Was that a threat?"

"Just keep your distance."

"Guaranteed," the detective smiled and walked away, leaving Howard alone with the suitcase.

The living room of the Price house was brimming with police officers. A group of technicians dabbled with phone equipment at the back of the room, in front of them five plainclothes officers buzzed, one took notes, one studied photographs, another read over some letters, the other two stood drinking a cup of steaming coffee as they admired the photos and drawings that decorated the walls.

"Want one dear?" Elizabeth asked, holding a plate of sandwiches invitingly in front of her husband.

"I'm not really that hungry."

"Go on, there's plenty."

"I'm sure there is but I'm still getting over breakfast."

"You hardly ate breakfast. There was loads left over."

"That's because you cooked enough for five hundred."

"Nonsense."

Howard looked at his wife's face. Despite the depression and anxiety of the moment she had attached a look of ignorant calm to her features, standing by the notion that if she didn't think about it, it wouldn't hurt her. It seemed to be working, although the ten milligrams of Diazepam she had swallowed with breakfast also played a part.

"What's in them anyway?" Howard asked.

"Ham and mustard—"

"I don't like ha—"

"And these ones have cheese and jam," she continued. "These ones are egg. And there's tuna and mayonnaise in the kitchen."

"I'm not really that hungry."

"Do you want a cup of tea then?"

Howard paused. The sandwich plate was still in his face and he could smell the wall of English mustard pushing at him. All the police officers, except the detective, had taken advantage of Elizabeth's generosity—some still munched on sandwiches and collected more from the manic-sedated woman who danced around the living room like a Stepford wife with a short circuit.

"I'll have a cup of coffee," Howard said.

Elizabeth smiled, nodded, and then retired to the kitchen.

When she left his side Detective Brown ghosted in front of him. In his right hand Howard spotted a cordless phone, taken from his own living room. Behind the detective the technicians had stopped fiddling with the phone base; their attentions were firmly fixed on Howard.

A deathly silence fell over the room, interrupted by the silent whirring of a kettle in the kitchen.

The detective held the phone in his outstretched palm, "It's time to make the call," he instructed.

49

The sound of the ringing phone silenced both occupants in the room; one watched while the other answered.

"Hello . . . what . . . no— . . . no— . . . look! You fucking twat, I don't want another mobile phone. I don't care how many fucking free minutes you're going to give me . . . stop swearing? You phoned me, you invaded my fucking privacy. Give me your home phone number . . . why? So I can phone you when you're at home and annoy the fuck out of *you* that's why. Who the fuck do you think you are—"

Johnny Phillips paused, his mouth open in mid-argument. He grumbled, dropped the phone onto the arm of the sofa and threw his body onto the plush leather. "The fucker hung up on me."

Richards grinned from the comfort of the armchair, "Are you surprised? You swore at him; poor sod is just doing his job."

"Telemarketing isn't a fucking job. A job requires some skill, talent, or at least the ability to do something that most can't. Anyone can dial a list of numbers and repeat the same bullshit patter."

"Not anyone."

Phillips raised his eyebrows.

"A deaf-mute for instance," Richards said. "You can't make a telephone call if you can't speak, and you can't clinch the sale if you can't hear."

"The majority of them can't speak English, they manage all right."

Richards shrugged. He rose from the armchair, grabbed a game controller and sat back down. He used the wireless controller to bring the console into life. The documentary vanished and was replaced by a screen displaying various trademarks and designs.

Phillips took another controller from the back of the sofa, wedged behind a cushion.

"People with no hands," Richards said.

"What?"

"Telemarketing. If you have no hands you can't dial a phone, can you?"

"Can't say I've tried."

"Goes without saying."

"You could use a stick."

"How would you hold it?"

Phillips pondered this briefly, "An attachment maybe, like a hook, but, well . . . a stick."

"You would get a stick implanted into your stub, just so you could use a phone?"

"You could use it for other things," Phillips said.

"Like?"

"Pointing."

"Pointing?"

"You know, like a school teacher or one of them dicks who stands in front of the orchestra and waves a stick around."

"Still limited career choices though," Richards reasoned.

"It beats a hook. Imagine trying to wank with one of them things."

"I have the image of a handless mute operating as a teacher and a composer in my head. The last thing I need is someone masturbating with a hook."

"Makes you wonder though doesn't it?" Phillips said.

"Wonder what? How they wank? How they pick their nose? How they wipe their ass, how they finger their girlfriends, hold their children, play the drums?"

"No . . . but," Phillips's face creased with thoughtful amusement as he mulled over what had just been said. "Although that's some thought-provoking information right there. I mean, why don't they get a giant Swiss army knife attached instead? They could have the works on there: a knife, corkscrew, scissors, tweezers, mini torch, nail file. They'd be like Inspector Gadget, the idea of it makes losing a hand seem appealing."

"Why would someone with no hands want a nail file?"

"I meant people with just one hand missing."

"Hmm."

The game loaded up on the television screen and the console exploded into life, both men leaned forward, their controllers grasped, poised for the whistle.

"Enough of the intellectual conversation," Richards said. "It's time to kick your ass."

50

Morris waited for the mobile phone to ring twice before he acted. Roach, sitting opposite, looked on anxiously.

"Good afternoon," Morris picked up the phone and spoke in a pleasant voice, devoid of tension.

"I have the money," Howard Price said, his voice dry and almost whimpered. "Now I want my daughter back."

"All in good time Mr. Price. I want you to pack the money into a black duffel bag or rucksack," Morris instructed.

"It's in a titanium case," Howard said. "Practically indestructible."

"A titanium case? You expect me to lug a million dollars around in a titanium case? Did you bring the sign along as well?"

"Sign?"

"The one that says, 'look at me I'm up to no good and I'm carrying something incredibly valuable.' The money needs to be stuffed into a bag."

"Okay."

"Tell the cops not to come within one hundred feet of the drop-off or I'll cut your little bitch up and flush her down the toilet along with the other crap."

"The police are not involved," Howard lied.

"Don't fucking bullshit me Mr. Price, you're not dealing with an amateur, you are dealing with someone who has your daughter and doesn't give a fuck whether she lives or dies. Choose your lies carefully."

Howard paused, "The police won't come anywhere near the scene."

"You better fucking make sure they don't," Morris warned. "At four this afternoon, you are to come alone to Roucester Park."

Howard nodded to himself. He knew the place well, he used to take Lisa there as a child. It was rich with trees and gardens, some days they would climb a small tree and sit amongst the bed of leaves and just watch the day drift away.

"Okay," he confirmed.

"We will have people watching the roads leading into the park and the park itself, so don't try anything cocky. This isn't your day to be a hero, okay?"

"I just want my daughter back."

"Slowly walk twice around the basketball courts and sit down by the net closest to the road. Wait there for five minutes and then leave—leaving the bag by the net. I want to see you in your car, driving away from the scene within three minutes okay?"

"Understood."

"Have a nice day," Morris hung up the phone, tossed it onto the couch and shot Roach a row of pearly whites, "We're sorted."

51

Despite Howard's composure on the phone, when the line went dead his eyes fired red and he shot an evil glance at the detective, "He fucking knows you're here."

The detective—who had been listening into the call via a set of headphones—looked at Howard with an apologetic smile. "It was an educated guess."

"How the fuck do you know?" Howard demanded.

"There was no one watching the school and there is no one watching the house. Both were checked before we arrived and after we left. He called your bluff Mr. Price. He knows we'd get involved despite his warnings."

"How?"

"My guess is that this is not their first time. We don't have much to go on, and I'm sorry that I can't offer more than a simple educated guess myself, but I would bet my mortgage on them having priors, maybe for assault or fraud."

"Can you check?" Howard asked.

"I'm afraid not. We have no fingerprints, DNA, or conclusive photo fit."

"How many people do you think are in on this operation?" Howard asked.

"At least two—your daughter was taken by one man while another handed her friend a letter—but there could be more."

"How many more?" Howard was pacing up and down.

"It's hard to say. Not many, I don't think we're dealing with a gang here. If we were, they'd have asked for more than a million. One million split twenty, ten, or even five ways isn't much. I would guess two, maybe three, experienced, highly trained professionals."

"What makes you think that?" Elizabeth—who hadn't been listening to the phone conversation—appeared from behind the kitchen door.

"Amateurs would ask for more, they'd want enough to set themselves up for life, something along the lines of twenty million."

"I haven't got that much; I can't get that kind of cash," Howard was in shock.

"Exactly," the detective said. "But if you read what all the magazines and papers print about you it's easy to believe you can afford to wipe your ass with fifty dollar bills. Pardon my French. They see your successful business and your assets, not your bank account. But these men—" he paused. "They're smart enough to know you don't have that much money and cocky enough to risk a high-scale kidnapping for a share of two, three, or five hundred thousand each."

Howard fell back in disbelief. The armchair behind him cushioned his fall and he sank into its soft fabric.

"I cannot believe this is happening," he said, his eyes fixed on the floor. "I take a short holiday to relieve some stress and—" he stopped himself and merely shook his head. Elizabeth left the kitchen and walked to his side, laying a comforting hand on his shoulder.

"Still no trace?" Detective Inspector Brown asked the small group of technicians at the back of the room. All three of them shook their heads.

"The phone had a faint signal," one of the men said. "Which indicates they could be some distance away from the nearest tower."

"That's a start, isn't it?"

The technician sucked in air through his teeth and sighed it out, "Not really," he said, disappointed. "It could be a crappy phone or poor service."

The detective shook his head in disappointment and looked at the clock.

52

James Roach appeared from the bedroom where the troubled Lisa Price lay. He had fed her half a bar of chocolate, some chips, and had given her plenty of water.

Darren Morris was in the living room, sitting in silence. He looked at his watch when Roach returned. "Three hours away from a million bucks," he announced happily.

Roach suppressed a smile.

"This is a big moment for both of us," Morris said.

"Something could still go wrong," Roach said.

"What's got into you?" Morris asked, "You're normally the unfeeling zombie of this partnership. You have the face of a man who drowns kittens and beats his grandmother. You kill without thinking twice, you would happily commit genocide if the money was right, and I bet even then your expression wouldn't change. Yet now, because of a simple kidnapping, you start worrying? You bewilder me, you really do."

"Kidnapping is different to killing."

"Yes, it's easier."

James Roach opened his mouth to reply but he quickly slammed it shut again. A loud thud echoed throughout the apartment, it seemed to be coming from next door. More minor noises vibrated the room in which the two hitmen-come-kidnappers sat. Roach was the first to react. He bolted to his feet—his face now the intimidating picture of old—and rushed to the door to see if he could hear any sounds.

Darren Morris remained calm.

The sounds soon dwindled and Roach crossed from the door to the wall in an attempt to hear any noises from the apartment next door.

"Well?" Morris asked.

Roach shushed him and shook his head to indicate he couldn't hear anything.

Morris smiled, "There's nothing to worry about—"

His words were cut short as the front door burst open. The wood cracked and sprayed shards of wood. The deadbolts, padlocks, and chain ripped free from the door and wall, bringing a hail of plaster and wood with them.

Six men rushed into the room, four headed straight for James Roach who was as ready as ever. The intruders, all dressed in black, got more than they bargained for.

Roach swung his fist hard as the men rushed him, his wrist reverberated as his knuckles slammed into the jaw of one of them, instantly cracking three teeth and sending him sprawling to his knees—gargling blood and spitting enamel.

He ducked a full-blooded punch delivered by another intruder; the man twisted his body to put his full power into the swing. Grabbing his outstretched elbow—inches from his face—Roach pushed it inwards until he heard it crack. His attacker screamed in horror as his forearm snapped and his wrist broke inwards. He threw himself onto the floor, horrified to see that bone from his arm had torn through his skin and had pierced his sweatshirt.

Morris, sitting in a relaxed position, didn't have as much time to fend off his attackers. As the other two men rushed him he lifted his feet from the chair and, drawing both legs back to his chest, kicked out hard, sending it flying into them. It tripped up one of them, sending him sprawling—his chest slammed into the back of the chair on his way to the ground and he reduced the hard wood to splinters before smacking the back of his skull on a rotted base board.

Dodging a shoulder barge from the second man Morris side-stepped quickly, picked up another chair and slammed it over the second attacker. It snapped as it cracked on the top of his head and he collapsed in a heap, blood seeped through his black ski mask and he keeled over.

Morris rushed to help Roach, who was trying to break free from the grips of the final two assailants. Grabbing one from behind by the neck, he held onto him until the intruder released his grip on his colleague, then he kicked hard into the back of his calf; the darkened intruder yelped and lost his footing.

Dragging him to the floor, Morris repeatedly jabbed him in the face, erupting sprinkles of blood with each well-placed punch.

Roach broke free of the other intruder's grasp and managed to gain the momentum in the battle by delivering a swift hook to his abdomen. The man recoiled as the blow hit. Roach gripped the top of the man's head as he dipped forward in pain.

He heard mumbles of worry and fear as he held the masked head over the kitchen counter. He slammed his face hard onto the laminated top, the sounds of broken bone, shattered cartilage, and pained screams filled the air. He forced the man's head into the counter again and again, repeatedly smashing his skull onto the wood until he ran out of breath and the muffled screams had stopped.

The body fell to the floor, landing alongside the attacker that had died beneath the crushing fists of Darren Morris.

Breathing heavily, both men looked towards the shattered doorway. What they saw made their hearts sink.

Peter Sanderson stood in the doorway of the decrepit safe house, two heavyset bodyguards either side of him. In his sweaty right hand, clasped in his chubby fingers and aimed at James Roach, was a 9MM pistol.

"Shit," Morris uttered.

The two bodyguards stepped into the room, allowing a gap in the doorway through which another three men appeared, all carrying automatic pistols. Three of them trained their weapons on Morris and Roach while the other two restrained the pair of kidnappers.

"What's this all about?" Morris wanted to know as one of the men grabbed him and walked him into the living room.

Sanderson trudged through the door and slammed it shut behind him; it jarred in the damaged frame and popped back open. "I thought I would pay you a visit," he said. "See how you've been doing."

"We're doing fine," Morris assured as he and Roach were forced into the two unbroken hardback chairs.

The defeated attackers moaned and groaned around the apartment, one managed to drag himself to Sanderson's side. He mumbled an apology and tried to propel himself to his feet but his boss stopped him with a kick to the jaw.

"Stay on the fucking floor," he bellowed. "Lie there with the rest of the fucking filth." He snarled in disgust before rocketing another hard boot into the wounded intruder's ribs. He turned to Morris and Roach and smiled, "If you want a job done I guess you do have to do it yourself."

"What the fuck do you want?" There was a sense of urgency in Morris's voice.

"What do I *want*?" Sanderson seemed to mull this over as one his bodyguards grabbed a chair for him and escorted his wide derrière onto it. "I want many things, but I'm not here for what I want. I'm here for what I command. I command respect and loyalty. You see, my dear friends, I believe in trust and honor among fellow criminals, especially the ones working for me. So you can imagine my shock when I found out that you two . . ." he eyed both the men with hatred, "have been fucking me around."

"We haven't—" Morris began.

"Don't bullshit me Darren," Sanderson interrupted. "I know what you've been up to."

"What are you talking about?"

"This is what I'm talking about," Sanderson waved his arms around, indicating the apartment.

"We just wanted a change of pace that's all," Morris said.

"Kidnapping is certainly a change of pace, I will agree."

Both Darren Morris and James Roach felt a ten-ton weight crush their hearts and an icy chill speed up their spines.

"We've been watching you," Sanderson continued with a wry smile.

"We?" Morris said, the sarcasm gone from his voice.

"Like I told you on the phone Darren, I have more men on this cartel case. It just so happens that these men ran into Pearce's contact, the man you promised me was dead and empty of information. Luckily for me, and very unluckily for you, he was very much alive and *full* of information."

"Pearce probably had more than one contact," Morris said, trying to snake his way out of trouble. "The one we found was dry, so we killed him."

Sanderson sighed and shook his head. He rapped his fingers on the butt of the pistol which had been lowered slightly. "Another lie," he said finally. "My men saw you check into a bed and breakfast. They watched you all night."

"We couldn't get in touch with Pearce's supplier that night so we waited—"

"They saw you meet up with that duck-ass convict Linders and drive away in a freshly resprayed car, then they followed you here. It disappointed me, it really did, after so many years of good service. But, you see boys," his fingers became unsteady on the trigger. "I wouldn't mind so much if you wanted to pull a little side job, but kidnapping is a step beyond and I'd be against it, you know that. And for that, there's a price to pay."

"If you want a cut of the ransom money you can have it," Roach spoke for the first time.

"I don't want money, James. You know how the game works, you break my respect, you lose my trust; if you lose my trust, I break a leg . . . or two."

"You came here to break our legs?" Morris asked.

Sanderson raised his weapon. "Maybe. Maybe not. Maybe I think you deserve more than a broken bone or two. You've done so well for me over the years, but I don't like liars. I don't like to feel cheated. I don't—"

A pained, desperate scream stopped him. It was soft, distant, scared. Sanderson lowered his weapon, turned to look at his bodyguards and then turned back to the two hitmen. "I almost forgot. The object of your affections. Your reason for deserting me."

Sanderson nodded to his bodyguard and gestured to the bedroom door and the source of the noise.

Roach and Morris exchanged unspoken words, before they turned back to the front and Morris spoke. "Leave her out of this. Do what you want to us, but she doesn't have to suffer.

Sanderson's face was stoic. "You're a martyr for the greater good, now are you? These past few weeks have really changed you. From murderer to saint, what are the odds." He laughed.

Morris could hear the girl struggling in the other room. He could hear the sound of her restraints being ripped off. Next to him, Roach was getting fidgety, but Morris kept his cool and focused on Sanderson. "This was about the money, not the girl," he said. "Do what you have to do with us and leave her where she is."

Sanderson stopped laughing and yelled at the pleading man in front of him. "Get off your fucking cross! You're a filthy fucking hitman. A down and out like all of us. Stop trying to pretend you're anything but."

Morris met his boss's stare. Sanderson was nearly foaming at the mouth following his outburst, but there was a calmness there.

He was angry, but he was also getting a kick out of this. The hit-man was the first to break contact, his chin sinking to his chest.

"I thought so," Sanderson said.

The bodyguard dragged Lisa Price into the room and Sanderson ushered her over with his pistol. She was weak, tired, scared, but she didn't react to the weapon as the crime boss expected her too. She didn't scream or try to run away. She merely shuffled over to him, helped by the firm hand of the bodyguard in her lower back.

When she was in front of him, Sanderson got down on one knee, to her eye-level. "How are you doing, darling?"

Lisa Price raised her head to acknowledge him, but she didn't answer.

"Have these men been giving you hell?"

Still she didn't say a word. She followed Sanderson's eyes and looked at Morris and Roach, the former seemingly deflated and defeated, the latter looking even more agitated by the second.

"Have they been hurting you? Have they been torturing you?"

This time Lisa Price shook her head, but not convincingly.

"I bet they've been touching you, haven't they? Is that what they've been doing?"

At that moment Roach bolted to his feet. The movement was quick, but the sound of the chair kicking back underneath him alerted everyone in the room. Sanderson tried to respond, a moment of panic lighting up his face. He wasn't quick enough, but his bodyguard was. A shot rang out, deafening in the small room, and Roach dropped, his leg buckling underneath him as the bullet tore through his thigh.

"You bastard!" Roach screamed. "How dare you fucking say that! Leave her alone!"

Sanderson was shocked. He straightened, laughed. He tried to shake off the panic and surprise that had clearly been on his face moments earlier, but it was evident in his voice. "What the fuck happened to him?" He asked Morris, nodding to Roach who was frothing at the mouth as the armed bodyguard aimed a gun at his forehead. "You guys really have changed. Both of you. I mean. . ." he shook his head. "Fucking hell."

Roach was panting heavily, in pain and angry; Morris was silent, looking at Sanderson. They both saw the look on his face, the way his features changed. An idea had occurred to him and both of them suspected what was coming. "I tell you what," he said. "Let's see how much you have really changed." He gestured to the bodyguard who had yet to fire his gun, before whispering in his ear. The bodyguard retrieved a large double-edged knife from a sheath on his leg. After Sanderson gestured to Morris, the bodyguard walked over and gave him the knife.

"Let's see how much these guys really care about you," Sanderson said to Lisa Price. "Go and see your new friend, darling."

Lisa looked at Morris, Roach and then at Sanderson. The crime boss nodded, his eyebrows raised, and Lisa carefully walked towards Morris. She smiled at him—a desperate, pleading smile.

"What the fuck is this," Morris said, looking at the knife and then the girl.

"This is a test," Sanderson said. "Kill her."

"What?"

"You heard me. Kill her. Prove your loyalty. Prove to me that you are the same guy you have always been, and I might let you off. One last kill, Darren, and you're a free man. Both of you, he waved his gun between the two hitmen, "You're free to go."

Lisa began to cry as she looked into the eyes of her captor. Morris looked to Roach, both of their faces alive with anger, disgust, and desperation. Sanderson thought they were reaching a conclusion about the girls' death. He thought that their stare was a morbid agreement between two men who had killed for money, pride, and freedom many times before.

He was wrong. And he was still smiling when Morris quickly jumped to his feet, pushed the girl out of the way and then threw the knife as hard as he could at the gun-wielding psychopath.

As Lisa toppled over, falling into Roach's open arms as Morris had intended, the knife found its target. It hit Sanderson's hand. The handle landed first, as Morris had feared it might. But it was thrown with enough force that it was still enough to knock the gun out of his hand and cause him to recoil in shock.

Both of the remaining guns turned on Morris, but before any triggers were squeezed, he was already on the first bodyguard. His strength and his agility was gone, but he still had his weight and his desperation and hopefully that was enough. He tumbled into the guard, throwing his forearm forcibly into his head as he did so. He felt the impact as the man hit the floor, heard the crack of his head and felt the resistance disappear in an instant. Morris scrambled back to his feet, taking longer than he would have liked and suffering with each movement.

He turned to Roach, hoping to see that his friend also had the better of his chosen target. But what he saw drained every last bit of hope out of his body, because Roach was already on his knees, the gun already pointed at his forehead. He had failed, unable to fight through his injuries, unable to overpower the bodyguard. Morris caught his old friend's stare and in a split second he saw a look that was filled with more self-hate, hopelessness, and regret than he had ever seen on his partner's face.

Morris turned to Sanderson just as his friend was executed. Lisa's screams could be heard through the fading echo of gunfire. But as bad as he felt for her, he knew there was nothing he could do. Sanderson was one step ahead; his gun was pointed at Morris's head.

Another shot rang out, and the screaming grew louder. When the echoes of gunfire had ceased and both hitmen were dead, the screams continued. They were fading, tiring, but they were still there.

Sanderson didn't even lower his gun. He simply moved his aim to the little girl and squeezed until the screams stopped.

"Didn't I tell you to fucking shoot first?" Sanderson said to his bodyguard, his voice shaking with fear and anger.

"He came at me, boss."

Sanderson was silent for a few moments, giving himself time to recover as the voice of the gunfire rang in his ears. He then shook his head, and put the gun away. "Such a shame," he said. "They throw away all those years of loyalty for one fucking kidnapping. It makes me sick it really does."

"Clean up this mess," he ordered to the only bodyguard still standing. He walked over to the wounded man in front of him and prodded them with his foot. "Get these fuckers on their feet and away from the scene."

The bodyguard nodded.

"Take their bodies," Sanders instructed, nodding at Morris and Roach. "Dump them in their car out front and drive it off a cliff, or burn the fucker. If the kidnapping is linked to them it might come back to me, so dispose of them."

"What about the other car sir? The BMW?" the bodyguard asked.

"Burn it before you leave the scene, it'll get blamed on fucking joy riders and arsonists. This area is full of the bastards."

Sanderson left the building with a smile on his face.

53

"Are you sure you don't need our assistance?"

Detective Inspector Brown sat beside Howard Price smoking a small Hamlet cigar. Howard didn't allow smoking in his house; he despised the smell and the way the stench clung to the fabrics, but he hadn't minded when the detective spark up the cigar. He'd asked Howard if it was okay, and he had nodded a vague agreement, the smell of his house and its belongings seemed unimportant.

"We can keep tabs on the area. Our men can be very discreet," the detective insisted through a thick stream of smoke.

"I said no, okay?"

"That's okay Mr. Price, I'm just warning you. If something goes wrong, you'll be on your own. If *we* were there we could resolve the situation."

"Nothing will go wrong," Price was confident. "I'll give them the money and they will give me my little girl back."

"And if it does go wrong?"

Howard shot the detective an evil stare. A draft of thick smoke cut across his face and slowly dissipated into a blur; their glances remained menacing through the gray smoke. "What are you trying to suggest detective?"

"Sometimes, in cases like this," the cigar smoking officer began using small hand gestures. "The kidnappers can get a little greedy; get a little bit out of control."

"What do you mean?"

The smoking man paused. "Let's say they are spying on you when you arrive in the park. If they are, then they know you're alone, if they think you're alone, one million might not be enough for them. They know how desperate you are to get your daughter back; they might take the money from you, keep your daughter and demand more." His words, although softened, cut through Howard like a knife.

The idea scared him, the thought of his little Lisa being in the hands of criminal madmen was horrid enough for his troubled mind, but the idea that they would play such horrific games terrified him.

"Okay," he said at last. "Then that's where you come in."

The detective smiled, "Excellent," he said. "We'll hook you up with a small microphone. It'll catch all incoming signals and send them back to us. We'll be able to hear every word spoken between you and them."

"What if they check me for bugs?" Howard asked.

"Not likely," he was quick to reply. "They'll want to get the money and make a quick exchange. They know we're involved so they won't want to waste any time or make any mistakes." He beckoned a police officer—standing in a group of tea-swilling officers which included the bright-faced Elizabeth—over and the man reacted immediately. "This is Officer Devon," Brown proclaimed, then to Devon he said: "Get Mr. Price hooked up and ready to go." The Officer nodded and within minutes he was sewing a small device inside Howard's chest pocket.

"If you need help, if they flee or if they start beating you or your daughter, just call, we'll be able to hear everything from the microphone and we'll have six police cars stationed within a one-mile radius. When the deal is done and your daughter is safe, watch them, see where they go, and speak the directions into the microphone, okay?"

Howard nodded as the officer finished setting up the gadget.

54

"What a fucking life," Michael Richards drove the pool cue hard into the white ball, sending it slamming into a red, which in turn hit another red before both balls dropped into the pocket.

"What are you moaning about now?" Phillips said.

They had returned to the pub where they had spent last night drinking and playing pool. It was empty, quiet, and cheap.

Richards paused, rested his cue against the table and picked up his glass. "This," he said, as if in confirmation. He took a long drink. The heavy taste of alcohol in the final dregs of the drink stung his taste buds and he creased his face accordingly.

"This?"

"Getting pissed, playing pool, playing video games, getting pissed again. That's all we seem to do nowadays."

"Don't you like getting drunk?"

"Of course."

"And you like pool, and video games."

"That's beside the point."

"Why do you always get philosophical on me when you've had a drink?"

"I'm not being philosophical."

"Maybe philosophical isn't the right word. Hmm," Phillips stroked his chin. "Annoying, that's the word I was looking for."

"I'm just saying that's all."

"You're always *just saying* it though. There's nothing stopping us doing other stuff, we have the money, we're young, if you're so bored why don't you think of something to break that boredom. Snap out of the mold."

"I like the mold."

"You just said you hated it."

"No, I didn't. I said, what a fucking life."

"Okay, so you implied it then."

Richards paused and shook his head, "I'm not sure what I want to be honestly," he said, lining up his cue to take another shot.

"Money," Phillips spoke for him. "That's what we both want. With money, we can take things to the next level. With enough money, we can take it to the highest level, quit the game, and live the high life."

"We'd need one hell of a con to make that kind of money," Richards said. "The betting shop could bring us that sort of cash I guess. If we ever get around to opening it," he paused mid-shot and looked across at Phillips. "Quit the game? You would quit the game?"

"Sure, why not. If we have money coming out of our asses why risk exchanging that money for a fat fucker's dick in the prison shower room?"

Richards smiled, "Good point," he agreed. "I just—" he paused again.

"You just what?" Phillips pushed.

"I just never imagined you . . . well I never thought you would ever give up the game. Come to think of it, I never thought I would either."

"We've been doing it a long time, but I'm sure we'll manage without it."

Richards shrugged, took his shot and as the black ball slammed into the pocket he grinned cockily.

Phillips said, "Another game?"

"Of course, it seems to be my lucky night."

Phillips mumbled a curse under his breath and turned his back on his friend "I'll get the drinks in," he said, vanishing from the pool room.

Michael Richards dug in his pocket for some spare change to feed into the table. He found three quarters and began pushing them into the silver slider on the side of the pool table. After setting up the balls using the plastic triangle he glanced up at a large wall clock. The time was 3:42; they would make this their last game, take the bus home, stay there for a few hours, and then hit the clubs in the evening. He was feeling lucky.

55

Howard's mind jittered on a stimulant fusion of hyperactivity and nervousness. He wanted the deal over with; he had left the house early, unable to stare at the stuck clock any longer as time refused to budge.

He had made sure the police would not interrupt the proceedings, threatening to take legal action against them if he found they had been spying on the park or keeping tabs on him. How he would sue the police he didn't know, but he was rich, powerful and worried, he hoped the threat would be enough to keep them at bay.

They were on standby in case the delivery didn't go as planned. He hoped to God it did.

He drove to the park himself, checking his rearview mirror cautiously all the way. As far as he could tell, he wasn't being followed.

Leaving the car in a graveled car park he trotted nervously for about two hundred yards. He passed a bus stop where a group of kids gathered; they eyed him suspiciously as he passed and his nerves cut sharper with each stare. One or two mumbled something, probably aimed at him, but he ignored them and as he turned the corner away from the bus stop a large bus pulled to a screeching halt—making his skin crawl—and the youngsters clambered on.

He reached a row of trees and slowed his pace. He stared at the foliage with a deep longing, he and Lisa had spent many hours playing among them. A smile crossed his face, a smile devoid of worry—it didn't last. He wondered if he'd ever see her again, if he'd ever see her soft eyes, her gleaming smile, and her sweet, beautiful face.

He had to keep positive, of course he would see her again. Things might be different after all this, she's a young girl and this would be traumatic, but he would help her through. He would even quit work to make sure she was attended to always. Since she had disappeared he had regretted all the hours he had worked at the office, hours that could have been spent with her.

With those thoughts came anger, anger at the people who had taken her away, and anger at himself.

His feet touched concrete. He was on the edge of the basketball courts. He paused where he stood; surveying his surroundings to see if he could catch sight of his daughter's kidnappers, but there was no one else around.

Taking in a deep breath, readying his body and mind, he walked slowly around the basketball courts.

"Have we got enough to drink at home?" Johnny Phillips asked Michael Richards as both men left the pub.

"You're the expert on that. You buy it and you drink most of it."

"You drink your fair share."

"I'm normally flat out on my back after six cans, to you that's just a warmup."

"Good point," Phillips agreed. "I think there might be a few more in the fridge," he continued. "I'm not too sure. We still have that bottle of red wine the old lady next door bought us for Christmas. Can't stand the stuff but if it's all we've got—"

"It isn't," Richards interjected.

"What?"

"You drank it on New Year's."

"Did I?"

"You and that skinny porn star from up north. The same slut you fucked in my bed."

Phillips nodded, "You were out that night."

"And on the sofa."

"We didn't make a mess."

"And on the kitchen table."

"I cleaned it after."

Richards shook his head and smiled wryly. They continued towards the bus stop as a large bus screamed past them.

"We also did it in the bathroom," Phillips admitted after a while.

"Why on earth would you want to fuck her in the bathroom when you have a bed and a couch?"

"She was a kinky bitch. She wanted to fuck in every room. It's not easy to please a porn star you know."

"Actually, no, I don't know," Richards said. "Bath or the shower?"

"Toilet," Phillips replied without hesitation.

"You fucked her on the toilet?" Richards asked with disgust and more than a little curiosity.

"She was a very flexible and very dirty girl."

"You're fucking crazy you know that?" Richards laughed.

They crossed to the bus stop and waited in silence. Richards rested against a wall, taking some pressure of his feet while Phillips walked around in front of him and scanned the area.

"Hey," Phillips said eventually. "Isn't that that rich guy?"

"What?" Richards asked, bemused.

"Over there by the basketball courts," Phillips thrust a finger beyond the bus stop and over to the fields.

Richards studied the slowly moving figure for a while. He was walking with his head held high in anticipation; in his left hand, he held a large duffel bag. "Howard Price," he confirmed.

"That's him," Price remembered. "From the magazine. What the fuck is he doing around here?"

"Taking a walk maybe?"

"People like him don't take walks in places like this, he'll get mugged." A smile began to crease his face as he uttered those words and he looked at Richards.

"Hell no," Richards said immediately. "I'm not mugging him."

"We don't have to. We can con him, pull a quick one."

"He'll find out, and we haven't got a car."

"A bus will be along any minute, we could take it to a different place, and then hitch another ride home. Or, failing that, we could just run, he's old and fat, he isn't going to catch us. I'll distract; you steal, we've done it loads of times, it's easy enough," Phillips said with an almost giddy excitement.

Silence fell between them—Richards was thinking. They both watched Price and, to their surprise, when he had walked full circle around the courts he sat down on the concrete and lay the bag by his side.

"Rich men don't carry money," Richards said.

"They carry Rolex watches," Phillips said. "And a duffel bag . . ." he contemplated this for a moment ". . . which could be full of goodies."

"Or laundry."

"Which self-respecting millionaire does his laundry himself, or at a laundromat?"

"Good point."

"Well, He's just sitting there. Want to give it a shot?"

Richards's eyes flickered from Howard Price's slumped figure to Johnny Phillips's alert and somewhat excited expression. "Okay," he said rather belatedly. "Let's go over and see what we can do."

The cold concrete below Howard Price's backside irritated him. He had spent the majority of his life sitting in office chairs and his body had adjusted accordingly—giving him lower back pain. Now, without anything to lean against, he was in great discomfort.

He checked his watch for the fifth time in three minutes. He had been waiting by the side of the basketball courts for one hundred and twenty-three seconds—he had been counting, he couldn't help himself. The kidnappers had told him to leave after five minutes, but he wanted his daughter. That was the deal, one million for Lisa, she was worth it; she was worth every penny to him, but it shouldn't have come down to this.

His heart skipped a beat when he saw two men leaving the bus stop and striding his way. One of the men, the larger one, looked like a criminal. He had a hard, rugged face and a strong build, the other looked weaker but still intimidating in an intellectual way. To Howard they certainly didn't look like the normal riffraff that patrolled these streets, they looked different somehow, more professional.

They crossed gazes with Howard a few times and he was sure they were heading straight for him. He stood up and waited.

"Howard Price, right?" the rugged man asked.

Howard nodded. His whole body seemed to be suffering from tremors of anger and fear.

"It's nice to meet you," the rugged one walked up to him and shook his hand. Unbeknown to Howard, Michael Richards had drifted away as his friend took center stage.

"Really?" Howard stuttered.

"Sure," Phillips said. "You're a big man in this town. Hell, probably even the country. No doubt one of the richest too, eh?" Phillips nudged Howard who smiled, more out of bewilderment than anything else.

"It's not about the money," Howard replied.

"That's what all rich people say," Phillips said.

"The money doesn't matter. I just want my daughter to be safe," the emotions were rising inside of him.

"Your daughter? I'm sure she'll be fine. With the amount of money you've got to throw around, you can afford to keep her safe. Am I right?" Phillips asked, lightly nudging him again.

"Is she okay?"

"Who?"

"Don't play games with me. You know who I'm talking about."

Phillips shook his head, "I guess the craziness comes with the money. So, how's the business?"

"Why do you care?" Howard spat.

"I'm just being friendly. No need to get hostile. Can't an honest citizen have a chat with a famous local?"

Howard paused. Something inside him told him he should play it cool and calm. The last thing he needed was to outrage his daughter's kidnappers.

"You're right," he softened. "The business is fine."

"Good. Good. Can't say I use your programs, not much of a computer person myself."

"Really?" Howard said with an incredible amount of disinterest.

"Yes," Phillips replied, ignoring the dull reply. "I'm more hands on. I play some video games now and then; browse the internet every so often, but only for porn, of course," he winked. "I don't suppose your company gets involved in any of that?"

"Porn?"

"Video games."

"We have a few titles lined up," Howard's words were slow; he had stepped closer to the man, allowing their conversation to flow easier into the microphone.

"I'll have to look into them. More of a console man, but I play the odd PC game too, if it involves stripping models and cards," Phillips grinned again. "So what sort of games are you making?"

"Nothing really big—"

Howard paused and looked past the quizzical criminal. Michael Richards had retreated towards the bus stop, the cash-filled duffel bag in his hands. His retreat was turning into a desperate sprint as he tried to leave in a hurry.

Phillips also turned to see his fleeing friend, "What the fuck?" he whispered.

"What are you doing!" Howard screamed in Richards's direction. "I want my daughter!" he moved forward, past Johnny Phillips who was still looking in the direction of his runaway friend, somewhat bemused.

Gathering his senses Phillips stepped forward and grabbed the businessman, grasping a clump of material from his shirt he pulled him back.

"What the fuck are you doing?" Howard raged. "I want—" his words transformed into a muffled clutter as his jaw met Phillips's right fist with crushing precision.

He stumbled backwards. A pain instantly exploded across the left side of his face and he tasted blood. He lost his balance and fell, landing on the uncomfortable concrete.

His world turned black momentarily. Through blurred, blue, and starry vision he glimpsed a bus roaring along the road towards the bus stop; his blurred attacker sprinting quickly towards it.

56

Phillips reached the bus stop just as the bus screeched to a stop in front of him. He reached forward and grabbed Richards who was ready to step onto the vehicle.

"What the fuck do you think you're doing?" he demanded to know.

"Get on the bus," Richards said.

"You fucking ran on me. That wasn't part of the plan. When has deserting ever been part—"

"Just get on the bus."

"Anything could have happened back there," Phillips continued, ignoring his friend's pleas.

"Get on the bus, I'll explain."

"All those years together and you fucking run on one little scheme?"

Richards turned and grabbed his friend by the collar. "Johnny," he hissed through clenched teeth, "get on the fucking bus!"

Phillips, taken aback, obliged and they both hopped on the bus, empty except for an old man sitting at the front.

"What the fuck is this all about?" Phillips asked as the two men sat down at the back. "You were supposed to sneak a look, take a few things of value—if any—give me the signal, then leave. We never mentioned running away. We've done this trick dozens of times, Mickey, what the fuck are you playing at?"

Michael Richards smiled; a vision that disturbed his friend.

"What? What is it?" Phillips asked as the bus pulled away from the scene. "You manage to pick his pocket or something?"

Richards shook his head.

"You steal his watch?"

Richards shook his head again.

"What then?" Phillips was growing impatient.

He opened the duffel bag and allowed his friend to peek inside.

"Holy fucking hell!" Phillips bellowed. The old man at the front of the bus turned hastily—almost losing his balance—and sneered at Phillips. The bus driver shot a similar scorn through the rearview mirror.

Phillips ignored them and kept his attention on the contents of the bag.

"Between five hundred thousand and one and a half million," Richards said. "Probably. I haven't had time to check, but I think they're all fifties."

"Holy shit."

"Looks like our friendly local is involved in something bigger than computer software."

"Probably fucking drugs," Phillips said. "I can't believe it, we're fucking . . . Jesus."

"I tried to catch your eye after I snuck a peek but you weren't looking," Richards described with a smile engraved on his face. "You were busy talking. I hesitated and ran. I kinda hoped you would follow, not too sure what I thought would happen to be honest. It's not every day you find a bag full of cash."

"Fucking hell," Phillips said again.

Richards laughed giddily, "How did you get away?"

"What?"

"How did you get away from Price?"

"I knocked him out," Phillips said, before returning his attention to the open bag. "We're rich!"

"You knocked him out?"

Phillips turned to his friend, his mouth open, his mind couldn't push the thought of the money away but it managed to grasp the question "I didn't know what else to do."

"So you hit him?"

"Pretty much. He seen you running away and tried to run after you so—"

"So you whacked the poor fucker?"

"Does it matter? He gets a sore jaw; we get a bundle of cash. I think we win on that one."

Richards laughed again, "Good point."

After more moments of admiration and more random outbursts by Phillips, Richards sealed the bag and clutched it tightly to his chest.

"We'll get off at the next stop, then walk to the apartment," he said. "We need a safe place for all of this."

Phillips nodded, his jaw still practically on his lap.

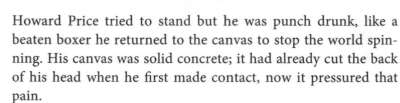

Howard Price tried to stand but he was punch drunk, like a beaten boxer he returned to the canvas to stop the world spinning. His canvas was solid concrete; it had already cut the back of his head when he first made contact, now it pressured that pain.

Initially, his nerves had mixed with the sleep deprivation and left him unawares, the punch had completed the task of turning him into a vegetable. His jaw ached, but he didn't mind; his back, backside and head ached, but he didn't mind. As he stared up at the blue skies, the only thing he saw, thought, and cared about, was Lisa. He had let her kidnappers escape.

He felt rage and depression combine to form a void of emptiness.

The swap hadn't gone as planned, it wasn't even a swap, they had his money, he didn't have his daughter. They had retreated, he couldn't catch them now but he would certainly try to hunt them down.

The police will be here soon, he thought as he watched a blackbird hover overhead before perching on the rusted rim of the basketball hoop. They would want to take control of the operation, and he would let them.

He had agreed to the swap and had kept the police away from the scene, but they had broken the ransom agreement, they had beaten him and taken the money.

He tried not to think of the safety of his daughter. He only hoped that the detective had been right and that the kidnappers would become greedy—he didn't mind them asking for more money as long as his daughter was safe. He didn't want to even contemplate the possibility that they had killed her already.

Through the roaring rivers of blood that screamed through his ears he heard the sound of at least three cars halt on the nearby road. No sirens had sounded but he knew it was the police, they promised they would be discreet. They had kept their promise.

Within minutes, he was surrounded by plainclothes officers offering their support, each of the officers had a sorrowful look on their face. They took pity in him, they had listened to the conversation through the microphone and now found him flat out on the concrete with no money and no daughter.

They took pity on him because they thought Lisa was dead.

Howard dabbed his jaw with a tepid ice pack that had been handed to him by one of the officers. It did little to soothe his discomfort.

"What about the bus?" he asked, each syllable a strain on his jaw.

Detective Brown answered the question as he paced the floor, wearing a tread into the living room carpet.

"We have men looking into the route the bus takes, if we're lucky we may find some security footage at one of the stops," his words offered little hope. "We may be able to get some information from the driver as to where he dropped off the men but we don't even have their descriptions."

"Like I said. He was a rugged, hard type, about 5'11 to 6'2, something like one hundred and fifty to two hundred pounds."

"That's just one of them," the detective noted.

"I didn't get to see much of the other. They were together though; one description should be enough to put forward to the driver, right?"

"Well, the description is pretty vague. In fact, you just explained half the population of this town. There's also the possibility that the men took several bus journeys before jumping into a car. They might not have even got on the bus. You said your vision was blurred at the time?"

"I saw them waiting at the bus stop," Howard's words were slow and deliberate, anger was hiding deep down inside of them.

The detective paused thoughtfully, "It seems a bit strange that kidnappers would use public transport. Especially with one million dollars in their possession."

Howard sighed. This conversation had been going on for the last ten minutes. In that time, the only comments he could hear from the officers ranged from, "It seems strange," or "That doesn't fit in," to "It's certainly not a straightforward case." He wanted his daughter back and they weren't doing anything to help him.

"Is she dead?" Elizabeth appeared from the kitchen. Howard hadn't seen her since his return. He had left her with a hopeful look—albeit drug and ignorance induced—in her eyes. Now her eyes were filled with tears, red with pain, and black with sorrow.

The detective did the wrong thing. He paused, hesitated. Howard was the one who eventually answered, "She'll be okay darling," he assured her while giving the detective the evil eye. "We'll catch them next time."

"Next time?"

This time Detective Inspector Brown spoke, "We believe, and it is highly possible, that the kidnappers will call to demand another ransom. They'll get greedy. That's when we'll take them down."

Elizabeth nodded, looked solemnly at Howard then retreated up the stairs. Her footfalls were slow and heavy; everyone in the living room listened to the quietly whimpering women as she ascended the stairs and crawled into her bedroom.

"Do you think they'll phone again?" Howard asked after Elizabeth's sorrow had faded.

"Of course they will," Detective Brown said.

"But why don't we have them now?" Howard wondered. "You said you'd be on standby if anything went wrong. Something went wrong and you were nowhere to be seen."

"We kept our distance as promised Mr. Price," the detective said sternly. "We still have men scanning the area for any witnesses. Things like that take time, in the meantime we need to wait on another phone call. Hopefully, by the time they arrange the next drop off, we'll have enough information on them to be ready and waiting. That is, of course, if you'll let us this time."

Howard nodded. "I want those bastards dead."

57

The two conmen eagerly climbed off the bus and began a walk to their safe house apartment, taking a shortcut through a dense field.

"It still doesn't make much sense," Richards said.

"I know what you mean," Phillips agreed, "but who gives a fuck? We have a bag full of cash and we did practically fuck all to get it."

"He could have seen us. He could be giving descriptions to the police as we speak."

"Maybe. But if it is drug money, I doubt he would involve the police."

"And if it isn't?"

Phillips dodged out of the way of a melancholic bee on a rollercoaster ride to find flowers in a field full of weeds. "Well, he didn't get a good look at you and you were the one that ran off with the money."

"You knocked him the fuck out," Richards reminded his friend.

"We'll just have to hope I knocked some short-term memory out of him as well," he joked. "Plus he seemed distracted. He was nervous, sweating, almost scared. I doubt he had full control of the situation, he probably can't remember what I look like."

Richards nodded, "But still. Why all this money?"

"Like I said. Drugs, rich businessmen like their drugs. Drugs and hookers, it helps them de-stress I guess."

"That doesn't fit though," Richards said. "He's a respected man. He has a big company, a beautiful wife, and a young daughter, he doesn't seem the sort."

"You'd be surprised."

"Maybe . . . but, why so much money for a single drug deal? Surely only top-end dealers would be using all of this cash to buy drugs."

"Maybe he does a little bit of dealing on the side," Phillips said. "Who cares, we have the money. That's what matters," he smiled and wrapped his arm around his friend. "We're fucking rich, buddy," he said loudly.

Richards smiled and nodded but his smile soon faded, "What if it's laundered," he asked. "A big company like that—crime syndicates would be all over him to filter their dirty dealings. The last thing we need is a group of gun-toting thugs after us."

"It's nothing we can't handle," Phillips paused. "Well, it's nothing I can't handle."

They continued in silence. Phillips's mind was on the money, how much there was and how much would be left over after buying their dream business. He acknowledged that there could be enough for them to scrap the business idea and retire; Richards's mind was in less of a dream world, he was plagued with the origins of the stolen cash.

In the apartment they both felt a rush of exhilaration. As Richards deactivated the explosives, Phillips hotfooted it behind him like a child in desperate hunt for a toilet.

They stumbled eagerly towards a cabinet under the sink where they stored an electronic money counter. They sat it down on the floor in the living room and carefully stacked the money into one end of the device.

Richards's hand hovered over the start button, "Are you ready?" he asked.

Phillips was sweating at an incredible pace; his heart kicked a speedy rhythm in his chest. "Go for it."

Richards pressed the button and instantly the money began flipping through the system, their eyes were fixed on the LCD screen. When it stopped, they each took a sharp intake of breath, stunned into silence by the seven-digit figure displayed on the screen.

58

Two hours had passed since Howard Price had been robbed of a million dollars. He had been hopeful that he would see his daughter again; he should be with her, embracing her, telling her everything was going to be okay and making sure nothing like this ever happened to her again—now he was in a worse position than when it started.

Two hours without contact from the kidnappers who ran away with his money. Two hours of mind-destroying thoughts; questioning his daughter's safety, desiring revenge, and responding to an onslaught of police questions.

The officers were still in his house, they were waiting on another call, another ransom demand. People had been brought in to analyze the conversation that had been recorded by Howard's hidden microphone, but nothing had come of it. Experts had been brought in to try to draw descriptions of the kidnappers based on Howard's memory, but he had been too nervous, angry, and worried to concentrate on what they looked like.

He had been informed that the police were searching the area for clues and asking locals for any information about the attack, but he hadn't received any word back on that either. He was in limbo, as the detective had lightly described it, he just had to wait. Nothing was sure.

Elizabeth had retired to her bedroom half an hour after Howard had returned home unsuccessful. She had taken a further dose of sedatives and that, along with the addition of her favorite movie, would help to take her mind off the situation. He hadn't checked on her but he guessed she would be asleep, lost in a sedated slumber. He only hoped he would have good news for her when she woke.

In the corner of the room, Detective Brown's cell phone played the soundtrack from Knight Rider and glowed neon blue in his pocket. Reacting immediately, he stopped his conversation with a fellow officer, walked a few steps back, pulled out his phone, and answered the call.

Price could only hear snippets from where he sat. He wasn't particularly interested in the officer's conversations, but then the detective shot a worried glance and a nod his way and he gained an interest.

The detective felt the businessman's eyes upon him and turned away to admire a portrait on the dining room wall. Howard tried to hear what he had to say to the unknown caller but his headache, his state of mind, and the space between him and the detective—filled with chattering police officers—didn't allow much to get through. He heard the detective mumble and saw him nod several times before he hung up the phone.

Howard's heart stopped and his mind hit gridlock when the detective made his way over. His eyes averted from Howard and his face filled with what appeared to be sorrow.

Bad news was coming.

"That was the station on the phone," the detective explained, trying to make eye contact but failing to do so for more than a few seconds. "There has been an incident in an abandoned group of apartment buildings a few miles down the road," he furthered with more unease. "Neighbors reported shots being fired and our men were rushed to the scene."

"And?" Howard urged.

"Three bodies were found inside one of the unused apartments. Two Caucasians, around thirty to forty-five were found dead in the living room. It appears there was a fight of some sort, and—" Another pause.

"Just fucking tell me!" Howard bellowed.

"I'm sorry Mr. Price," he sympathized, his head held low. "A young girl matching Lisa's description was found dead with them."

He wanted to cry but it was too early for tears. He wanted to scream but his anger wouldn't release. He wanted to die, but death was not an option. He wanted to wake up, but he wasn't dreaming. What he did do was deny that it was Lisa's body that had been found, with that faith came happiness; he needed her alive, and he had to force himself to believe she still was.

"So what?" he said. "It could be anyone, right?"

The detective nodded but his agreement was unsettling. "It's possible; although the men on the scene seem sure it was—"

"This is nonsense," Howard declared. "She isn't dead; why would they kill her? Like you said, they want more money, I *have* more money. They *can't* kill her; she means the world to me," his voice became distant and soft. "I need her; they can't do this to me."

"There is still a possibility it wasn't your daughter," the detective said, a fabrication of his own conclusions to comfort the grief-stricken man. "But . . ." another uncomfortable pause.

"But what?" Howard asked, his eyes growing heavy.

"The two men found dead in the apartment could have very well been the kidnappers. They had a lot of supplies with them, they had the door bolted and appeared to be sleeping there."

"That doesn't prove anything."

"Maybe not," he gave a sharp nod, held Howard's glassy stare and then applied a gentle and instinctive shake of his head.

"Although, they had a great deal of money on them, too much for people squatting in a rundown apartment."

Howard shook his head, "How can that be?" His mind drifted to a state of dissociation, it didn't want to be in this reality anymore. "They're dead already?"

"The reports of the shots were phoned in by an anonymous caller around the same time you were attacked," the detective explained. "It's possible," he halted to suck air in tightly through his teeth. "Highly possible . . . that this was a hijack."

"Hijack?" Howard wasn't even sure why he was still speaking. He wanted to die; he wanted the world to swallow him up. He wanted to hold Lisa in his arms again.

"It looks like someone found out about the kidnapping, raided the flat, found all the information they could, including the meeting place, and then executed the real kidnappers, before stealing the ransom money."

Howard couldn't take any of it in. His eyes were beginning to fill with tears, his head throbbed worse than it did before and he felt like he was going to pass out.

"I need to know if my baby is okay."

"I understand," the detective seemed sympathetic. "They have her," he stopped and callously corrected himself. "The body, at the coroners waiting for you to identify it."

Howard nodded. Despite the possibility that the dead child might not be his daughter, a part of him had already died.

59

"It's been secure enough in the past," Michael Richards looked at Johnny Phillips who had a worried edge to his expression.

"I know, but this is one million fucking dollars," Phillips replied. "In the past we've stored eighty-thousand here tops. The rest is split into bank accounts and whatnot—we need to do that with the million."

"We can't open another account and deposit one million straight away," Richards argued. "And we can't stick it in the other accounts. If this *isn't* drug money, and Price *does* report it missing we won't last a day if we try to stick it in the bank. They'll get word from the police to be on the lookout and they'll snag us when we get there."

Phillips deflated, "It's just—"

"It's just a lot of money I know," Richards cut in. "An amount that we'll probably never see again as long as we live. But we need to play it cool, otherwise we'll be trading cigarettes for the rest of our lives."

"What if someone breaks in."

"The place is wired."

"Exactly. Which means our money will blow up along with the intruder."

"We have a certain amount of respect around here," Richards noted. "Everyone who lives here has an unwritten immunity to crime. No one snitches, no one pisses in their own backyard, and no one, police included, cares where these people end up or what they do. Even though they're all criminals. They won't touch us."

"I'm just worried that's all."

Richards laughed and sat down on the sofa, "You're normally the calm one."

Phillips smiled and settled back into his own chair, "I guess we can cancel our night out then?"

Richards pondered this for a moment, "Not really," he said. "We don't need to babysit the money, do we? And we did just pull off a big score, so I think a celebration is in order."

Phillips seemed to wise up to the idea in the silence that unfolded, "Shoddy Simon," he blurted.

"What?" Richards asked, bewildered.

"When I was down there he had a ton of suitcases, he tried to pawn one of them to me." Phillips was in a dream world—smiles and wide-eyed glints.

"And your point is?"

"You know what he's like. Even if he knows he ain't got a chance of selling you something he still shows it off to you."

"Yes," Richards agreed. "I still remember the three dozen faulty toasters."

"Well, he showed me a collection. Special ones they were, he only had a few. He said they were practically bomb proof."

"He said that?"

"Well, not in so many words, but that's what we need. We stick the cash in a couple of 'em and hide them in the apartment. If some fucker walks in here and blows the place up, we wipe the blood from the cases and move on."

"So let me get this straight," Richards said to his smiling friend. "If someone breaks in here, they trigger the wires and the explosives . . ."

"Yes."

"The explosion that follows not only obliterates the intruder, but also the entire apartment and our neighbors. Leaving about six apartments under ash and rubble, but, underneath that rubble, will be two cases with our cash in it."

"Exactly."

"Are you fucking mad?"

"Look, I know it isn't the best plan, but it'll help put my mind at ease."

"Fine," Richards agreed.

"Excellent. Simon should be at home getting ready for his evening soap operas by now; I'll head over there and buy the cases."

A few hours later, he returned to the apartment and dropped two thick, silver cases on the floor. They were still glorious although they had clearly been used.

"Not bad," Richards nodded.

"Two hundred bucks," Phillips said.

"Is that all? These things fetch a fucking fortune."

"I know and he was selling them for a fortune too," Phillips informed his friend. "But that was when he was sober, or as sober as Simon can get. He's so whacked out of his head right now I could have swapped him his house for a packet of Skittles and a Jolly Rancher."

"He'll remember when he's sober."

"More than likely, but this isn't Marks & Spencer's. No receipts no refunds, a deal is a deal, and this my friend," Phillips flicked the locks on the cases and opened them up to expose a heavy steel interior which had been lined with fine leather. "Is one hell of a fucking deal."

Richards nodded in agreement, "Okay, let's get the cash out of the bags and into the cases then."

They both grabbed bundles of cash and lined it neatly into the cases.

"I was thinking, when you were out . . . about this money."

"Don't start your shit again Mickey, the only thing that matters is that we have it."

"I know but we still have to move with caution, just in case. Just in case what we took was real money due for a legitimate transaction right?"

Phillips agreed.

"So, it would be nice to know don't you think?" Richards queried.

"To me it wouldn't make a difference, but if it would shut you up I guess so."

"Exactly. So, like I said, I was thinking about where the money came from, what it was for, and why he was there. I don't think it's for drugs, he doesn't look the sort. And I don't think he would buy to sell, why risk losing a business worth millions for an illegal side gig that'll get you locked up for the rest of your days?"

"Good point," Phillips agreed. "So what are you getting at?"

"I'm not sure. There are many options. He could have been blackmailed for a start."

"One million is a lot, someone would have to have pictures of him having anal sex with the pope while fingering the Queen of England to ask for so much."

"I thought about that too," Richards agreed. "What about a hit?"

"A hit?"

"He could have been paying to have someone killed."

"Dodgy location to meet a hitman who asks for a million a head. And who in Price's life would be worth killing for that amount of money? He's a businessman, and a good family man," Phillips paused and stopped putting the money into the cases.

Richards noted this strange act and shot him a quizzical glance, "What?"

"Nothing," he paused, "I don't think, it's just—" another pause and an effort to remember something.

"Just what?" Richards wanted to know.

"Well, when I was speaking to him," he said slowly, still recollecting the moment. "He was acting a little more than strange."

"What do you mean?"

"Well, at first I didn't think anything of it. I thought he was hopped up on drugs. I mean he was shaking, his eyes were bloodshot and when I shook his hand I got a handful of sweat, weird at the time but when we found the money it all clicked that he was on drugs, only he kept mentioning his daughter . . ." Phillips looked at his friend. "He said he just wanted her to be safe, he wanted her back."

They looked at the piles of money simultaneously.

"You don't think . . ."

"He was nervous, tired, a little scared. It wasn't drugs, and the money—" he paused and bit his bottom lip.

"Ransom," Richards blurted, he felt like he had a brick lodged in his esophagus, his words came through his throat as a harsh, barely audible gurgle. He found it hard to swallow.

"*Holysweetfuckingmotherofgod,*" Phillips cried softly. A note slipped from his grasp, he watched it float to the floor where it settled on the upturned duffel bag which still bore mud stains from the park. "We're fucked."

60

All hospitals stink of death. The stench clings to fabrics and walls; it's everywhere and it's unavoidable. The smell is always overshadowed by a sickly, lemony antiseptic odor, but beyond that, death lurks; poking through the walls, hanging around the wards, lying beside the patients and grasping in hope at the visitors.

Howard Price hated hospitals, and the smell was just one of the reasons. He had seen his father die in hospital. He had also watched the slow demise of his grandfather as a child, a memory that had stayed with him through the years.

The hollow halls, the echo of unseen footsteps, the brightly painted, spacious walls, and the spreading sickness—he hated it all. He had only been to his local hospital twice since his move to the countryside. The first time he was forced to go by a doctor who wanted to use the hospital equipment to run some detailed health checks; the second time was two years ago, he had been playing soccer with Lisa and she had taken an awkward tumble, fracturing her arm.

This time—his third time—was for Lisa again. Detective Brown drove him there, an awkward journey of silence and pitying glances, fragmented by heavy breaths and sighs as the detective tried and failed to start a conversation or offer any words of consolation.

As they walked through the front doors Howard didn't flinch as the stench hit him like a brick. He barely noted the people walking around the halls: nurses, doctors, patients in gowns, injured people waiting to be examined, and the countless visitors.

He caught the eye of one small girl who was playing in the empty halls with another child. She smiled at him and he returned the gesture with tears in his eyes.

Detective Brown walked through the swing doors of the morgue and ushered Howard inside. Shaking, tears still in his eyes, Howard slowly moved forward, walking into the wall of cold as his shoes tapped the blue tiles of the morgue floor.

The doors swung shut behind him, the room was blanketed by a deathly silence. Death, unsurprisingly, weighed heavily in the air.

He paused, his feet rooted to the spot, his body didn't want to move. He didn't know if his daughter lay in that very room, minutes from now his world could crash down on him.

Elizabeth had been asleep when he left the house. He had taken a quiet walk upstairs, sobbed gently over her sleeping figure, kissed her softly on the forehead and then left.

He didn't want her here, her tearful, sorry self would only make him more melancholic. He realized that he was probably being selfish, but he didn't want her to have to see her own daughter lying dead on a table.

How he would break the news to Elizabeth if it was Lisa hadn't crossed his mind. He didn't want to imagine a world where his daughter had been murdered and he was the one who had to break the news to her mother.

"Just over here, Mr. Price," the detective stood beside him, both men were still. Brown was pointing down a corridor in the long room where a man in a white jacket stood over a slab near a child-shaped sheet.

Howard nodded, feeling somewhat unstable he managed to walk to the white coated man.

His expression was sorrowful, and—like Detective Brown had done at the house—he tried to smile at Howard, offering his sympathies in expression without actually holding his gaze for more than a few seconds.

The somber face of the man in the white coat, the placid face of the detective and the depressed face of Howard Price all looked down at the sheet. The body underneath looked unbelievably small and fragile.

With a nod from the detective the mortician reached out his hands and grasped the top of the sheet. Howard found himself subconsciously grabbing the detective's arm.

The mortician lowered his head and slowly pulled back the white sheet to unveil the beautiful, cold staring face of Lisa Price.

Howard loosened his grip on the detective's arm and collapsed with a sob. His legs turned to jelly at the sight, his mind whirled and he crashed to his knees. Crying loudly, he wrapped his arms around the cold head of his little girl. He stroked her hair, he kissed her, and he spoke to her with rivers of tears streaming down his face.

She was gone, he had lost his daughter. Only now did he fully realize it.

He'd never felt so much pain.

61

"Wouldn't something like this be on the news?" Michael Richards paced the floor of the apartment. The television blared in the background. The channels, along with the internet news sites, had already been fully scoured.

"Obviously not," Phillips replied as the current news program was concluded with a minor piece on recycling.

"Wouldn't the police have been there?" Richards questioned again, his tone filled with worry. "They should have been watching the park, keeping tabs on Price and whatnot."

"Maybe."

"There could have been fucking marksmen on the roofs of the local houses," he worried.

"You've been watching too many movies."

"But it still happens, right? A high-profile kidnapping like this, the armed response unit would be all over."

"Maybe," Phillips repeated.

"What if we were caught on camera? Maybe the area was rigged; they could have been tracking us to this very location. They have the equipment to do that sort of thing, right? What with all this satellite bullshit."

"Maybe," Phillips muttered for a third time.

"How could this happen anyway? What happened to the real kidnappers? Aren't they supposed to have been nearby, checking out the area?"

Phillips shook his head in a defeated manner, "Look, Mickey," he began. "I don't have a fucking clue okay? I can honestly say I've never kidnapped anyone before, this is all new to me."

"This is not a time for jokes."

"If we can't laugh when we find a million bucks when can we laugh?"

"That money isn't ours."

"None of the money in this apartment is ours," Phillips reminded his partner in crime. "In fact, if you want to look at it that way, this apartment isn't even ours. Neither is the house, the car, or the clothes on our backs. We're fucking criminals Mickey; everything we own belongs in someone else's bank account."

"But we're not kidnappers," Richards asserted.

"We didn't kidnap anyone."

Richards held his stride in the middle of the room and stared at his friend. "We took the money, Johnny," he said sternly. "Then we beat him up and escaped the scene. We didn't kidnap anyone but I can guarantee we'll be prime fucking suspects."

"They have no proof against us."

"What about that!" Richards gestured to the two cases on the floor and the notes still scattered around them—the job of unloading the money hadn't been finished.

"So we stole a bag, big deal. Petty theft that's all."

"And assault," Michael Richards recalled.

"We'll get a warning and a fine."

Richards nodded and calmly took a seat beside his friend on the sofa, both turned their attentions to the money on the floor.

After a long thoughtful silence Michael Richards spoke slowly, almost in a trance, "If we hand over the money, we'll get away with minor charges."

Phillips nodded.

They both continued to stare lustfully at the money, it seemed to call to them. In Phillips's eyes, he saw the money being transformed into the betting shop of his dreams. He saw all his plans for high-paying cons being pulled off. He saw expensive cars, crates of champagne, big houses, and loose women. He saw the life he had strived to achieve since he was a teenager.

Richards's mind circulated with the same ideals. They would only need a small amount of the stolen money to put to the rest of their cash to get the lease to the betting shop. The rest of the money could easily be used to cover their tracks. They could live the high life while building up a strong, highly profitable business. He saw a change, a break from the mold, and a snap into a comfortable life. The money would transform their lives for the better.

They both looked at each other.

Richards spoke first: "We can't give the money back," he said. "We've been waiting for this all our lives. We need this."

Phillips nodded; his head moved methodically, his mind was elsewhere.

Richards pursed his dry lips and wet them with the tip of his tongue; he could feel an anxious lump swell inside his throat. "What do you think?"

Phillips turned his attention from Richards to the money and then back again, "I think we should keep it."

62

Walking back through the hospital, Howard's face was a creation of anger and despair. His body had been drained as he had struggled through the day and the ordeals that had been thrown his way. On seeing Lisa, he had been fueled with sadness. Soon, that fuel ignited, and anger flared inside him, anger at the bastards who had killed his daughter. They had taken her life and taken a part of his, he wanted to avenge her death, and he wanted her kidnappers to die by his hands.

After seeing her body, he requested to be alone with her. He had smothered her in his arms, crying into her beautiful blonde hair. Half of him hoped he was dreaming, the other half hoped *she* was dreaming, and she would suddenly wake up and forgive him. All of this was his fault, that much he was sure of, and for that he apologized as he cried into her fading locks.

On her forehead, above her cold stare and below her matted fringe, someone had carefully attached a thick white bandage. Howard knew this for his sake, she had been shot in the head, and he didn't want to know where else. The bandage covered up the nasty wound and would reduce the horror in his nightmares.

His rage grew when, after lifting her upper body from the table to hug her more intensely, he noticed ligature marks around her wrists. Inch-thick blackish blue marks wrapped around her tiny wrists like sadistic bracelets.

His time alone with her didn't last long, after five minutes he was escorted—half carried—out of the morgue in fits of tears and screams of rage.

Outside the hospital, Detective Brown paused as Howard grasped onto a nearby wall and unleashed the contents of his stomach onto the tarmac below. He wretched until his starved body was dry and could offer nothing more than its own bile. His body was sent into spasms as his stomach tried to expel something that wasn't there. His chest burned and his throat ached as the motions of sickness continued.

Many people walked past, pretending not to notice—their eyes fixed on the roads ahead of them. Some people nearby—visitors and a few residents of the hospital—were standing around a side door smoking cigarettes. Their conversation halted as Howard continued to gag.

The smokers spared a moment as they put themselves in his place. They didn't know if he had received a bill of bad health, a threat to the health of a loved one or if his was suffering from the death of a loved one, but they shared a mutual and respectful silence as they watched him spill his guts.

Minutes later he finished; his face red as fire, his stomach pained and empty.

Inside the unmarked police car, a slouching Detective Brown offered Howard a mint which was gratefully accepted.

His mouth was dry and he could taste a slimy sickness encroaching on his stomach every time he swallowed. Popping the mint straight into his mouth, he sucked on it erratically, covering his taste buds with a layer of strong peppermint.

Taking a mint himself, the detective pushed the packet back inside the glove compartment and started up the engine.

"I know there is really nothing I can say or do," he began, in a consoling tone. "But I truly am sorry for your loss."

Howard nodded and wiped a stream of perspiration from his forehead. The detective acknowledged his actions and, pressing a switch near the steering wheel, he opened the passenger side window. The cold evening air rushed into the car.

"What did they do to her?" Howard asked as the detective started the car. "I saw marks on her arms, cuts, bruises . . ." as he recalled the sight he felt another storm of sickness and he pushed his face closer to the open window.

The detective paused; using the junction ahead as an excuse for his hesitant attention. "She was tied up," he said eventually, his eyes on the road ahead. "Her wrists and ankles were tied; she was fixed to a mattress in the apartment."

"Why tie her up so tightly though?" Howard asked, "She's just, *was* just, a little girl."

"The rope was loose when her body was found. Chances are the rope was over-tied at one point or another, causing the bruising, but generally she seemed well looked after."

"*Well looked after*?" Howard gasped. "She was kidnapped and tied to a fucking bed!"

"I'm sorry Mr. Price," he apologized. "That wasn't the right way of explaining it. You see, in cases such as this; the kidnappers usually take little, if any, care over the safety of their hostage. They normally strap them up with tape, tie them down and gag them. They force them into dark rooms; cover their eyes, mouth and even their ears. Often the hostages are beaten in sadistic outbursts."

"You're not helping."

"What I am trying to say is that Lisa was well looked after, *considering*. We believe she was fed and given water during her detainment."

"How could you know that?"

"Bottles and wrappers found at the scene," the detective spoke at a calm and leisurely pace. "They made sure she was kept alive and well. They may have initially hurt her when snatching her from the school or dragging her into the apartment as minor marks were found on her feet and legs, but she wasn't beaten. Another thing worth noting is that her eyes and ears were not covered, only her mouth. She could have easily seen and heard her intruders, a fact that clearly didn't bother them."

"What does that mean?" Howard demanded to know.

"It could suggest that the two men didn't have any previous convictions. And they probably weren't locals. There is also a good chance they were involved in the criminal world, we found a number of illegal weapons on them. It's safe to suggest that they're well known in the underworld and had already hatched a plan to leave the country after the kidnapping."

Howard shook his head; he wasn't hearing what he wanted to hear but he let the detective continue nevertheless. "You know all of this yet you can't find two men jumping onto a bus with a bag full of money?"

The detective shot Howard a weary glance. "That matter is still being looked into Mr. Price. The reason we know so much about the kidnappers is because the scene has been fully scrutinized. Forensics are giving the apartment a full check over as we speak. Fingerprints of both the executed men have been found in various places around the apartment, on Lisa's restraints and on the mattress where she lay. It's clear they were the people we were looking for. The description given to us by the young girl at the school, although vague, fits both the men."

"So who killed them?" Howard's voice had sunk with his mood. It was thick, gravelly.

The detective shrugged. "If they *were* involved in the criminal underworld, there's a good chance that another gang found out about the kidnapping and hijacked it. Criminals fight criminals; thieves steal from thieves, it's commonplace."

Howard pushed himself back on the chair and let his head loll to one side. He watched out of the side window as the car raced along a dual-carriage way, bypassing a number of other vehicles at a pace only an unmarked police car could get away with.

The image of his daughter lying there cold and dead played on his mind. Inside he felt hollow; he felt like a part of him had died. Only the thought of vengeance remained.

He slowly turned his attention back toward the driver as something niggled away at him. He was carrying a weight that was growing heavy inside him.

"You say she was treated well?"

"Not first-class care, but as far as kidnappers go they seemed to treat her okay."

"Did she—" Howard paused; he was frightened to ask. "You said you found marks on her skin."

"That's right."

Was she sexually abused in any way?" he asked, his voice fluctuating heavily as he asked.

The detective immediately shook his head, "Highly unlikely," he was quick to reply. "We found nothing to indicate such a thing. She was still fully clothed in her school uniform when we found her."

Howard breathed a sigh of relief but before the sigh fully escaped he questioned his reason for doing it. He had lost his daughter; she had been strapped to a bed for twenty-four hours and then murdered. He shouldn't feel any relief; his baby was dead.

"We will conduct a post-mortem on her body tomorrow," the detective added. "Then we'll know for sure. In the meantime," he swung the car right down a small country road which would eventually lead back to Howard's home. "I suggest you tell your wife. She may want to see the body."

Howard's heart sank again, just when he felt he couldn't feel any lower he felt the barrier for ground level break. He had forgotten about Elizabeth; she still didn't know if Lisa was dead or alive and it was his job to tell her.

63

Michael Richards and Johnny Phillips were stuck in the middle, between a rock and a hard place, happiness and despair.

"So what do we do?" Phillips had settled on the sofa; his mind was tired. At the start of the afternoon it had been overcome with excitement, now it was flooded with doubt.

Richards, sitting on the floor beside the two metallic cases—filled with cash and securely locked—looked up at his friend, an expression of wonder creased his face, "We wait I guess."

"Wait for what?"

Richards looked across at the television which was tuned onto a twenty-four-hour news channel. A short woman in her mid-thirties stood near the London Underground, talking to the many people who were rushing on and off the trains. Her words were not fully audible but Richards heard her say, "Anniversary," a few times. "The news," he stated with his eyes still on the television. "If this is a kidnapping, and we did steal the ransom money, surely it'll be on TV."

"Do the police publicize kidnappings to the press?" Phillips wondered. "Wouldn't that be a dumb thing to do? What if the real kidnappers saw the broadcast? They'd go berserk."

"Maybe they already have," Richards realized. "If Howard was there to drop off some ransom money and we ran away with it, there's a bloody good chance the kidnappers would be pissed off."

"But they'd just demand more, right?"

"Probably," Richards nodded. "But by then the police will get suspicious. Either way, they'll be looking for us."

"We ran away with the money," Phillips agreed. "You don't think they think *we* did it, do you?"

Richards looked at his friend. Their eyes locked for several seconds "Let's hope not."

They watched the television as the broadcast changed to local football results. "I think we need to get the fuck out of here," Phillips said. "If they were tracking us they'll be down on us any minute. They could be watching the place right now."

"Where would we go?"

"We could head back to the house."

"It's not exactly safe. The neighbors know what we look like. If a news channel shows our faces it'll be seconds before one of the nosey fuckers calls the police on us. We need to go somewhere safe and secluded. Wait this thing out."

Phillips nodded and they both looked at each other, expecting the other to speak.

64

Elizabeth was asleep when Howard found her. Still in her drug-induced dream world, her head resting lightly on plush pillows, her body covered with a thin silk sheet. She had a smile on her face as she slept, she always smiled when she slept.

Howard stared at her for a while, lightly touching her cheek and running his fingers through her hair. When she woke, she was unsure of her surroundings. Part of her had hoped that the whole kidnapping had been a dream and she had woken to a world where her daughter was safe. Howard had to tell her the unfortunate truth.

She asked where Lisa was. She could see the sorrow in Howard's eyes; she could see the dried tears—she knew he had been crying. She could practically smell the despair and emptiness that reeked from his soul.

She began to cry before he even had the chance to tell her what had happened.

He told Elizabeth that Lisa had been killed while he held his wife in his arms. He whispered, sobbing, that he had identified the body while his face was nestled in her hair.

After a while he could feel his shoulder growing damp where her tears soaked into his shirt. She didn't speak, she just cried and held him tight.

After trying to console her, something Howard had no experience in, he lay her back on the bed and gave her more tablets. She sobbed herself back to sleep where her dreams would do the consoling, before the waking world dragged her back to despair.

He headed for his office and opened his liquor cabinet. Inside he found half a bottle of thirty-year-old whiskey and a slightly dusty tumbler, he took them both to the desk.

He filled his first glass and drank it immediately. He did the same after refilling it. He continued until only a quarter of the bottle remained, then the telephone rang.

"Hello?"

"Mr. Price," the voice on the other end of the phone was marbled with static. "This is Detective Brown."

"Hello Detective," Howard said, sarcastically adding, "What can I do for you today?"

"I'm outside your house. I've been ringing the doorbell for ten minutes."

He could never hear the front or back door from the office, which was why he chose it as a study. He hated being disturbed.

"Really," he said, disheartened that the effects of the alcohol hadn't diminished his despair but had made him apathetic.

"When I dropped you off I received a phone call from headquarters," the detective explained.

"Really," Howard said again, his tone dull and uncaring. "Did they want to know what topping you wanted on your pizza?"

The detective paused, "Mr. Price," he said through the thick coat of static, "Some interesting leads have developed on the case. I thought you would like to know about them."

"Case?" Howard was confused. "What case? My daughter is dead. The kidnappers are dead, there is no case Mr. Brown."

"Don't you want them found?" the detective persisted. "Don't you want justice? These people murdered your daughter. They shot her in cold blood, beat you up and then ran away with the money. Don't you want justice for what they did?"

Price paused and downed another glass of whiskey before hanging up the phone.

He stared at the desk for a moment. It was filled with scattered papers, random sticky notes, pens, pencils, and business cards from people he didn't even know.

He thought about what the detective said and remembered his anger when he had seen his daughter dead. The detective was right, he did want justice, but he wanted a different kind of justice. He wanted vengeance, an eye for an eye. If he could hold her killers by their throats and watch them die he would be satisfied that justice had been served. Real justice.

They took away his daughter's life; he wanted to take away theirs.

The detective was ushered into the living room, but before he could speak Howard walked out of the room. He returned seconds later with the bottle of whiskey and his glass. He offered the detective a drink which was politely declined. Howard filled another tumbler full of the amber fluid and flung himself onto a chair opposite his guest.

"Well?" he started.

The detective shifted uncomfortably in his seat, "We have some vital evidence regarding the kidnappers."

"That much has already been established." There was no compassion in Howard's voice. "Tell me more."

"A bus driver came forward," he stated after some minor deliberation. "We missed him initially because he was covering for a friend, taking a route he shouldn't have been taking." Brown looked at Price but the features of the grieving father didn't even flicker. "He was driving the bus that picked up the suspects. He provided us with detailed descriptions and mentioned that they were carrying a large duffel bag with them."

Howard was somewhat impressed, but sarcasm fueled his expression.

The detective continued after a short silence, "We also have another witness, an elderly gentleman who was on the bus at the time. With his, and the driver's, descriptions we can now complete an accurate description and sketch of the two suspects."

Howard nodded.

"We'd like to run them in tomorrow's papers and on the local news channels," he added, grabbing Howard's attention. "And we'd like you to give an interview, a plea if you like. We just need you to stand in front of the cameras and tell your grief to the world and ask that the killers hand themselves in."

Howard was already shaking his head. "No chance."

"May I ask why?"

"You want me to appear on live television—"

"It doesn't have to be live."

"You want me to appear on *television*," Howard corrected, "the morning after I lost my daughter?"

"I know it sounds—"

"Fucking ridiculous."

"Excuse me?"

"It sounds fucking ridiculous and it won't happen. You have my blessing to release whatever you want about the bastards that killed my daughter and I might be willing to sit for a newspaper interview later in the week, but I will not go on television and plead to the fuckers who shot her the morning after they did it."

Brown nodded, "I understand."

"But I want to be with you on this," Howard said.

"What do you mean?"

"The case, I want to be involved."

"I'm afraid we can't—"

"Of course you can," Howard disagreed. "I'm not asking to hold your hand through it all, I just want to be kept informed."

"You *will* be kept informed Mr. Price."

Howard nodded and smiled wryly.

"I know you must feel angry and frustrated by what's happened," Brown said, reading Howard's thoughts. "But you must understand that we have full control of the situation now. We aren't taking any chances with these criminals. But this is not Hollywood Mr. Price; despite your anger you need to stand back and let the professionals take control."

Howard laughed.

"I must get going now," Brown said, standing up. "We will be sure to keep you informed. Keep an eye on your television, Mr. Price, the nine o'clock news will be running the story across the country; after that it will be a media circus, all news channels will have access to the story."

Howard nodded and watched the detective leave the room.

He looked at the clock. In less than an hour and a half the story would be unleashed upon the nation.

With a bitter smile, he drained the rest of the whiskey and let the empty bottle fall to the floor.

65

"Maybe we got away with it," Phillips suggested.

"It can't be that easy," Richards disagreed.

They had decided that alcohol would help them think the situation through and had been knocking back cans of beer between bouts of contemplation and idle stares directed at the money.

"Something like this would be on the news by now though," Richards said, making an argument against his own statement. "Surely."

"You're right," Phillips agreed. "It's been like four hours since we took the cash. It would have taken Price minutes to get in touch with the police and it would take them less than an hour to track down the bus driver, find out where we went, and drag our asses to jail."

Richards nodded. The drink had taken most of his worries away. "Maybe it wasn't a kidnapping after all," he said in hope. "Like you said: the police would have been at the scene if it was. They would have chased the bus and stopped it."

"I think," Phillips paused to burp. "I think we've gotten away with this. Maybe the money was for drugs or some other dodgy shit. Maybe the reason he was calling for his daughter was because he was so fucking whacked out of his head."

"Or he could have killed her," Richards offered, a statement his sober self would deem completely irrational. "Or was paying to have her killed, the money could have been for a hitter who he hired to kill his daughter and wife. He might have been having an affair on the side; she found out, he didn't want to lose face, so he had her killed."

"The daughter could have gotten in the way," Phillips offered. "Maybe he only wanted to have his wife killed and the reason he was so distraught was because his daughter was caught in the crossfire." The drunken reasoning had stretched beyond the ridiculous but they hadn't noticed.

They both settled back into their chairs with smiles on their faces, happy that they had relieved the majority of their tension. They had been watching the news channels all day and had seen nothing regarding Howard Price or a bag full of money. Phillips finished his drink and placed the empty can on the floor. Richards did the same and when he looked up he saw his friend smiling at him.

"What?"

"We have no more drink."

"Haven't you got any stashed anywhere?"

"Nope, or at least not that I know of," Phillips said, pondering. "We should head to the pub."

"Are you sure that's wise?"

"Why not? We've established that we'll be safe, along with the money, so why not go and celebrate? We can hit the pubs and clubs like we were going to do before all of this started. We have something to celebrate, now don't we?"

Richards smiled, "I guess so."

"All right then," Phillips grinned, rising. "Take a few dollars from the stash, I'll get my coat and the car keys."

"You've been drinking, you shouldn't drive."

"Good point. You drive."

Richards nodded and took the keys, "Wait," he said, pausing in the center of the room. "I've been drinking too."

"Ah."

"Taxi?" Richards offered.

"We could walk. It isn't cold and the pub isn't that far away."

Richards agreed, "The pub is close to the nightclub as well," he added. "And by then we should be so pissed that the walking won't bother us."

"That's the spirit!" Phillips removed his coat from the back of the chair as Richards rummaged underneath the sofa and found a small stash of twenty-dollar bills. "Take more than that," Phillips urged. "Stick it all in your wallet and wave the fucker around like you own the place. That way we might be able to get you laid."

"What time is it?" Richards asked, raising his voice over the sound of the television in the bar.

"There's a clock behind you."

"Nearly nine already," Richards said, slurring his voice.

"We best get going. Get into the clubs as they open. We don't want to get lumbered near the back next to a sweaty teenager high on drugs and wanting to hug everyone. If we get in early enough we can get a seat near the bar," Phillips explained, draining the last of his beer.

Michael Richards nodded, he too drank the remainder of his drink.

The pub was beginning to fill. The occupants had more than doubled since they had entered. Most of the drinkers were young teenagers readying themselves for a night out; some were old men who had been in the pub most of the day.

The pub only had one main room and despite its size it was quickly becoming claustrophobic.

All eyes seemed to be on a large television above the bar, it was playing a soccer game: Arsenal was playing some team they'd never heard of.

As the two friends rose and walked towards the bathroom at the far end of the pub, the noise from the television diminished as the channel cut to a news broadcast.

The way to the gritty bathroom was through three heavy wooden doors and a long corridor. As they found their way to the urinals, filled with cigarette butts and other trash, the noise from the bar faded to a background hush.

"Fucking hell," Phillips spat. "Look at this," he ushered Richards's view to his urinal. Richards leaned across and looked inside to see a used condom floating around inside a small pool of water.

"That's fucking disturbing," Phillips muttered, moving to the next urinal.

"You've never fucked in a pub toilet?" Richards questioned with his eyebrows raised.

"Of course I have," Phillips said unzipping his pants. "A few times, but those places were the fucking dog's balls compared to this shit hole. "Look!" he gestured towards the floor.

Richards found himself looking at a streak of feces along the side of the far wall. "Okay," he agreed. "That is pretty nasty. Looks like they don't clean at all."

"It's a family business, but the family is an alcoholic mother, a five-year-old child, and a fucking greasy old man."

"How do you know?" Richards asked. "You seem to know everybody. We, or at least I, haven't even been in this pub before."

"Neither have I," Phillips confessed. "But I slept with the owner a few months back. She was doing the rounds at the clubs. She mentioned she owned a pub an' all that; I just didn't take much of it in at the time. If I'd have known I wouldn't have come here."

Richards laughed and zipped up his pants. "Is that why she stopped you for a chat when you were getting the drinks in?"

"Yes," Phillips answered in disgust. "She said she was waiting to see me again, wondering when I was going to stop by and all that shit. Then she dragged me into a conversation about her son and her father. I had to tell her I was busy and promised I'd phone her later."

They left the toilets and walked back through the long corridor. The noise from the television had been drowned out as the volume from the customers increased.

"Have you got her number?" Richards asked as they reached the door.

"Fuck knows," Phillips said putting his hand on the door. "But I certainly ain't fucking calling her."

As they pushed open the door and reentered the pub, the crowd grew quiet. People who had been standing near the bathroom door watched the two men enter and shushed their conversations.

As Phillips and Richards made their way to the front door the noise levels decreased further until only the noise of the television interrupted the heavily populated pub; neither of them noticed the change in their surroundings and they strode out of the pub, oblivious to the ominous silence behind them.

"So you fucked a single mom then left her?"

"I didn't know she was a mom at the time. Hell, I didn't even know her name."

Inside, one of the men ended a call on his cell phone and stuffed it back into his pocket. All the customers turned his way.

"The police should have them in ten minutes," he said. "I told them where they were headed."

A younger man by the front door turned to the speaker, "D'you really think it was them?"

"It certainly looked like them." He looked around the pub at the sea of faces. "Right?" he asked for confirmation.

The people in the pub nodded and spoke in turn. Soon the volume was turned up to its maximum again as the drinkers talked excitedly among themselves.

66

"Five minutes you said," Richards mumbled as he and Phillips strode down a pavement, sided by a line of shops; some derelict, some shut for the night.

"It was a guess. Like I said, I ain't been to that pub before, how was I to know how far away from the nightclubs it was?"

"If you didn't know you shouldn't have guessed."

"Sorry mother," Phillips laughed. "Anyway, you said you'd be too pissed to care about walking by this stage."

"Well, I ain't," Richards moaned. "And I need a drink."

"We'll be there soon."

Richards shot his friend an intimidating sneer.

"—*ish*" Phillips corrected, "Soon-*ish*."

"What is—" Richards began to moan again but his words were strangled by the sound of roaring police sirens.

The noise came from nowhere, a fact that Richards casually pointed out to his friend.

"They probably had the sirens off for a while. They don't turn them on as soon as they leave the station you know," Phillips explained. "Maybe they're near the crime scene and want to go unnoticed."

"You call that unnoticed?" Richards said, his voice barely audible over the screaming of numerous sirens.

"They have to turn them on eventually, don't they? Let the civilians know and whatnot. The suspects won't be able to escape by now you see."

Richards nodded and they both watched as four police cars screamed around the corner further down the dark, empty road. The cars were closely followed by two large vans. They grimaced at the sounds of the deafening sirens piercing the thin night air.

The red and blue lights flickered with epileptic mania and littered the horizon with discotheque quality; bringing bright light onto the dull street.

"Someone's in trouble," Phillips smiled. "Probably some druggie at the club, no doubt—" his words lodged in his throat and he froze.

The cars skidded to a screaming halt in front of them. Two officers jumped out from each vehicle and took cover behind their doors, aiming handguns at the pair.

Behind them the doors of the vans swung open and eight heavily armored officers swarmed out, all cradling guns. As if they were preparing for war, they stood in formation in front of the vans.

"Stop right there!" one of the officers screamed, his gun aimed at the two men.

Michael Richards and Johnny Phillips looked at each other simultaneously and spoke concurrently: "Shit!"

Howard Price felt empty, lonely, and unsure what to do with himself. His wife was still fast asleep upstairs; he didn't want to disturb her and even if she *was* awake he doubted he would be able to speak to her. His world had been ripped apart; nothing seemed real, right, or normal anymore.

The alcohol had done little to drown his sorrows, and it hadn't knocked him out or killed his memories like he'd hoped. Everywhere he looked he saw Lisa. He saw her by the television, watching her cartoons in the morning before school; he saw her on the sofa, wrapped up in his arms, begging him to let her stay up late; on the floor he saw her, and him, playing board or card games; he saw her on the dining room table and in the kitchen.

She was all he saw when he closed his eyes.

Standing up, feeling surprisingly mobile, he grabbed his coat and left the house, not bothering to lock the front door, but taking care not to slam it.

The cold air helped him. It ran through his body and his head, it also seemed to force the alcohol into action. He could feel the warming sensation he had expected to feel.

Standing in the doorway he thought about his daughter's killers. Every time the thought crept into his head it was closely followed by anger. The more he thought about them, about hurting them, the less he thought about Lisa—anger seemed to push despair away.

He pulled out his car keys and headed for his Mercedes.

The two conmen were frozen in place, their feet firmly gripping the concrete. They watched a blaring light show: blues and reds interchanging and flashing gloriously, almost blinding them from the human horrors that stood in front of the pulsating lights, pointing guns directly at them.

Their ears were pounding with the sound of their own blood, blood they could feel pounding unnaturally through their veins at supersonic speed.

They turned and looked at each other. The shouts from the police were increasing; demands were being issued, they were being told to put their hands above their heads and kneel on the ground.

Neither of them moved.

Phillips—closest to the road—turned his head and looked past Richards. An alleyway, darkened by night, stretched as far as his eyes could penetrate; he nodded towards at Richards to indicate this, and his friend returned the gesture.

The officer began shouting again, "I will not repeat myself, put your—" he paused as the two suspects fled down the alleyway.

They ran as fast as their feet could take them, noticing how quickly their fear had sobered them up. They skipped over empty bags of chips, beer bottles, and shopping bags of waste as they sped through the dark alleyway.

"I can't fucking believe it!" Richards bellowed, slightly out of breath.

"Start!" Phillips said, sharply ducking into another alleyway. He pushed his friend over. Richards fell with a clatter; his land-

ing softened somewhat by collection of cardboard boxes. Phillips
soon joined him, diving next to him onto the pile of boxes.

"What the fuck did you do that for?" Richards demanded to
know.

"Need time to think."

Nestled in the cardboard they were obscured from view by
two large trash cans on either side of them. Ahead of them, a short
jump into the darkness, past a tight squeeze down the side of one
of the cans was a small drop. In the drop was a door leading to
a basement apartment, lights flooded from underneath the door.

"What the fuck are we going to do?" Richards begged to know.

"We've got to get out of here."

"Good plan."

Two gunshots exploded into the quiet night, making both
men jump. The warning shots—fired into the skies—were followed by more shouting.

"Then again," Richards said, panting. "Maybe we should just
give ourselves up."

"Think what they'll do to us if they catch us. If they find out
our history they'll throw away the fucking key. Not to mention all
the cash we'll lose."

"You're right," Richards nodded, still in shock. "We need to
get out of here."

More shots were fired into the air and a final warning was
issued.

"On the other hand . . ."

"Look!" Phillips snapped, roughly grabbing his friend by the
collar. "We can get out of this. We've been through fucking hell to
get this far, we ain't going under now, okay?"

"Agreed."

Behind them the police were separating and spreading out
through the alleyways. Phillips put his finger to his lips, warning
his friend to be quiet as the sound of slow footsteps encroached.

Richards felt like he was going to have a stroke, watching Johnny Phillips—poised by the end of the trash can—his heart and mind had run off course. A fun night out had turned into his worst nightmare.

The footsteps echoed louder on the pavement as the cautious officer approached their hiding place.

The tapping feet proceeded with a slow, deliberate pace. The conmen heard his breathing, heavy and fast—clearly they weren't the only nervous ones.

The sound of the heavy footsteps stopped short of the fugitives' hiding place. Richards and Phillips exchanged hesitant glances as they both strained to hear the sound of moving feet.

Another step sounded and Phillips pounced. Like a fox in the night he sprang upon his prey, he grabbed the officer and twisted his wrists, forcing him to drop his weapon. After the semi-automatic pistol fell to the floor, he delivered a strong head-butt to his face.

The ambushed officer's nose exploded from the impact and he screeched in shock and anguish, droplets of his blood sprayed from his wound and splashed onto the wet cardboard near Richards, who looked at it in revulsion.

Phillips grabbed his head with his left hand and swung at it with his right fist. His knuckles cracked the officer's jaw, spilling teeth and blood in his mouth; he instantly coughed out a stream of saliva-soaked blood that coated Phillips's jacket. With a soft mumble, he fell from Phillips's grasp, hitting the floor and crumpling up like a ragdoll.

Phillips reached down and picked up the gun. Checking down the alleyway he noticed an armed officer aiming a gun directly at him, in a flash and a rush of adrenaline he dove back to his position behind the trash cans. A shot exploded and slammed into the ground, skimming off the solid surface and chipping away at the concrete; missing Phillips's flying feet by inches.

Three more shots fired into the direction of the invisible suspect. They all missed, screeching and rebounding off the floor and walls.

"They're fucking shooting at us!" Richards screamed.

"No shit," Phillips said, releasing the magazine cartridge from the pistol and checking the bullet count—it was full. "Come on, we need to get the fuck out of here."

Keeping their heads low they scraped past the bin and jumped down the drop. Phillips fell against the basement door awkwardly, his feet slipping from the tarmac above. The lock on the door cracked and the door burst open. He clattered to the floor inside the grimy kitchen of a musty crack house.

67

Richards looked around in distaste. His nose recoiled from a terrible smell that swam through the kitchen; its origin was a broken sewer pipe below an unused washing machine.

"What *is* this place?" he wondered.

"Crack house," Phillips replied firmly, pulling himself to his feet with a grunt. "Kinda."

"How the fuck do you know that?"

Phillips put his finger to his lips to hush his friend, "I used to date, well, fuck a crackhead. She came here a lot; I came with her when I was pissed. It's owned by a dealer who likes to *spread the love*. Through that door there," he pointed to a door directly opposite the one he had just crashed through, "is the main room, probably a few people in there." He walked to the other side of the kitchen and to another door, "Through here," he said with his hand on the doorknob, "should be the hallway."

He pushed the door open; it squeaked and brought with it another stench: decay.

It was a dimly lit, poorly kept hallway. The walls hadn't been painted, papered, or plastered. They were chipped in numerous places and adorned with poorly penned graffiti.

They could hear hushed voices coming from all over the apartment, seeping out of the walls like the stench that turned their stomachs. They were unsure if the voices were the police or the occupants and didn't want to wait around to find out.

Phillips quickly ushered Richards to another door. They opened it to embrace the open air again, this time on another, similar street. They could hear the noise generated by the police two streets back, as they frantically searched for the suspects in the alleyways.

"Now what?" Richards asked, surveying the roads ahead.

"We wait," Phillips said, pulling his friend out of full view of the road and the houses opposite.

"Wait for what? What the fuck are we going to do?"

Phillips didn't answer; he watched and waited as a car slowly turned down the street. Its headlights picked them out as it slowly advanced towards them. Phillips pulled the handgun he had taken from the police officer into view, "Now we hitch a ride."

The effects of the alcohol were strong in Howard Price's body. He had left the house somewhat sober, but since embracing the fresh air and taking on the task of driving through the winding streets, the effects of the substance had become more prominent. He could feel his face getting flustered, his body tingling and his motor functions relaxing.

The streets were empty and he was still sober enough to drive, there wasn't much of a fear that he would hit anyone. There was a good chance the alcohol would get the better of him and he would crash into a tree or a wall and kill himself, but he didn't think that wouldn't be such a bad thing.

The drive had helped to clear his head but it also allowed more thoughts to pass through. He thought about work, he couldn't face going back there, not now. And the prospect of staying in the house scared him; Lisa was a part of that house. Maybe he would get away for a while; he and Elizabeth could travel to their holiday home in the south of France. He even pondered giving up work, investors had already inquired about buying the company, maybe it was finally time to sell.

Contemplating all of this, he continued to drive on at a steady pace, shocked when the figure of a man, standing in the middle of the road, was highlighted by his headlights. He slammed his foot on the brakes, his reactions were slow but he managed to stop in time.

Johnny Phillips smiled. Standing in front of the Mercedes, his gun lowered by his side, he squinted his eyes to strain out the beam from the headlights. His face — bright in the yellow shine — was obscured from the driver's view, just as the driver was obscured from his.

He raised the gun, making sure it could be seen through the windshields by the invisible driver. Then, moving carefully, he walked around to the passenger side of the car. Michael Richards appeared out of the shadows near the same side.

Phillips put on his meanest expression, took a deep breath and then yanked open the passenger door. He pointed the gun directly at the driver, "We need a ride—" he paused. "Mr. Price . . .What a surprise."

Howard Price felt his blood boil, the man who had beat him and had a hand in killing his daughter now had a gun pointed at his face.

68

The engine of the expensive Mercedes burst into life on the quiet dark street, with the police officers less than thirty yards away. It accelerated quietly before picking up speed further down the road; traveling almost twice as fast as it had before.

Howard Price drove with Johnny Phillips in the passenger seat holding a gun to his head. Michael Richards had slipped into the back of the car when his friend hijacked the vehicle.

"Head to Rokers Court," Phillips demanded, the barrel of the gun still inches from Price's temple.

"Okay," Howard agreed. He tried to peer at Phillips through the corner of his eye but saw only the glint of the weapon. "And then what?"

Phillips paused and thought for a second, keen to hide his trembling hand and growing fear from the man he had technically just kidnapped. "Just go there and shut the fuck up," he said. He had no idea what he was going to do, but he knew that he wanted to get far away from the chaos he had left behind.

"Why did you do it?" Howard asked as the car pulled turned away from the spaghetti streets and hit a long country road.

"Money," Phillips said simply, without paying attention, his mind was on his next move.

Richards kept his gaze away from the pair in the front, choosing to concentrate with an agitated nervousness at the roads behind them, dreading a police car pulling into view and giving chase.

"How could you do such a thing?" Howard wondered.

"What?" Phillips said, distracted.

"It's sickening, how could you do something like that?" He could feel Phillips's breath, he could smell his presence and taste his evil thoughts, each passing second sent more bolts of rage through him.

Phillips ignored the comments. He was stuck in a void, as a con man all of his actions were usually plotted for him; especially when it came to avoiding the police and escaping with the money. Confidence tricks take time, practice, and skill, the situation he found himself in required pure intuition and luck.

Howard struggled to maintain calm. He was sharing the same breathing space as the people who had executed his daughter without remorse, people who valued money over the life of a little girl, *his* little girl.

"You bastards," Howard said again, spitting his words with ferocity. He turned to look at Phillips, who was lost in thought. "You fucking bastards!" he growled, his mouth had taken on the form of a pit bull; he was snarling with deep hatred. "You have no right—"

Phillips snapped out of his trance and straightened the gun; reaffirming his intentions. "Keep your fucking eyes on the road old man!"

Howard paid no heed to the words of warning. The car, touching onto sixty miles an hour, wobbled from lane to lane.

In the backseat Richards felt his body clench as his heart began to beat a multitude of warnings. He tried to offer his own words of warning to the driver but his meek voice was overshadowed by Phillips's sudden outburst.

"Look at the fucking road!" he bellowed. His voice rocked through the car like thunder and the currents of threat that coursed through it even sent a chill to Michael Richards's bones.

Howard relented momentarily and returned his attention to the road, settling the car back onto a straight line.

"Do not try to make this any fucking harder for me," Phillips warned again, his tone much softer. "Or I *will* shoot you," he pushed the gun against Howard's temple and held it there for a few seconds, hoping the older man would pay attention, even though he had no intention of pulling the trigger.

Vengeance continued to boil up inside Howard like some venomous bile. He pressed his foot down harder on the pedals and watched as the speedometer crawled past seventy.

"My daughter went through hell," Howard spoke again, his hatred masked by a somber tone. "She should be with me now, but instead you killed her, and for what? Money? Is money worth more to you than the life of a child?" the car continued to pick up speed, in the distance the large block of Rokers Court stood out like a gray blotch on a black canvas.

Phillips looked at him, baffled, "We didn't fucking kill your daughter old man."

"Fuck you!" Howard shouted, lost in anger. "You're sick, she was just a little girl, she wouldn't have harmed you."

Howard turned the wheel sharply and dragged the car off the road. The suspension rocked as it bounced over thick grass, clumped mud, and wet rocks.

Phillips screamed random obscenities and tried to focus the gun on Howard's head, but even when he had the shot he didn't want to take it.

"You took her away from me!" Howard screamed as the side of the car stripped the bark from a tree with an aggressive screech.

"We didn't!" Phillips shouted. "We didn't harm her. Get back on the fucking road!" he pressed the gun hard against Howard Price's temple.

The older man ignored the weapon, brushing the feeling of cold steel away like a minor headache.

"She didn't deserve to die," Howard called with the gun now deeply imprinting the skin on his head. "I hope you rot in hell!"

Phillips saw the large wall ahead and he was quick enough to see that the car was heading straight for it, the gun fell from his loose grasp as his mind scurried to find a survivable solution. Moving from his seat he tried desperately to dive across the driver's side, he didn't know why.

Maybe part of him wanted to try to grasp the steering wheel and swerve the car away from its impending doom, maybe he wanted to take the cushioning effect of both airbags or maybe he hoped that Howard's body would somehow save his; maybe it was a last-ditch attempt to attack the man who was trying to steer him into the wall.

He didn't make it across in time.

With one final shout of horror from Richards in the backseat, the car crashed hard into the concrete wall. The front of the Mercedes crumpled like an aluminum can.

cribe.

Phillips, halfway off his seat at the time of the impact, flew from the car. His body careered through the front windshield; the glass exploded on impact and showered him in glittering shards as he soared.

The shrapnel peppered his skin and cut into every inch of him, some chunks sliced and parted, other bits imbedded themselves like clear splinters. The transparent knives severed various tendons and muscles in his body.

The car had been doing over fifty miles per hour over the rugged woodland terrain and the force of the crash was enough to demolish the front end and then rebound it. Phillips suffered a similar fate, his journey through the air ended when he hit the wall head first and collapsed back upon the crushed hood.

The crack of his skull reverberated through the night, following on echoes left by the destruction of metal and brick; adding an organic touch to the catastrophic cacophony.

His mangled body folded in on itself as blood leaked from every pore, his body had been ravaged by wounds, covering him from head to toe. The crack in his skull had splashed blood and pink matter over the wall, like paint on the canvas of a flamboyant artist.

His left arm was hanging by a thread of skin and drooping loosely across his bloodied body, his forearm and hand dangled over the edge of the car. A river of blood ran down his arm, onto his hand and through his palm, before dripping a steady line of crimson from the end of his little finger onto the soggy ground below.

69

Michael Richards was stunned, his world shook before him in a hazy glow, a glow that had been dotted with stars, fuzzy lines, and a feeling of shock and confusion.

He had noted the shouts and the commotion in the front seat and had reacted upon it, nervously twitching his vision between

Phillips, Howard and the dimly lit woodland beyond the windshield. He remembered shouting in horror, he remembered his own screamed obscenities that had stuck in his throat.

He hadn't seen the wall until the last minute; it seemed come out of the darkness like a deer in the night. He had seen Johnny Phillips move and grow increasingly agitated, he had worried that his friend might get jumpy and pull the trigger.

Seconds later he was rocketed forward and dragged back with a crushing thump as the locking features on the seatbelt took effect. It knocked the wind completely out of him and sent his vision into a starry abyss.

He heard a crash, a smash. Something had shattered one of the windows.

Whatever had happened he knew he needed to act fast, Price or Johnny could be injured or dying. He pulled himself out of his trance and tried to focus as hard as he could, he tried to see past the blotted blur that had covered his vision and when he did he caught sight of the trauma.

Howard Price was still in the driver's seat, he was leaning forward against the wheel, his chest resting on the port of an unexploded airbag. There was no Phillips in the passenger seat, only sprays of blood.

As Richards became more aware he discovered blood on himself, spattered on his cheek and hand. He wiped at it and studied it, instinctively checking his face for wounds. The blood wasn't his.

What disturbed him most was the collection of torn flesh still dripping from the shards of glass that protruded from the shattered windscreen. A three-inch line of flesh hung from the top of the windscreen like meat in a butcher's shop, it had been snagged by a splinter of glass that had remained rooted into the fixtures and it dangled there, still dripping.

With his heart beating like an amphetamine addict, he unlocked his seat belt—feeling the kinks it had left in his skin—and staggered out of the back door.

Johnny Phillips, once a strong figure and his best and only friend, lay in ruins. His body was crumpled on the front of the car, slowly sliding off as a pool of blood lubricated the metal underneath him. Richards's heart stopped and so did his legs, he wanted to run to his friend but he knew it was too late. He saw the gouge in his skull; he saw the ripped arm and the shards of glass that had pierced his entire body.

"Johnny . . ." he muttered, his mouth suddenly very dry.

He took a step forward but quickly retreated. He couldn't bear to see his friend like that. His emotions tried to take over but it wasn't a time to mourn. He had to get away, escape the scene, what the ghost of Johnny Phillips would be screaming at him to do. But he was rooted; his best friend lay dead and destroyed a yard away from him and he couldn't look, or run, away.

A breathless mumble alerted him and he turned to see Howard Price waking up inside the car. He was cursing into the rim of the steering wheel in a disoriented fashion while trying to propel his body upwards.

Richards stood and stared for a while, unsure what to do. He watched as Price lifted himself and returned to his seat, for a moment he didn't seem to know where he was or what had happened but Richards saw the realization cross over his features. The older man first looked at the shattered windshield, then at the destroyed corpse of Johnny Phillips, then his tired eyes turned to Michael Richards.

The pair looked at each other for what seemed like an eternity, none of them sure what to do next. Then Richards saw a glint in the old man's eyes, a look of anger and a lack of remorse, he had killed Johnny Phillips, his body within touching distance, yet he barely bat an eyelid.

Richards turned and ran, his feet suddenly capable, his mind thinking straight. He powered through the rough ground and the dark night, trampling through unseen bushes and dodging his way around a succession of trees.

Howard snapped back into reality with a pounding headache. His head hadn't reached the steering wheel but the force of the crash had shot his brain through his skull. He caught sight of the man in the backseat running away and he noted his direction.

They had locked eyes, Howard had seen fear in the eyes of the younger man before he had watched him leave. He wanted to chase him, to catch him, and to kill him. Doing to him what he had done to his friend and what they had done to Howard's little girl.

But he didn't run after him, he probably wouldn't catch him and he didn't need to chase him anyway; he had a good idea where he was going.

Still with his seatbelt on Howard struggled to free himself. When he moved, he felt a sharp pain—starting in his lower back—shoot through his body with agonizing efficiency. It felt like a bolt of lightning had sliced through his central nervous system.

He paused to control his breathing, he was wheezing, his chest had taken a hit and his breaths were suffering. Sinking back into the seat he stared at the dead body of Johnny Phillips, he didn't smile, he didn't frown; he didn't react at all. He had no reason to feel sympathy for the crumpled killer, but he didn't delight in his death like he had hoped he would, the weight of vengeance was still on his shoulders, there was still another killer out there. He didn't know which one of them pulled the trigger but he wanted them both to pay for it.

70

Howard climbed out of the car. The door had jammed and squished into its own frame, it needed two kicks to encourage its release.

He paused to rest against the damaged roof, gritting his teeth as a stabbing pain incessantly worked through his lower back. Straightening up he slammed the door shut, it crashed into the hinges, rebounded, and then dropped off.

He looked into the distance, the building of Rokers Court was partially lit, unlike the grayed scenery around it. He knew the second killer would be going there, if only for a brief time.

He walked away from the car but only made it a few feet before stumbling and reaching for the support of a nearby tree. His body had almost been crippled in the crash, pain roared through him like an angry virus, settling in every cell.

He removed his hand from the tree and allowed his shoulder to fall against it, then he reached inside his pocket and fumbled around for his cell phone. He stared at the blue screen and considered his actions.

He knew he should call the police and he certainly needed to call an ambulance. The police would deal with the second killer and the ambulance would be able to help him.

He dialed the first nine.

He knew that he wouldn't be happy sitting inside a hospital while he waited for incompetent police officers to inform him of the current situation with the runaway kidnapper. He closed his eyes and rested his head on the tree.

It wasn't all about him, he had to think about his wife. Elizabeth still needed him and she certainly wouldn't approve of him trying to chase down a murderer while in his fractured state. She would want him safe, she would want him healthy; together, armed with the knowledge that justice had been done, they could try to move on with their lives. Lisa's life was over but that didn't have to mean that their lives were.

He dialed the second digit while nodding to himself.

He paused. He knew he could never live with himself if he let this moment pass. The police would take their time in arriving and would probably only stop to ask questions about the wreck and the dead kidnapper, wasting precious time while the other man made his getaway.

He pictured his future with Elizabeth. A future where they both sat in separate worlds, ignored each other and rarely spoke; their refusal to bring up the subject of Lisa's death and the killer that had gotten away would place a tension between them that was so thick it would surely cause their early demise.

He cancelled the call. Inside the car was the gun that the dead kidnapper had held. Howard reached in through the door-less driver's side and picked it up, tossing it from hand to hand. Looking through the trees ahead of him he slipped the handgun into his pocket and set off at a steady jog.

Pain ravaged his body and each step perpetuated it, but he ignored it, he pushed it to the back of his mind and increased his pace.

The trees and bushes ripped at Michael Richards's skin, opening small wounds and grazes, but he continued running. The last thing on his mind was the pain being inflicted on his body; it was the pain inside that was destroying him. He tried to take the images and thoughts out of his mind, concentrate on the moment, but no matter how hard he tried, part of him wanted to settle down, relax, and mourn; part of him needed to think about the death of his friend.

Instincts were needed too; he needed to escape to avoid the same fate. He rushed on. He couldn't see much in front of him but he had a good idea where to go.

Ahead he heard the sound of a car rushing past, it startled him at first, almost stopping him in his tracks as he instantly thought about the rows of police cars that had halted him earlier, but the worry dissipated as the vehicle sped away.

The road was near and beyond that lay Rokers Court. As he continued onward he could see its lights breaking through the trees ahead, the sight forced him to pick up his speed, he was nearly there.

Howard Price fought back the pain. Adrenaline rushed through his body and stirred up the sleeping alcohol that had rested during the time of distress; everything combined in a rush of endorphins that eased his suffering and allowed his tortured body to keep going.

He hadn't run in years, neither his job or his social life called for it, he was a desk man not an athlete, but now he had a goal.

He could feel crumpled fauna underneath his feet and the thought that he was treading the same path as the man he was chasing spurred him on even more, he felt like a predator chasing its prey.

He never thought that vengeance wouldn't provide the solace he needed, because he needed *some* solace and revenge was the only thing he could think of. Lisa's death had destroyed him and time would be no healer, nothing ever would. Just the thought of hunting down her killers and dealing out his own justice was enough to relieve his despair.

He never thought of how the police would react. They would certainly arrest him and that would only make things worse for Elizabeth, she had just lost a daughter to a thoughtless murder and now she would lose a husband to an equally thoughtless act of personal justice.

He could see the road. Light broke through trees ahead, somewhere further down he could hear the fading roar of a car engine. He stopped and rested against one of the trees, checking his surroundings to make sure the criminal wasn't waiting to ambush him.

The moonlight and the light from the huge apartment building ahead provided him with a grayed, shortened view of the woodland around him. Shadows and shapes danced in the dark, jumping with the wind. Behind him he heard the ground settling, the mud floor was peppered with weeds, trigs and scraps of bushes, all of which had been trodden on or kicked out of place.

A beam of silver light fell overhead and landed inches away, highlighting a broken chunk of tree which had bled sap that had dripped and dried.

He inspected the gun in his hand, pushing it underneath the stream of light to study it closely. The weapon was dull and scratched; it showed signs of heavy use. He wondered how many times it had been used.

He tried to catch his breath as he studied the deceptively heavy gun.

How many shots had it fired?

Turning it over in his hand he saw a small switch above the handle which indicated that the safety was off.

How many families had been destroyed because of this single piece of metalwork?

He had never held a gun before now, he didn't even know how to load the weapon or how to check if it was already loaded.

How many lives had it taken?

He was sure it would be ready to fire. The man lying dead on his car was a murderer, he would have never held the gun to Howard's head if it wasn't already loaded and ready to kill. If it *wasn't* loaded, he had his hands, he had his spirit, he possessed the strength of a man who had nothing to live for but vengeance.

Was it the gun that had killed Lisa?

He opened his jacket and, with the handle still gripped firmly in his right hand, he slipped his hand inside; out of sight of any unwanted attention but ready to aim and fire in seconds.

At a jogging pace, he made a move for the final row of trees.

71

Richards was panting and struggling to breathe, barely suppressing the need to rest against a wall or sit down and take the burning out of his legs and lungs. The consumption of alcohol probably didn't help, but it was something he could barely feel anymore.

He looked behind him, his eyes flickering hesitantly towards the wooded area which was now in complete shade. He couldn't see Howard Price but something told him that the old man was hunting him down.

Richards stopped briefly as his eyes tried to focus. Past the entrance to the apartments, over the empty road, there was a slight incline into the forest. It was normally used as a hideout for teenagers or drunks, anyone wanting shelter while trying to hide suspicious activities from prying eyes.

Now something more sinister lurked inside the looming mass of trees, a destroyed car, a mangled friend, and an angry father seeking revenge on the wrong criminal.

Turning away from the road he studied the semicircle of apartments in front of him. The area was empty, most of the locals were at the pubs or clubs, the kids that littered the corridors and corners through the day would be on the streets or finding shelter. Signs of life shone from a few of the visible apartments, flickering blue lights that bathed in orange glows.

He allowed his twitching legs to take control and he set off across the car park, his feet thudding against the solid tarmac as he drove forward.

He noted that only his Vauxhall occupied the large space. He acknowledged this with passing relief as he headed up the flight of stairs—being careful not to draw attention from any curtain peepers—and crossed to the apartment.

Howard knew he was aiming for a long shot but it was all he had. The gun-toting kidnapper, now lying dead in the woods in front of a savaged car, had mentioned Rokers Court. He had said he needed to go pick something up. The kidnappers wouldn't have given up so much information if they'd planned on keeping him alive. They probably planned on using him and his car for as long as possible before shooting him like they had done to Lisa.

They wanted to keep him, toy with him, and then toss him away. He was another pawn in their game, another life to waste in the pursuit of money, Lisa had been their ticket to money; Howard would be their ticket to freedom.

He entered the court breathing heavily. He had to stop, lean over, and rest his hands on his knees. He spat out dry saliva and took in as many deep breaths as he felt he had time for. He was tired, the day had been long, he'd had too much whiskey, and he had never been a good runner.

He had felt better in the woods, but now, out in the open and ready to exact his revenge, he felt a sickening anxiety; a rush of blood and a rumble of his stomach. He still felt angry and he still didn't feel remorse but something niggled away at his nerves.

A single car occupied the spacious area where he stood. His eyes fell on the vehicle instantly, he wanted to make sure the kidnapper wasn't inside, he wanted to make sure he wasn't trying to make his escape.

It was empty.

Glancing around he was sure he sought what he was after. He pulled the gun out from his jacket and continued.

A short walk across the dimly lit parking lot took him to a flight of metal stairs. He walked at a slow and deliberate pace, making sure to scan every niche before he took each step.

The rusted stairs clinked and moaned underneath his feet. In the silence of the night the sounds were like echoed gunfire and he found himself grimacing, as if his twisted features would stop the aging metal from groaning.

At the top of the stairs he waited and listened, there was a blind spot leading to the second-floor balcony, the killer could be hiding around the corner, waiting to ambush him.

Raising the gun and drawing his elbows into his chest to steady his shaking hands, he walked forward on silent feet, careful not to make a sound and give away his position.

Reaching the corner, he burst out and thrust the gun forward, his finger on the trigger.

There was no ambush. He relaxed and eased his grip on the gun, he had been holding it so tight it had imprinted itself onto his skin.

There weren't many occupied apartments on the second floor, but one of the few that *wasn't* boarded up looked occupied and the front door was wide open. There was a straight line between him and the apartment and with the balcony on his right-hand side and a few closed apartments on his left, he could concentrate on his objective and not worry about being jumped.

As his heart tried hard to escape out of his chest his feet walked on at a faster pace than they had done on the stairs. His eyes never left their destination.

The lights had not been turned on inside the apartment. The kidnapper must have rushed in to try to hide, or maybe he didn't know he was being chased and was collecting a few items before trying to make a getaway. He had been rushing, he hadn't had time to shut or lock the door.

Howard felt a throb of anticipation course through his body, his heart palpitated and his sweaty hands gripped the gun even tighter. He stopped before the door to listen but he could only hear the sound of his own blood throbbing through his ears.

He entered the apartment with haste, holding the gun out like he had seen in numerous cop shows, he stepped one foot inside the hallway. It wasn't as bad as he expected, he expected a pungent odor or a sickly, cold décor but he didn't get any of that. The hallway was dark, as was the living room, which he could see to his right.

Slowly, trying not to make a noise, he moved another step, enough so he could see into the living room. His finger pressed the trigger tightly, ready to be pulled. Out of the corner of his eye, just past the entrance to the living room, he saw the duffel bag that had been used in the kidnapping, the one that carried the money that had cost his daughter her life.

He had the right apartment. There was a good chance that the person who had escaped his grasp was still inside.

Revenge was finally going to be his.

Holding his stance, he waited for his eyes to adjust to the darkness. When they did he couldn't pick out the suspect. He let out a long breath that he hadn't realized he had been holding, it wheezed out of his lungs with unnerving volume.

He ignored the sound, it wouldn't matter, he had the gun and the advantage. With his concentration tight and his eyes on the room ahead he took two steps forward. His right foot was the first to trip the laser wire.

72

Michael Richards grimaced at the noise. The explosion was colossal; he knew it would be. Sitting on the hard pavement, with a concrete pillar behind his back, he shifted his position so he could catch a glance at what was once his and Johnny's apartment.

The domicile was completely devastated. The front door and the walls of the hallway lay in chunks in the parking lot. The railing outside of the apartment had warped and sliced in half, its two sections hung from the second floor, dangling and swaying in the shock waves.

The apartment itself was entirely hollowed out, as were the apartments on either side. The apartment below—unoccupied—looked like a dollhouse, the roof ripped off for everyone to see inside.

Fragments of cement and plaster rained a thick dust cloud over the court. Material from sofas, mattresses, and carpets swirled in the air and blocked the moonlight.

Richards brushed a tear from his right cheek and slowly rose to his feet. The police would arrive soon, even if the lawless locals didn't call, the explosion would have been heard for miles around.

Fires had started in the building and a thick smoke soon joined the material in the air.

Tears still streamed down his cheek but Richards tried to ignore them. He had lost a friend tonight, a friend that had been like a brother. He and Phillips had been family, together from an early age, never apart. They had no one else, they relied on each other. Now, Phillips was gone and Richards was alone.

He had to dispose of Price and the belongings in the apartment, he didn't have time to collect all the stashes and he didn't want Price on his back. He had now actually committed murder, but in his eyes, it was justified. That bastard had killed his friend, his brother, the only person he ever felt safe with.

Wiping more tears away, he bent down and picked up the two metallic cases from behind the concrete pillar. He took one in each hand and walked through the shaded estate. He closed his eyes as he made his way through the thick atmosphere at a deliberate pace.

People were opening their curtains on the other side of the exploded apartment building, trying to catch a glimpse of carnage, but they wouldn't be able to make out the shape of the retreating, lonesome millionaire, trudging his way to the dusty Vauxhall.

He was a ghost in the synthetic fog, a shadow in the snow.

His ears were still ringing from the explosion, but he could hear occasional popping and crackling sounds through the high-pitched whine as fire turned its deadly attention to electronics and dusty remnants, setting off a chain of mini eruptions.

He reached the car and opened the trunk, taking his time to drop the cases inside. His eyes turned to the apartment for the last time, through the dusty veil he could see the fierce red of crackling flames covering what used to be a bedroom, or a kitchen, he wasn't sure.

After placing the cases in the trunk and covering them with a quilt, he gently closed the door and clambered into the front seat. He pulled the car keys from his front pocket, grabbed hold of the rearview mirror and stared at his face.

He was still crying and he couldn't stop himself. He also looked worn out and deeply depressed. But something else lingered there, a sparkle in his eyes. After nearly a minute of staring at his own face he smiled. "One fucking million," he said aloud.

The area was still quiet; he knew he had enough time to escape. He could head up north and stay with some acquaintances for a while, people he and Phillips used to hang around with, they would keep him safe. When it all blew over he would leave the country, maybe America, maybe Australia, it didn't matter where, he had the money and had no ties, not anymore, he could go anywhere.

Starting up the engine he looked to the roof of the car, his eyes on the skies. "Maybe I'll even open a betting shop," he said proudly.

Despite his constant smile, tears still rolled down his face.

Acknowledgments

To Nicole Frail and Emily Shields, whose hard work brought this book to life; to Peter Beren, who has been a valuable asset throughout; to Marion Schwaner, for her work in publicity; and to everyone else at Skyhorse Publishing.

To all the authors who inspired me to write in this genre and others; to all the clients who pay me to write on a daily basis; and to Anthony, Jon, and everyone else at Palamedes, who will help to make sure this book gets read.

Last, but not least, I also owe a debt of gratitude to my mother, who loved and supported me to her final days, and to my partner, who still does.